Saradindu Bandyopadhyay

The Mystery of the Fortress and Other Stories

An author is always haunted by the character be creates. A character, that he brings to life and takes care to paint to perfection with his thoughts- invariably comes back to prey on his mind.

I have written thirty-one episodes on Byomkesh- planning out the plot of each story, one at a time, but when I have been stuck not knowing how to proceed, it is Byomkesh, who has come forward and showed me the way. This is not a ghostly affair, it is purely a psychological phenomenon. It happens to authors, who write many stories about a single character.

I often think that Byomkesh is now sixty and he should be allowed to retire. But the next moment the faces of a million readers float before my eyes and I ask myself, how can I disappoint them?

But one day I shall release Byomkesh very suddenly. Even if the readers want him, I do have some obligation to Byomkesh. How long can he go on?

Saradindu Bandyopadhyay

In an interview by Partho Chattopadhyay, published in Ananda Bazar Patrika in 1968

The Translator

An engineer and a retired Bank executive, Shankar Sen (b. 1936) took up writing for pleasure after his retirement. He composes prose and poetry in both English and Bengali, and his first full-length publication *The Best Poems of Shamsur Rahman* comprising English translations of more than a hundred poems written by one of the greatest contemporary poets in Bengali literature was released in 2005. The effort took two years and was acclaimed by the poet himself as a masterly reproduction of his best poems in English. Shankar Sen's second published work *Poetry of Changing Times* was an English translation of some rare poems written in Bengali by Utpal Dutt, the famous Indian stage and film actor, which were found after the thespian's death and compiled in a book *Din Badaler Kobita*. In 2006 *Down Memory Lane* a collection of Shankar Sen's own poems in English was released in Kolkata and this was followed by the publication of a collection of his Bengali poems, named *Shei Bakul Bicchano Pathey* in 2006 itself. *The Mystery of the Fortress* and Other Stories A Byomkesh Quintet is Sen's second publication in prose, following *First Love and Other Stories*, which was released in 2008, comprising English translations of some of the best short stories written in Bengali by Buddhadev Guha. Shankar Sen and his wife Rita live mostly in Kolkata, sharing their time with their two sons in the USA and Mumbai.

a BYOMKESH quintet

Saradindu Bandyopadhyay

The Mystery of the Fortress and Other Stories

TRANSLATED FROM BENGALI
BY **SHANKAR SEN**

NEW AGE

Saradindu Bandyopadhyay
The Mystery of the Fortress and Other Stories
Translated from Bengali by Shankar Sen.

Publisher
New Age Publishers (P) Ltd
8/1 Chintamoni Das Lane, Kolkata 700 009

First Published in English
by New Age Publishers (P) Ltd 2009

10 9 8 7 6 5 4

Illustrations and Cover design by Anup Roy.

ISBN 81-7819 065 6

Price Rs **450.00**

Contents

When Man grew ambitious, God destroyed the Tower of Babel and everyone began to speak in different tongues.
However, in His infinite grace, He also created people to rebuild those bridges to enable dialogue and the diffusion of human thought.
That person, whose name we so rarely take the trouble to notice when we open a foreign book, is the translator.

Paulo Coelho
in *The Other Side of the Tower of Babel*

Introduction

Even today— nearly four decades after Saradindu Bandyopadhyay's death his collections are rated as the number one bestseller in Bengali fiction— an unprecended record in a state, where the readers are as critical as they are obsessed with creative arts. Saradindu wrote poetry, novels, short stories and screenplays. But one of the most remarkable achievements of his literary career, which has perhaps contributed to a large extent in retaining his popularity at the highest level till today, is the creation of *Byomkesh Bakshi*, the super sleuth, a character which might have been inspired by Sherlock Holmes, but was flawlessly 'Indianised' through the literary genius of the author.

Byomkesh preferred to call himself *a seeker of truth*. Tall, slim and sharp-nosed, he possessed unique powers of deduction and could analyse complex situations to solve mysteries by using his keen intelligence. Saradindu never went beyond the realities of life in weaving a romantic web around his favourite character; rather, it is within the ambit of real life that *Byomkesh* thrived, growing from strength to strength and thrilling the hearts of many readers spanning across several generations. And yet *Byomkesh* is not a stereotypical super-hero. He blends with a middle-class background and in many ways, could be said to serve as a common man's conscience. He is gifted with extraordinary intelligence and analytical powers and had he not been a detective, he could have easily become an outstanding scientist or a brilliant mathematician.

The first *Byomkesh* story appeared in 1932 and the last— the thirty-third, was found half-finished after the author's death. Many of the thirty-two stories written on the adventures of *Byomkesh Bakshi* have already been translated in English, Hindi and other Indian languages. I am thankful to Prabir Chakravarti for providing me a list of hitherto 'untranslated' stories, from which I picked up this quintet with his kind permission. I acknowledge my gratitude to

Santanu Bandyopadhyay as well for his keen interest and appreciation of my effort to translate the work of his illustrious father. I have tried to reproduce the backgrounds and dialogues as close to the original Bengali version as I could, adhering, out of necessity, to the commonly used address of *Babu* after the names of gentlemen — an expression equivalent to *Mister* in English. But I must, without hesitation, plead my inadequacy in matching the absorbing page-turners composed by the author in his inimitable style.

Saradindu Bandyopadhyay died at the age of seventy-one. Three years before his death he was awarded the Rabindra Purashkar for his novel, *Tungabhadrar Tirey* (On the banks of river Tungabhadra). In the same year he was honoured by the Calcutta University with the Sarat Smriti Purashkar. But the greatest reward that he received during his lifetime and continues to receive till today, decades after his death, is the adoration of his readers, the people of Bengal. And in the midst of the creative world of Saradindu, *Byomkesh Bakshi* stands tall and high— immortalized by the pen of the master storyteller.

Ladies and gentlemen, welcome to the world of *Byomkesh*.

Kolkata **Shankar Sen**
February 2009

The Invisible Triangle

I had heard this story from Police Inspector Ramanimohan Sanyal. Byomkesh and I had gone to a town in Bihar on some confidential Government business and it was there that we became acquainted with Ramani Babu. Unwinding the red tape of Government files was taking time and we were thus obliged to spend many idle hours at the Dak-Bungalow. Ramani Babu used to call on us almost every evening for chitchat. '*Ramani*' in Bengali means a female and '*mohan*' implies a charmer and his appearance and demeanour were well-suited to his name, as he was both charming and soft-spoken. But that was merely a disguise. In reality he was a very shrewd and experienced officer of the Police Department. He was a little younger than us, not over forty, but similarity of temperaments made our evening sessions most enjoyable.

It had struck us, of course, that such frequent visits were perhaps not solely out of selfless compassion. We waited with the expectation that the true purpose of his visits would be revealed to us in due course.

Then one day he recounted a story to us. It was not exactly a story, rather a few sequences of a murder case. But the isolated events could be put together to draw up a well-composed anecdote.

After finishing his narrative Ramani Babu said, 'Byomkesh Babu, I know who committed the murder and I also know why he committed the murder; but I am still unable to send the man to the gallows because there is no proof. The only means to nab him is through a confession; the guilty man has to be made to admit his crime. You are capable of conjuring up such tricky ruses, can't you think of some trick to trap this man?'

Byomkesh smiled and said, 'I shall think over the matter.'

The story had drawn my interest. It might have made an impression on Byomkesh as well. That night after Ramani Babu had left, Byomkesh asked me, 'Can't you compose a story with all the ingredients which Ramani Babu provided to us?'

I said, 'I can. The ingredients are good. If only the psychology of the characters can be inserted, there can be a proper story.'

Byomkesh said, 'Then, go ahead. But there is one condition. You can't change the events for the sake of making the story more interesting.'

It took me two days to write up the story. When it was completed I gave it to Byomkesh, who read it and said, 'It seems to be all right. Let us show this to Ramani Babu and see what he says.'

When Ramani Babu called on us that evening I gave him my handwritten pages. After reading through the whole story, he seemed delighted and said, 'This is it! The psychology of the individuals has been perfectly matched with the incidents. But ...'

I am reproducing the story below ....

Shibaprasad Sarkar had become a prosperous man in the town through his wine business. He had a deep attachment for accumulating wealth; so in addition to a large house and an expensive motorcar, he had also amassed a lot of money. People used to call him a miser, but he preferred to think that he was frugal. The margin of difference between these two concepts is very narrow; however, we shall not try to go into all that.

But in Nature's kingdom there is always a balance. When Shibaprasad's only son, Sunil, who had lost his mother at an early age, reached adulthood, it was found that his character was just the reverse of his father's. He was a spendthrift and an extravagant youth. He had no attachment for money, but he was very fond of the many lawful and unlawful pleasures that could be acquired with the help of money. He went on squandering his father's money with reckless abandon.

Although not a blindly supportive father like King Dhritarashtra, Shibaprasad did have a lot of affection for his only son. Observing the son's wayward conduct, he got him married to a very pretty girl. But this failed to accomplish any permanent remedy. Sunil remained attached to his wife for some time but then reverted to his old habits.

The bride's name was Reba. She was not only good-looking, but also intelligent with a sound worldly sense. On top of this she was educated and possessed a modern outlook in keeping with the prevailing trend. Ignoring her husband's waywardness, she devoted herself to looking after her aged father-in-law with all earnestness. Shibaprasad had continued to manage his business himself till his old age, because his son was good-for-nothing and he did not trust his employees. Reba started taking over most of his responsibilities. She used to drive her father-in-law to his place of work, where she helped him in many ways and then drove him back home. In this way, Reba gradually took over the virtual role of Shibaprasad's son.

Four years after Reba and Sunil's marriage Shibaprasad expired. After his death it was found that he had left a Will, bequeathing all his possessions to his daughter-in-law.

Immediately after inheriting the estate, Reba sold out three-quarters share of the wine business, retaining a quarter share in her control. She also sold off the large house and purchased a small, compact house in a solitary location at the edge of the town. After disposing of the big car she bought a small Fiat for her own use. She then told her husband, 'You shall receive three hundred rupees per month towards your pocket expenses. I shall not be responsible if you borrow money in the market. I have already had a notice to this effect printed in the newspaper.'

Then they moved into the small house and started living there. They had no children.

Here ends the prologue of the story.

Sunil was around thirty. He had a firm, thick body and his face was round and flat like an owl's mug, which at first sight gave the impression that he was devoid of brains. It is seen that those who enjoy the pleasures of life by squandering their father's money are ruled more by their passion than through their intelligence. This is more or less a self-evident truth and needs no proof. Everybody took Sunil to be an intemperate, imprudent and stupid person.

But Sunil was not really stupid. He might have been devoid of good sense but he possessed plenty of mischievous craftiness. When he found after his father's death that the control of the estate had passed on to another hand he did not express any bitterness or anger. He seemed to become somewhat dull and unresponsive. As long as Shibaprasad was alive, it was he who had paid up the many debts incurred by Sunil in the market. But now that Reba had inserted a notice in the newspaper nobody was prepared to loan him money. What pleasure could one have with a mere ten rupees a day? So Sunil started spending his time at home like a good boy. He went out in the evening once or twice a week but spent the remaining days at home reading English thrillers. His relationship with Reba became merely a tie-up demanded by social custom. They had separate bedrooms. From outside they were seen to live in close proximity under the same roof, but in their minds they were separated by insurmountable barriers.

Reba used to drive out in her car in the morning. She used to go through the accounts of her quarter share of the wine business every day. Coming back in the afternoon she used to go out again in the evening — but not for work; she had joined a small ladies' club, where she spent time in games and chitchat and occasionally she went to the movies. Then she returned home. Sunil stayed at home all the time.

They had a middle-aged maidservant, named 'Anna', who attended to all domestic duties, including cooking. There was no other servant. Reba had curtailed her expenses in every possible way.

One evening Sunil was in the sitting room reading a mystery novel. Reba returned home at eight and locked up the car in the garage. She then changed her clothes and came and sat down on a sofa in the sitting room with a Bengali book in her hand. There was no conversation between husband and wife. It was not yet time for dinner. Reba opened her book and started reading. The name of the book was *Byomkesher Kahini* (The stories of Byomkesh).

Sunil's dull face was expressionless. He raised his face to glance at Reba; then lowered his eyes to his book. After a moment he cleared his throat.

'Reba.'

Reba raised her eyebrows and looked at him.

Sunil asked hesitantly, 'Have you noticed a man roaming about in front of our house?'

Reba folded her book and stared at Sunil's face for a moment, before saying, 'No. Why?'

Sunil spoke very slowly, 'For some time I have been noticing a man walking down the street staring at our house. Then he turns back and again goes past looking at our house.'

Reba pondered for a while and asked, 'What does the man look like?'

Sunil said, 'He looks like a thug. A dark, strong and robust fellow, wearing a turban.'

There was no conversation for some time. Then Reba made up her mind and said, 'Tomorrow morning you must go and file a report at the police station. This is a lonely place and if he is really a thug, it is better to inform the police in advance.'

Sunil looked a little disconcerted for a while and then said somewhat hesitantly, 'You are the owner of the house, wouldn't it be better if you filed the report with the police?'

Reba said, 'But I haven't seen the fellow. – All right, we'll both go.'

Next morning they went to the police station. Rather than going to the small police outpost of their locality they went directly to the head police station in the town. The officer-in-charge of the police station was Ramani Babu, a Bengali, with whom they were slightly acquainted.

Ramani Babu received them cordially. Sunil's way of talking was slow and indistinct. So Reba took it upon herself to recount the incident. After the report was filed Ramani Babu said, 'Your house is at the extreme end of the town. But don't worry. I shall make arrangements for a patrolling guard to keep an eye on your house.'

From the police station Reba went to her workplace, while Sunil went home on foot.

That evening Reba said, 'I'll not go out today. I am not feeling too well.'

Sunil put down his book and stood up, saying, 'Then let me go out for a stroll.'

An expression of displeasure was noticed on Reba's face as she said, 'You want to go out? But don't take too long, come back early. You may take the car if you wish.'

Sunil said, 'No, no, that won't be necessary. I would prefer to go on foot. Walking keeps me fit.'

Even in the midst of her anxiety Reba felt somewhat relieved. She had become quite attached to her small car, which she looked after with great care. The thought of handing over the car to Sunil did not appeal to her.

Sunil went out, wrapping a grey shawl around his shoulders. It was the onset of winter. Dusk descended by five in the evening. It became quite dark by the time Sunil reached a narrow lane in the central part of the town. He knocked on the door of a ramshackle house. A strong, robust fellow came out. Sunil lowered his voice and said, 'Hukum Singh, I need your service.'

Hukum Singh greeted Sunil with a salute. Hukum Singh and his brother Mukunda Singh were two well-known wrestlers and thugs of the town. They had a long acquaintance with Sunil. A wayward son of a rich man and a thug are drawn to each other like soul mates and their relationship becomes cordial in a most natural manner.

In a low voice Sunil issued some fast instructions to Hukum Singh and then thrust some bank notes in his hand before rushing out of the lane. In the dim light of the evening nobody noticed the man draped in a grey shawl; even if he was noticed, nobody would have recognized him as Sunil Sarkar. And in that squalid slum who could have possibly known Sunil Sarkar personally?

When Sunil reached home Reba asked, 'Why did you take so much time?'

It was evident that she was relieved on Sunil's return. Reba did not have an ounce of affection for Sunil, nor was she burdened with any social attitudes, which made it obligatory to love one's husband. At heart she was now independent and fully in control over herself.

But howsoever independent a woman may be, she cannot ever disclaim the confidence, which she gains from the mere presence of a strong man.

Sunil looked at his watch and said, 'I have not even been away for an hour. All I did was just stroll around a bit, nothing else.'

There was no further conversation. They had their tea and then they sat down with their books.

But Reba could not remain still. The main entrance door was closed, but still she got up from time to time and peeked at the road through the window. The road, stretching down from the town, had crossed Reba's house and then gone a little further before losing its existence in open meadows, bushes and thickets. The last lamppost on the road stood almost immediately in front of the house, casting a melancholy light.

After peeping through the window once again, Reba came back and sat down on the sofa. She picked up her book and went on staring at it without reading a word. Then she enquired with feigned disinterestedness, 'At what hour does the police guard commence his patrol?'

Raising his expressionless face from the book, Sunil kept staring for some time and then said, 'I have no idea. Perhaps from ten or eleven in the night.'

Reba's face showed an annoyed expression, but she did not say anything more. They went back to their respective books.

Exactly at the stroke of eight Reba raised her face, looking startled as she heard some sound outside. She rose to her feet and again peeped outside after moving the window curtain by a few inches. A man was walking down from the direction of the town. He was indistinctly visible in the dim light of the street lamp. A thickset figure, his head covered by a huge turban, which shaded his face, he carried a long stick in his hand. The fellow had his face turned towards Reba's house and he went on staring at the house all the while as he walked past.

Reba took a sharp breath. Casting a glance in her direction, Sunil noticed that her face had turned pale and that she was beckoning him with her hand without speaking. Sunil got up and stood beside Reba.

Reba whispered, 'It is probably the same man whom you had seen.'

Sunil nodded his head. They remained standing by the window. After a while the crunching sound of *nagra* shoes treading on the road was heard again. The man was coming back. Reba stopped breathing.

The man was walking back towards the town looking intently at the house, as he passed.

After the sound of his footsteps had died down, Reba looked at Sunil, her eyes filled with questions. Sunils's heart was brimming with satisfaction, but he forced an expression of doubt on his face and said, 'Looks like the same man.'

They returned to their respective seats. Reba's face remained torn in anxiety. Sunil cast a sidelong glance at her and then opened his book.

The maid came and announced that dinner was ready. Then they sat down for dinner.

In course of the meal Sunil commented, 'There is probably no cause to be concerned. When the police have said that they would keep an eye on things … .'

Reba's anger was unleashed in an outburst of passion, 'The policeman is not going to stand guard in front of the house for the whole night, he would only pass by from time to time in course of his patrol. In between his rounds if a gang of dacoits break open the door and enter the house, what shall we do then?'

Sunil cast his eyes down and went on eating. In the end he asked, 'Do we have anything like a stick or a staff?'

Reba cast a look of utter disgust at her husband, considering it unnecessary to reply to his childish query. Even if a stick or a staff was available in the house, who was going to use it?

That night Reba carefully bolted the door of her room before going to bed. She knew that it was unnecessary to take such precautions because Ramani Babu had made adequate arrangements for her safety. But still she could not get over her anxiety. She remained awake for a long time while lying on her bed, her mind troubled by random thoughts.

It would have been better if she had not purchased this house in such a secluded area of the town, but who knew then that this was going to happen? Now she would lose face if she moved out from this house under the threat of thugs, ... her husband was devoid of worldly wisdom and was utterly useless, ... what could she do? Should she engage two able-bodied male servants? But how much could one rely on a male servant? The protector could well turn into a ravager. The dacoits could bribe the servants and get them to open the door at night for getting free entry into the house...from that consideration 'Anna', her present maidservant was a safer choice... there were some costly ornaments in the bedroom safe, but not a single weapon for self-protection....

Suddenly she remembered some thing and sat up excitedly on the bed.

Her father-in-law had owned a pistol. After his death it had been surrendered to the police about six months earlier. Could she get back the pistol? She would go and see Ramani Babu at the police station in the morning. With a pistol in the house what was there to be afraid of?

Considerably relieved of her worries Reba fell asleep.

Next morning Reba again went to the police station accompanied by Sunil. On the way she responded to Sunil's unspoken queries by saying, 'Father's pistol was surrendered to the police. Wouldn't it be a good idea to have it back?'

Sunil's eyes became wide as if the thought had not occurred to him at all and he pondered for a while, before nodding his head and saying, 'Good idea.'

At the police station Ramani Babu, on hearing the proposal, said, 'No problem. All you have to do is to make out an application. In whose name do you want the licence to be issued?'

Reba had not thought about this issue. She was a woman and had no experience in handling firearms. But not wishing to disclose this, she quickly responded by saying, 'In his name, of course,' and pointed towards Sunil.

Ramani Babu said, 'That can be done. Why don't you submit an application right now. I shall make a token visit to your house for an investigation just to comply with rules. You shall get the pistol tomorrow.'

Reba wrote the application and Sunil signed it. Ramani Babu asked, 'Sunil Babu, have you ever used a gun or a pistol?'

Sunil faltered and said, 'Umm—no — yes – a long time back I had taken my father's pistol without his knowledge and fired a few shots—I was very young then, — umm...'

Ramani Babu smiled and said, 'Your action had been illegal. Barring the licence-holder none else is authorized to use a firearm. But then no rules apply in an emergency. When faced with real danger any one is entitled to use a weapon.'

Ramani Babu came that evening to conduct his enquiry. He was served tea and light refreshments and chatted for an hour or so before taking his leave. He left with the impression that Sunil was stupid and dull and that Reba was dragging him around by his nose. A half-wit with money to squander becomes wayward and that is what had happened to Sunil, but he was now a reformed character. This was Ramani Babu's conclusion, but he had failed to recognize Sunil's true nature.

On the following day Sunil collected the licence and the pistol from the police station. He also bought a box of cartridges from a gun-shop.

When Reba returned home in the afternoon Sunil placed the revolver and the box of cartridges on the table and asked her to keep them in her custody.

But Reba looked apprehensively at the firearm and said, 'What shall I do with them? Keep them with you, since it is you who shall have to use the revolver if needed.'

That is exactly what Sunil had expected. He picked up the revolver and cartridges without a word and took them to his room.

Two days later the turbaned rogue was seen once again passing by the road. But thereafter his visits stopped.

When a week passed without any incident, Reba breathed a sigh of relief and said, 'Those people have probably come to know that we are now in possession of a firearm and that is why they have abandoned their plan.'

Nodding his head like a wise man, Sunil said, 'Hmm.'

Thereafter as days passed, Reba's mind became more and more calm and carefree. The household was restored to its normal routine. Reba went to work in the morning and in the evening she went out for relaxing with her friends. Sunil remained at home reading mystery novels, going out occasionally for an hour or so in the evening. He had no friends. Some times he went to the railway station to buy books from the bookstall and on a few occasions he went to the dingy part of the town to meet Hukum Singh. The job that he had in mind for Hukum Singh was not over yet.

Two months passed in this manner; the winter season was almost over. Fear of possible assault by thugs had by now disappeared from Reba's mind.

One evening two of Reba's friends called on her. She and her friends soon became engrossed in eating, chatting and laughter. When Reba's friends called at her house they had a tendency to ignore Sunil all together, not even giving him the recognition due to a domestic servant. So on their arrival Sunil either remained closeted in his room or went out of the house. On this day he first went to his room and then quietly left the house through the rear exit. He had been waiting for just such an opportunity for a long time.

Sunil walked down to the town and met Hukum Singh in the dingy lane where he lived. After listening to his instructions for about ten minutes, Hukum Singh said, 'I am informed that there is a pistol in the house.'

Sunil took out the revolver from his pocket and showed it to him. He then opened the chamber and showed Hukum Singh that there was no cartridge in it. He said, 'You can enter the house without fear.'

Hukum Singh opened his palm and asked, 'My reward?'

Sunil had saved six hundred rupees in the two previous months. Handing over the sum to Hukum Singh, he said, 'Here, take this. I do not have any more money with me at this time. After you finish your work you may take the ornaments that she is wearing. When I become the owner of the estate you shall receive ten thousand rupees. I am now going to the Railway Station. I shall return home after eight.'

Hukum Singh said, 'Very well.'

'Would you remember every thing that I told you?'

'Yes sir. You can put your mind at rest. I'll finish my make-up and proceed right away.'

Hukum Singh entered his hovel to apply soot on his face for disguise. Sunil did not go to the railway station, he started walking back rapidly towards his home.

It had grown quite dark. Drawing close to his house Sunil found that Reba's friends were still there. Feeling relieved, he took shelter behind a large tree by the roadside. He took out the pistol from his pocket. In his other pocket he was carrying the cartridges, which he took out and loaded the pistol. Then, fully ready, he waited behind the tree.

Reba's friends left after some time. Reba closed the main door from inside.

It was half past seven. Reba called Anna and asked her, 'Where is Babu?'

Anna said, 'Babu has gone out. When your friends arrived by the front entrance, Babu left by the rear door.'

'All right. Get on with your cooking.'

Reba was totally relaxed. She was no longer scared of thugs. Her thoughts turned to other matters and she felt content. She would have nothing to complain about if her life continued in this manner.

Sunil was lying in wait outside, hidden behind the tree. Hukum Singh was seen walking down from the direction of the town. He was treading softly; there was no sound of his *nagra* shoes on this occasion.

Standing in front of the main entrance, he looked up and down the street and then knocked softly on the door.

Reba thought that Sunil must have returned home; she opened the door. Hukum Singh rushed in and grabbed her throat with both hands.

Reba emitted a half-scream, after which there was no other sound. Anna had heard the scream from the kitchen and peeping out, she saw that a black-faced ruffian was squeezing Reba's throat. Without uttering a word Anna retreated to the kitchen and bolted the door from inside.

When Hukum Singh observed that Reba's body was lifeless, he laid her down on the floor. Removing the ornaments from Reba's hands and ears, he put them in his pocket. Then he went out by the front door.

Hidden behind the tree Sunil had been waiting for this particular moment. He came out screaming, 'Hey, who are you? What are you doing here?' As Hukum Singh remained standing in a nonplussed manner, Sunil raised the pistol and emptied all the bullets on his chest. Hukum Singh crumbled down on the ground and did not move again.

Sunil then rushed into the house screaming, 'What's happened?' Then at the sight of Reba, he cried out, 'Oh – Reba —!'

On hearing Sunil's voice Anna came out of the kitchen still shaken up. Sunil addressed her in an anxious voice, 'Anna, how did this happen? The thug must have killed Reba! But I too have killed the thug!' He jumped up, screaming, 'Police! I am going to inform the police.' And he ran out of the house.

The police arrived in due course. Anna reported to the police what she had witnessed.

Ramani Babu arrived on hearing the news. Sunil looked at him with a vacant expression and said, 'I had gone out for a walk. As I was returning home and had drawn close to our house I heard a scream. I came running and saw that man emerging from our house. I lost my head and shot him dead with the pistol. Then on entering the house I saw ...' He turned his eyes towards Reba's body and then covered his face with both hands.

After a few minutes' silence Ramani Babu enquired, 'You carried the pistol when you went for a walk?'

Sunil nodded and said, 'Yes. The pistol is held in my name. I always keep it with me.'

Ramani Babu said, 'Give me the pistol. I am confiscating it.'

Sunil handed over the pistol without protest. He did not need it any more.

Byomkesh said, 'Sunil Sarkar may look stupid, but he has brains.'

Ramani Babu smiled sadly and said, 'Byomkesh Babu, I used to think that I was intelligent, but Sunil Sarkar has proved me wrong. I had failed to grasp his strategy. Now there is no way that I can charge him with the murder of Hukum Singh. It has been established that Hukum Singh had entered his house, throttled his wife and snatched her ornaments; so Sunil had every right to kill him. He thus killed two birds with a single stone. He gained control over his father's wealth and got rid of the sole witness to his crime. Being the nearest kin, he has inherited his wife's assets after her death. Reba had left no Will. After obtaining an order from the court, Sunil is now in control of every thing.'

Byomkesh said, 'Hmm' and became engrossed in thought.

Ramani Babu said, 'Please think of some strategy, Byomkesh Babu. I find it simply intolerable to think that the crooked rogue shall merrily go on enjoying the rest of his life after fooling the law.'

Byomkesh raised his face and asked, 'Reba was fond of reading Ajit's books?'

Ramani Babu replied, 'Yes. I have searched their house from top to bottom, but could find no evidence, which would have served my purpose. But I did notice that the books on all your exploits written by Ajit Babu were there and they all carried Reba's name written in her hand. This would indicate that Reba used to love reading about your adventures.'

Byomkesh became immersed in thought once again. We lit up cigarettes and waited to see if any magical solution would emerge from his prodigious brain.

After ten minutes or so Byomkesh stirred and sat up in his chair. We looked expectantly at his face.

He asked, 'Ramani Babu, can you get hold of Reba's handwriting?'

'Handwriting?' Ramani Babu raised his eyebrows.

Byomkesh explained, 'Say, — her book of accounts or a handwritten note, from which we can get an idea of the style of her handwriting.'

Ramani Babu sat thinking with his face resting on his palm; in the end he said, 'I can try. But what is the plan?'

Byomkesh said, 'The plan is this. – Reba was fond of reading the stories written about my cases. So it was not impossible that she should write to me for my autograph. We get constant proof of this weakness among women. Suppose Reba had written to me six months ago; she had asked for my autograph, then informed me that her husband was planning to murder her and if I heard that she had met with an unnatural death I should investigate the matter.'

Ramani Babu thought deeply for a while and then said, 'Now I understand. You shall prepare a forged letter and then show it to Sunil for extracting his confession.'

Byomkesh said, 'I shall try to obtain a confession. If Sunil gets scared and admits the truth, then only he can be caught.'

Ramani Babu said, 'I only have to get a sample of the handwriting. Any thing else?'

Byomkesh asked, 'Did Reba have any printed letter pads in her name?'

'She did. You'll get that too. What else?'

'And – a tape-recording machine. If Sunil does confess it would be advisable to have it properly recorded.'

'All right. I shall see you tomorrow morning,'

Ramani Babu seemed quite excited as he took leave of us.

We had just got up from bed next morning when Ramani Babu arrived. He was carrying a leather satchel in his hand. He smiled and said, 'I have got what you wanted.'

Byomkesh offered him a cigarette and asked, 'What have you have brought?'

Ramani Babu opened the satchel and carefully took out a piece of paper, which he held before us, saying, 'Here, — this is Reba's handwriting.'

It was a torn portion of a letter on which a few lines were written in Bengali —'If a husband has no obligations to his wife, why should the wife have any obligation towards the husband? We belong to the modern era, there is no point in clinging to antiquated traditions –'

Byomkesh enquired, 'This is Reba's handwriting? But I notice that it does not bear any signature. Where did you get this?'

Ramani Babu took out a whole lot of blank notepapers from the satchel and said, 'And here are Reba's printed letterheads. Last night I went straight from here to Sunil's house and told him bluntly that I wanted to search his house once more. He raised no objections. – Now tell me, would this serve your purpose?'

Byomkesh was still examining the torn piece of the letter as he said, 'It would. And it shouldn't be difficult to copy Reba's handwriting. It is easy to copy the writing of people, who follow the style of Rabindranath's handwriting. — Have you been able to procure a tape-recorder?'

'I have,' Ramani Babu replied, 'I'll produce it whenever you want. – Have you decided on an auspicious date for launching the action?'

Byomkesh thought for a while and then said, 'Why not today? The sooner the better. I am addressing a letter to Sunil, which you may please get delivered to him by some one.'

Byomkesh wrote on a plain note sheet –

Shri Sunil Sarkar –

I had become acquainted with your wife through exchange of letters. She was fond of reading the stories written about me. I am sad to learn of her death.

I have come here some time back and am staying at the Dak Bungalow. If you could call on me at seven this evening at the Dak Bungalow, I can show you the last letter that your wife had written to me. The letter could be of importance to you.

Sincerely,
Byomkesh Bakshi.

Byomkesh put the letter in an envelope and handed it over to Ramani Babu, who got to his feet and said, 'I shall get the letter delivered to Sunil in a way so that he wouldn't even guess that you have any link with the police. I shall bring the tape-recorder in the afternoon.'

After he had left Byomkesh sat down with Reba's handwritten note. He went on examining it from various angles. He observed the paper after raising it against light and closely scrutinized the torn edge. Then he lit a cigarette and started smoking.

I asked, 'What did you find?'

Byomkesh blew smoke towards the ceiling and said, 'The letter was whole and has been torn recently. I am only wondering where the top and bottom portions of the letter could have gone.'

I thought for some time and then suggested, 'Reba might have written the letter to one of her girlfriends, from whom Ramani Babu collected it. Perhaps the girlfriend does not want her name to be disclosed.'

'Could be. May be Reba's girlfriend had laid out a prior condition to Ramani Babu that her name should not be divulged, which is why Ramani Babu evaded my query. Any way, — let the exercise in forgery begin. Ajit, please get me some paper and a pen.'

For the next two hours Byomkesh practiced copying Reba's handwriting. Then he handed over the original and his copy to me and said, 'See how it has come out. Of course, I had to do the signature by guess-work; it would have been helpful if I had a sample. But I think this would do.'

Placing Reba's note and Byomkesh's draft side by side, I observed that there was hardly any difference in the style of writing. To a layman Byomkesh's writing could easily be declared as Reba's handwriting. I said, 'It would do.'

Byomkesh then devoted his attention to composing a letter. He took a lot of time in slowly writing a letter on Reba's printed pad. The letter read as follows –

Respected Byomkesh Babu,

I cannot tell you how happy I felt on receiving your letter and autograph.

I know that there are many other readers like me, who admire you and bother you for your autograph. But despite all that, you have written a few lines to me, for which I am most grateful. I am carefully pinning down your autograph in my notebook.

Encouraged by your magnanimity I am writing some thing about myself. —

My husband is devoid of worldly wisdom and is a loose character, which is why my father-in-law left me all his wealth through a Will executed before his death. The estate is of considerable worth and I do not let my husband lay his hands on it. I suspect that my husband is planning to murder me; most probably he has engaged some thugs. I do not know what would happen. But if you suddenly come to hear that I have met with an unnatural death, do please investigate the matter. You are a seeker of truth. I am quite certain that you would not remain silent on the death of a helpless woman.

With my deepest respects,
Sincerely,
Reba Sarkar.

Byomkesh folded the letter and put it in an old envelope.

Ramani Babu arrived at three in the afternoon, accompanied by a young policeman. He was a radio-mechanic and was carrying a tape-recorder along with a microphone and other accessories.

After consulting Byomkesh, Ramani Babu told the mechanic, 'Okay, Biren, you may get on with your job.'

Biren said, 'Yes sir,' and started his work.

The mike was fitted to the suspended light above the centre table in the sitting room and the tape recorder was installed in Byomkesh's bedroom. When the tape recorder was run it made some noise, which would not be heard in the sitting room.

When everything was set, Biren went to the bedroom and closed the door. We sat around the table in the sitting room and talked in our normal tone. After a while we went to the other room. Biren re-winded the tape and switched on the machine. Then we could hear our conversation. The sound was quite distinct and we had no problem in identifying our voices.

Byomkesh was satisfied and he said, 'This is fine. – Have you sent the letter?'

Ramani Babu said, 'Yes, I have. He would come — most certainly. Some one with a guilty conscience shall be compelled to come when he receives such a letter. He would want to know if you are intent on blackmailing him.

Right then, we shall push off now and return after dusk.'

Ramani Babu arrived exactly at six, accompanied by Biren. A police van dropped them and went back.

Ramani Babu said, 'I came a bit early, just in case Sunil chooses to come before seven.'

Byomkesh said, 'You did the right thing. You and Biren shall remain in the bedroom in the beginning, so that Sunil does not know that we have any thing to do with the police. Ajit and I shall stay in the sitting room. After Sunil's arrival you may join us at an appropriate time.'

Ramani Babu said, 'That's a good idea.' He then took Biren to the bedroom and closed the door. Byomkesh and I remained in the sitting room, all set for the meeting.

Gradually it became dark. I got up to switch on the lights and sat down again. Byomkesh picked up the morning newspaper and started running his eyes on the pages. I lit a cigarette. Our ears had become very alert.

A few minutes before seven we heard the sound of a motorcar arriving and stopping in front of the main gate of the Dak Bungalow. Byomkesh and I exchanged glances. After two or three minutes Sunil Sarkar came and stood outside our door.

There was not much disparity with Ramani Babu's description; in addition, I observed that the front teeth visible between his lips looked vicious as a crocodile's snout. Sharp teeth on a blunt face; all together not a charming appearance. On top of which he was a depraved character. Reba's devotion to her husband may not have been anywhere close to that of Sita or Sabitri, but she could not be blamed for her shortcoming. Sunil Sarkar was nowhere near the likes of Ram or Satyaban.

Sunil stood foolishly for some time near the door, and then spoke in a broken voice, 'Byomkesh Babu —'

Byomkesh was sitting with his eyes fixed on the newspaper. He now lifted his face and said, 'Sunil Babu, please come in.'

Wearing a blank look on his face, Sunil came in like a clumsy dolt and stood by the table. Who would say that there was any semblance of brains in his head? Byomkesh stared at him from head to toe with hard, dispassionate eyes and then said, 'You are doing your play-acting quite well, but you are not as stupid as you are trying to act. – Sit down.'

Sunil plumped into a chair. Looking at Byomkesh with bulbuous eyes, he said in a faltering voice, 'What, what are you saying?'

Byomkesh said, 'Nothing. Since you are bent on acting like a fool, it is pointless to discuss that topic. – Sunil Babu, for the purpose of acquiring control of your father's property you have murdered two persons. The first was your wife and the second was Hukum Singh. I have conducted a thorough investigation after coming here. You got your wife murdered by Hukum Singh and then you killed Hukum Singh with your own hands. Hukum Singh was a partner in your crime, so you had to remove him. If he had been alive he would have exploited you for the rest of his life. You killed two birds with a single stone.'

Sunil was listening with his mouth wide open. Now, he started protesting loudly, 'What are you saying? I killed Reba! A thug, whose name was Hukum Singh, throttled my wife to death. Anna saw this with her own eyes, — Anna saw Hukum Singh throttling Reba and killing her.'

Byomkesh said, 'Hukum Singh was a hired killer. You had paid him money.'

'No, no, these are all lies. I did not get Reba murdered. She was my wife, I used to love her.'

'I have proof of how much you loved Reba here in my pocket,' as he said this, Byomkesh tapped his fingers on his breast pocket.

'What is it? Reba's letter? Let me see what she had written to you!'

Byomkesh took out the letter and while handing it to Sunil, he said, 'Don't bother to tear up this letter. I have several photostat copies.'

Sunil did not seem to hear the warning. Opening the letter he held it in both hands and went on reading it with concentration.

At this time Ramani Babu came out, quietly opening the door and stood beside Byomkesh's chair. They looked at each other and Byomkesh nodded his head.

When Sunil finished reading the letter and raised his eyes he first saw Ramani Babu. In an instant the mask of stupidity slipped off from his face. Exposing sharp teeth on his blunt face, he stood up and screamed, 'Oh, sò this is the game! A police plot to implicate me.—Byomkesh Babu, do you know who is responsible for Reba's death? That Ramani Inspector.' As he said this he pointed his finger at Ramani Babu.

We were not prepared for any counter-attack from Sunil. Byomkesh raised his eyebrows in surprise and enquired, 'Ramani Babu is responsible! What do you mean?'

Sunil said, 'You don't understand? Inspector Ramani was Reba's bosom friend, in other words, — her sweetheart. That is why he has such a strong grudge against me.'

There was a brief silence in the room. I looked at Ramani Babu. He had his eyes riveted on Sunil's face and his whole body seemed to have become taut and flushed like a piece of heated iron. I was filled with apprehension that there might be an explosion any moment.

Byomkesh spoke in a calm voice, 'Is that why you got your wife murdered?'

Sunil said, 'I did not get her murdered. You had thought of trapping me with this forged letter!' He crumpled the letter in his fist and then threw it down on the table.—'It is not that easy to trap Sunil Sarkar. I am off. If you have guts, arrest me. I shall then show you what I can do.'

We sat dumbstruck as Sunil left the room with the weaving motion of a reptile.

Within these last few moments Sunil's real character seemed to have taken a distinct shape before our eyes. Devious, deceitful and cruel as a deadly snake, which raised its head to strike in the blinking of an eye and disappeared into its hole the very next moment. An extremely dangerous person.

Ramani Babu released a deep sigh and sat down on a chair. Byomkesh spoke, somewhat to himself, 'He couldn't be trapped.'

Suddenly, we were startled as we heard a moaning sound from outside. Byomkesh was the first to move towards the door. We followed him.

Sunil's motorcar was parked in front of the Dak Bungalow and the body stretched near its front wheels belonged to him. The handle of a knife was protruding from his back.

In the agony of death Sunil tried to turn to his side. Byomkesh and I tried to assist him, but our assistance was of no use in his ultimate moments. Sunil opened his eyes once; it was not clear if he recognized us; but he spoke two words in an inarticulate voice, 'Mukunda Singh.'

Then his heart stopped beating.

I looked up and down the road, but could not see anybody. The road was empty. A single question went on whirling in my benumbed brain—who was Mukunda Singh? The name was familiar. Then I remembered, — Mukunda Singh was Hukum Singh's brother. He had taken revenge of his brother's death.

It was nearly half past nine by the time the body had been sent for postmortem and other legal formalities had been completed. Ramani Babu looked totally exhausted as he came and sat with us. Biren was still waiting in the next room with his equipment. Ramani Babu called him and said, 'You may go home. Let the machine remain here. I shall take it with me.'

Biren departed.

All three of us smoked silently for some time. Then Byomkesh said, 'Sunil may have eluded the law, but he could not evade the hands of destiny. Strange! Some times even thugs can solve problems involving moral issues.'

Ramani Babu said, 'One problem has been solved, but simultaneously another problem has come up. Now I have to arrest Mukunda Singh. My job is not over yet, Byomkesh Babu.'

After smoking in silence for some time, Byomkesh asked softly, 'Sunil's accusation was correct then?'

Ramani Babu sighed and said, 'Yes. Reba and I came from the same locality of the same town. I knew her from childhood, but there was never any love or anything like that between us.... Then after Reba was married to that monster, I happened to meet her in this very town.... she was not a bad sort ... I do not know how and what happened between us ... I had no suspicion that Sunil had come to know ... I had taken him to be a fool, but after Reba's death I realized that he was as deadly as a cobra ... I had tried to trap him, but failed ... then you came here and I made a last attempt with your help.'

Byomkesh said, 'The torn piece of the note that you gave me was from a letter which Reba had written to you?'

Ramani Babu said, 'Yes. We did not have much opportunity to meet. Reba used to write letters to me, baring her heart. She had written many letters. But let's not talk any more about Reba. Byomkesh Babu, tell me what should be done with the tape-recording.'

Byomkesh said, 'What is there to do with the recording? Let us erase it. Come.'

We went to the next room and switched on the recorder. The live voice of the man just murdered came over on the mike. Then the tape was erased.

Iron Biscuits

Kamal Babu said, 'I live in your neighbourhood, close to Hindusthan Park. I have seen you often and wanted to get acquainted, but I did not have the nerve to approach you. Today I had an excuse to call on you and I thought I would take this opportunity of getting acquainted with you as well. I am faced with a small problem.'

'Problem?' Byomkesh extended the cigarette tin towards his guest and said, 'Let's hear it. I haven't come across anything with the remotest hint of a problem for a long time.'

It was a Sunday morning on a hot summer day and this conversation was taking place at Byomkesh's house in Keyatolla. Kamal Babu was a chubby-looking person, but his features were sharp and intelligent. He accepted a cigarette with a smile and then started narrating his story, 'My name is Kamalkrishna Das. I work as a cashier in the nearby branch of the Indian Central Bank. I was transferred here from Purulia about a year and a half back.

'On my arrival at Calcutta I faced the usual problem of not finding a suitable living accommodation. Finally a gentleman let me occupy a single room in the ground floor of his building. Naturally I could not fetch my family to Calcutta. Leaving my wife and daughter at Purulia, I started living here all by myself in the single room.

'My landlord's name was Akshoy Mondol. His building was two-storied, having two rooms on the ground floor and two rooms on the first floor with separate access to each floor. Akshoy Mondol lived alone in the first floor, but he had frequent visitors. He was a soft-spoken person, but I had no idea about his occupation. He had an account with our bank and some times he used to come down to my room for chatting with me, but he never invited me upstairs. He also had no interaction with any of the neighbours.

'Around three months passed in this manner. One night I was a little late in returning home after attending a dinner invitation at a colleague's residence. On reaching home I saw Akshoy Mondol coming down from upstairs and then locking the staircase door. He had two packed suitcases near his feet and was somewhat startled when I accosted him and asked, "Where are you off to so late at night?" Carrying one suitcase in each hand, he came and stood close to me and said in a deep voice, "Kamal Babu, I am suddenly required to go out of town. I cannot say when I shall return."

'I noticed that his eyes were flushed. I asked, "But what happened? Where are you going?"

'There was a glimmer of a smile on his face, as he said, "Very far. Goodbye."

'As I kept standing foolishly, he stopped after walking a few steps and then came back to me and said, "Kamal Babu, you are an honest man and you work in a bank. Let me tell you some thing before I go. If I do not return within seven days, please take possession of my entire house. I have an account with your bank, where you may deposit one hundred and fifty rupees each month as rent. Now I have to be off. Goodbye."

'After Akshoy Mondol had left I stood there filled with confusion for some time. But when I got over my initial surprise it struck me that Akshoy Mondol had not left his door-key with me.

'I must admit that I was delighted with the prospect of getting possession of the whole house. I had a feeling that Akshoy Mondol had set out on an inauspicious journey and was unlikely to return soon.

'Next morning I sent a letter to my wife,— pack up and keep yourself in readiness; there are bright chances of securing a flat.

'I spent two days in high hope. On the third day I was hit by a foul stench. It was a terrible stench, the smell of decomposed corpse. Just like the stench that comes out from any fish or meat, which gets rotted in heat.

'I got suspicious and informed the police, who broke open the lock and climbed upstairs. I went up along with them. What we saw was a dreadful sight. There was a dead body lying on the floor, with hands and feet stretched out and a dark hole on the forehead. Akshoy Mondol must have shot the person dead on the evening when I was out for dinner and then fled with all his valuable possessions packed in two suitcases.

'Soon a large number of policemen surrounded the house. The body was sent for postmortem. The Inspector interrogated me. And then a full-scale search of the house was commenced. I and another resident of the locality were present as neutral witnesses.

'Nothing worthwhile was found in course of the search. Only a few small box-like articles, made of iron foils, were found in a drawer. The foils were longish in shape, somewhat like the silvery foils used for covering cigarettes in a packet; they were composed of very thin laminates of iron but were hollow inside. The Inspector picked them up and examined them closely for a long time, but no one could think of any purpose, which those light cartons of iron could serve.

'Any way, the investigation was closed for that day. The police left. But my mind was still not at ease. After three or four days I went to the police station and came to learn that the dead man had been identified from his fingerprints and other physical evidence as Harihar Singh, a criminal with a past record, who dealt in drugs and smuggling of gold and silver. The sources of his connection with Akshoy Mondol had still not been traced. A warrant had been issued in the name of Akshoy Mondol, but he had not yet been apprehended; he seemed to have simply disappeared from the face of the city.

'Before leaving the police station, I asked the Inspector a little hesitantly, "Can I now take possession of the whole house?"

'The Inspector told me, "Of course. Since the accused had put you in charge of his house before absconding, you are certainly entitled to stay there. But remember, if you get to hear any news about him, you must forthwith report the matter to the police station."

'Thereafter, a year or so passed quite peacefully. I fetched my wife and daughter from Purulia and after taking possession of the whole house, I have been living there in utmost comfort with my family. Every month I deposit the rent in Akshoy Mondol's account with our bank. I use his tables and chairs only, but not his almirahs or cupboards, which are lying just as they were left by the police after their search.

'Trouble cropped up all of a sudden about two months back. One morning I was in the ground floor, reading the newspaper, when a stranger arrived, accompanied by a woman. The man was middle-aged and had the look of a gentleman; the woman was obviously married. Pointing his finger at the woman, the man said, "This is Akshoy Mondol's wife and I am his elder brother. She has been putting up with me for all these days, but I cannot afford to maintain her any longer. Now she shall stay in her husband's house. You shall have to vacate this place."

'It was like a bolt from the blue. I looked blankly at them for a while. Then I had a sudden brainwave. I said, "I had never heard that Akshoy Babu was married. But if what you are saying is true, you may apply to the court and establish your claim. Then we shall see."

'The visitors had not expected such response from me. They went on arguing and abusing me for quite some time, but eventually they went away. I suspected that they were cheats and had wanted to occupy the house under false pretexts. The way rents have gone up these days, who would give up an opportunity of acquiring a house for nothing?

'I went to the police station and reported the incident to the Inspector, who said, "We have no information if Akshoy Mondol has a wife. Any way, if they come again bring them to the police station on some pretext. Meanwhile, we too shall keep a watch on the house."

'I own a pistol and I also have a pet dog, —a ferocious, mountain-breed, whom I call Bhuto. He eats only from my hands and from nobody else. I unchain him when I go to the bank and I also set him loose at night when he guards the house. No thief would dare enter the house while Bhuto is loose, he would tear the intruder to pieces. But still I felt some misgiving in my mind after this incident. Akshoy Mondol was not a good man, he was perhaps staging some crooked game while staying out of sight.

'After ten days or so I received an anonymous letter, "Leave this locality and go away, or else you shall be in grave danger." Obviously 'locality' implied the house. I showed the letter to the Inspector, who said, "Sit tight, don't budge. I am increasing the watch on your house."

'Since then, no one has called on me during the last one and a half months, nor have I received any further anonymous letters. I have been feeling a little secure now. But then another problem has cropped up. And that is why I have come to you. I could have gone to the Inspector, but he would have probably suggested some thing, which wouldn't have been to my liking.

'The situation is like this. I have a month's accumulated leave. My wife has been wanting since long to go on a pilgrimage to Hardwar, Hrishikesh and a few other places. An office colleague is also availing of leave. He is going on a trip organised by a travel agency and is pressing me to accompany him. Travelling in a group has many advantages. My wife has become very enthusiastic. My enthusiasm is no less. But... .

'If we decide to go we shall have to lock up the house before we leave. I shall also have to put Bhuto in some kennel for a month or so. The house shall remain unguarded. Supposing, in our absence Akshoy Mondol's wife, I mean, — that woman, breaks open the lock and takes possession of the house, what shall I do then? I have no other right save and except Akshoy Mondol's verbal permission. Because I am in possession of the house at this time they shall be required to go to court if they want to evict me. But if they manage to take possession of the house in my absence where do I stand?'

'This is my problem—purely a domestic matter—hardly worthy of your investigation. But still I came here, hoping to kill two birds with a single stone—making your acquaintance and telling you about my dilemma. Now, would you please tell me whether it would be advisable for me to leave the house and go on pilgrimage.'

Byomkesh sat for a while, with his hands on his cheeks. He then said, 'It wouldn't be proper to stop you from going on a pilgrimage and then again it is not desirable that you should lose possession of the house. Don't you have any able-bodied man among your acquaintances whom you can leave in charge of the house before going?'

'No, I can't think of anyone like that. Everybody has his own home. And those who don't—to tell you frankly—I dare not leave any of them in charge of the vacant house; I might end up digging my own grave'

'Then let's go and have a look at your house,' Byomkesh got to his feet.

Kamal Babu was elated when he heard this. He exclaimed, 'You'll come! Oh, that's wonderful! Let's go then. It's not very far.'

'Hang on for a moment. It may not be too far, but the sun is quite strong. Let me get my umbrella.'

Byomkesh went inside and fetched his favourite umbrella. Old and worn out, its iron handle and spokes had become rusted; the cloth was faded and contained several holes. But then walking in the streets with this umbrella, one could remain unseen while following any suspicious person. The suspect could be seen through the holes, but the outsiders could not see the face of the umbrella-holder. It was a befitting umbrella for one, who was dedicated to seek the truth.

'Let's go.'

Kamal Babu's house was at a distance of about five minutes' walk from Byomkesh's residence. Byomkesh had noticed the house some times while passing by that way. It was a small two-storeyed building. But it had a special feature, which caught the eye. The entire roof was covered by a frame of iron rods and strips, giving the impression of an enormous iron cage. It was impossible to approach the roof from outside.

On reaching his house, Kamal Babu said, 'Please come in.'

Byomkesh folded his umbrella and entered the house. Kamal Babu took him first to the sitting room in the ground floor. Barring a bed covered with a durrie and two canvas chairs there was nothing else in that room. Byomkesh cast his eyes all around, as if trying to find a clue, but in that almost bare room he could find nothing to serve as a pointer. He asked, 'Isn't there another room in the ground floor?'

'Yes. The second room was not used by Akshoy Mondol, but I have converted it into a kitchen. Would you like to see it?'

'No, that won't be necessary. And moreover, your wife is probably busy with her cooking. Let us go and see the first floor.'

'Please come.'

A narrow verandah ran alongside the room and the staircase was located at the end of the verandah. There was a door at the top of the staircase and a piece of iron, shaped like a horseshoe, was hung on the wall above the door suspended between three nails. Byomkesh stared at the object for some time and then pointing his umbrella towards it, he asked, 'What is that?'

'That is a horseshoe. The British have a superstition that a horseshoe fixed on the top of a door brings luck.'

The pointed end of Byomkesh's umbrella had got stuck with the horseshoe. Pulling it free, he asked, 'Did you install this?'

'No, it has been in existence since the time of Akshoy Mondol.'

Byomkesh seemed to become somewhat lost in thought while looking at the horseshoe. Kamal Babu broke into his reverie, saying, 'Please come inside.'

Sitting on a mat spread on the floor, Kamal Babu's ten year old daughter was engaged in her studies. Close to her and just outside the mat a fierce-looking dog was seated with his paws resting on the floor. He raised his lustreless, bluish eyes towards Byomkesh. Kamal Babu asked his daughter to go down and tell her mother to prepare some tea and snacks.

Byomkesh protested, but Kamal Babu did not pay any heed to him. The girl went down, followed by Bhuto.

Byomkesh stretched his eyes all around and inspected the room. He asked, 'Is there any furniture in this room which belonged to Akshoy Mondol?'

Kamal Basbu said, 'There were some items, but I have had them shifted to the next room. A bed and a table with drawers.'

The adjoining room was comparatively larger. The bed was set by the window and the table was placed at the other end. Byomkesh went close to the table and asked, 'Did the police take away all those iron cartons which were found in course of their search?'

'No, no, the police had taken only one carton, the rest are there in this drawer.' Kamal Babu opened one of the lower drawers of the table and said, 'Here they are.'

A few cartons were lying at the back of the drawer. Byomkesh took one of them out and then turned it around in his hand, examining it from various angles. In appearance and character it was very similar to a foil provided inside a cigarette packet. Putting it back in place, he smiled and said, 'Funny stuff. Place a couple of biscuits inside this and tie it up with a string and you have nothing to worry. Come, let us go and see the roof.'

'But there is nothing on the roof.'

'Doesn't matter. Perhaps the nothingness may become meaningful.'

There was really nothing on the roof. Covered by the iron framework, the roof stood like an empty tiger-cage. There was a red water-tank mounted on a raised platform in one corner. It was from that tank that running tap water was supplied to the house. Byomkesh went round the entire roof inquisitively and then asked, 'Don't you use the roof?'

Kamal Babu said, 'We come up and sleep on the roof when it is very hot. This is a very secure place, there is no way that a thief can enter here.'

'Hmm. Let us go down. I have finished my inspection.'

When they went down, Kamal Babu's daughter informed him that tea had been served in the sitting room,

While having tea and snacks in the sitting room on the ground floor, Byomkesh asked, 'What is the name of the Inspector whom you have been meeting at the police station?'

Kamal Babu said, 'His name is Rakhal Sarkar.'

There was a hint of a smile on Byomkesh's lips. He rose to his feet after finishing his tea and said, 'Well, I'll make a move now.'

Kamal Babu said, 'But what about our plans for going on the pilgrimage? You haven't told me whether it would be proper for us to go or not.'

'Of course you shall go on your pilgrimage. When does your leave commence?'

'From next Saturday.'

'Then book your tickets without further delay. You have no cause for fear. You shall not lose possession of your house. I guarantee that.'

'Oh! Thank you, Byomkesh Babu. Let me escort you home.'

Byomkesh said, 'No, that won't be necessary. I am now going to the police station for chalking out a plan of action with Rakhal.'

The police watch on Kamal Babu's house was lifted on Saturday morning. Kamal Babu took Bhuto to a kennel and left him there. Besides the police, another party was keeping a close watch on the house. They noticed everything.

A few hours later Kamal Babu left with his wife and daughter along with his suitcases after locking up the house. On his way he delivered the keys to Rakhal Babu at the police station and said, 'I have not closed the door to the side entrance as per your advice; now every thing hangs on my luck and your skill.'

The house remained vacant for the rest of the day.

At about eight thirty that night, Rakhal Babu took Byomkesh with him and proceeded towards Kamal Babu's house. Each of them carried a pistol and an electric torch in his pocket. They had surveyed the venue in advance. Climbing over the compound wall of the adjoining house, they entered Kamal Babu's house through the side entrance. Then, after closing the door of the side entrance from inside, they tiptoed across the staircase and reached the first floor. They stopped and listened; the house was silent. Rakhal Babu switched on his torch for a moment on the wall above the door. The horseshoe was in place. He then whispered to Byomkesh, 'It would be better perhaps to go up to the roof and wait.'

Byomkesh spoke into his ears, 'No, I am going to the roof; you hide in this room. If we both go to the roof, the door at the entrance to the roof cannot be closed from this side, which might make the visitor suspicious.'

'All right, you can go and hide in the roof. I'll close the door from this side.'

Byomkesh went up to the roof, Rakhal Babu bolted the door from inside and came down. He had no idea how long they would have to wait. In fact, no one might come that night. Entering the room on the first floor, he hid behind the door.

After making a round of the roof, Byomkesh sat down on the parapet a little away from the water-tank. There was no moon, only the stars were twinkling. Byomkesh blended with the darkness.

It was a long wait. Just like lying in wait on a shooting platform in a forest after tying up a goat or a lamb as bait. When it was almost two o'clock, Rakhal Babu started feeling restless in the closed room. The prey was probably not coming that night. But just then he heard a faint noise outside the door. Instantly his muscles became taut. Soundlessly he took out the revolver from his pocket.

The person, who had noiselessly entered the house and climbed up the staircase, had a canvas bag in his left hand and an iron stick in his right hand. A string of coarse silk of about three feet length was wrapped around the stick, just like a string draped around a fishing rod.

The man extended his stick towards the top of the door and took down the horseshoe. Then he tied the horseshoe to the open end of the coarse silk string and walked up the staircase to the roof. He had no idea that two men were lying in wait for him in two different parts of the house.

Byomkesh became alert as soon as he heard a faint noise from the door to the roof. A figure emerged in the dim starlight and then moving straight towards the water-tank, it got up on the parapet and climbed on the top of the tank. There was a metallic sound as the man opened the tank-cover and kept it on one side. Then he immersed the horseshoe tied at the end of his stick into the water.

In the dim light it seemed as if the man was catching some small fish with the help of a fishing rod. He was lowering his rod into the tank and lifting it up. Putting the fish in the canvas bag he was immersing his rod again into the water.

After about twenty minutes the man completed his fishing and got down from the tank. Holding the bag in one hand and the stick in his other hand, he had barely taken a step, when the sharp light of a torch was flashed on his face and Byomkesh's sarcastic voice was heard, 'Akshoy Mondol, how was your fishing?'

Akshoy Mondol was wearing a khaki half-sleeve shirt and a pair of khaki shorts. He was a dark, well-built man. Staring into the darkness with startled eyes, he lowered the bag on the floor very slowly and then moved his hand swiftly towards his pocket. Immediately Byomkesh struck him very hard on the jaw with the torch. Akshoy Mondol fell down flat on the roof.

Rakhal Babu had meanwhile come up on the roof. He squatted down heavily on Akshoy Mondol's chest and said, '*Byomkesh-*da*, he has a pistol in his pocket. Would you please take it out.'

Byomkesh removed the pistol from Akshoy Mondol's pocket and put it in his own pocket. Rakhal Babu put handcuffs on Akshoy Mondol's wrists and said, 'Akshoy Mondol, I am arresting you for the murder of Harihar Singh.'

Taking out a few wet pieces of iron from Akshoy Mondol's bag, Byomkesh examined them in the torch-light and said, 'Ah! Just as I thought, gold biscuits packed in iron cartons!'

Next morning Satyabati said to Byomkesh, 'If you know what is good for you, you shall forthwith tell me where you spent last night.'

Byomkesh said in a distressed tone, 'Please, your honour, Rakhal is my witness, — I have not committed any offence.'

'Birds of the same feather flock together. Are you going to tell me the story right away? Yes or no?'

'Yes, I shall, but before that I must have a second cup of tea. One cup was not enough to wash off the weariness of a sleepless night.'

*Byomkesh-*da:* The suffix *da* is an abbreviation of *dada*, which means an elder brother and is used for addressing a man who is one's senior.

Satyabati fetched a cup of strong tea for Byomkesh and then sitting down on a chair facing him, she said, 'Now tell me how you broke the torch. Were you engaged in a fight?'

Byomkesh said, 'Not a fight, only a knock out.' Taking a sip of tea, he started talking.

'Akshoy Mondol had made a lot of money through gold smuggling. He had built a house as per his needs in a decent locality of the city and had covered the roof of the house with a framework of iron rods and strips in such a manner that there was no scope for thieves to enter from that direction. He had a very special reason for securing the roof.

'Akshoy Mondol's occupation was to collect gold smuggled into India from other countries and release them in the market at opportune times. He stored the gold in his house, but not in any iron safe. He had thought up a unique device for hiding the gold.

'Akshoy Mondol used to live all by himself in his house. It is not known yet if he was married. He did not mix much with his neighbours, but lest they harboured any suspicion, he had let out one room in the ground floor to a gentleman named Kamal Das. He had employed some men for selling the gold in the market; one of them was Harihar Singh.

'Harihar Singh had probably been cheating Akshoy Mondol. The two had a big quarrel one day and in the heat of the moment, Akshoy Mondol murdered Harihar Singh. When he cooled down a bit, he started worrying about what he was going to do with the body. He could not possibly remove the body all by himself from that busy residential area. In the end he decided to leave the dead body in the house and make his escape with whatever gold he had there.

'But he could not take out all his gold. Gold is a very heavy metal, even heavier than iron. Women move around wearing gold ornaments from head to toe, but do you people have any idea about the weight of gold?'

Satyabati said, 'All right, all right, get on with your story.'

'The dead body was found a few days after Akshoy Mondol had made his escape. The police came, but there was no solution to the murder. There was no question that Akshoy Mondol had committed the murder, but he was absconding. Kamal Babu took possession of the entire house.

'Akshoy Mondol must have been hiding somewhere in the city; he decided to lie low for a few months. But he had been unable to remove all his gold, which still lay hidden in the house; he had to recover it. This was not an easy task. Kamal Babu's wife and daughter stayed in the house most of the time, on top of which they had a ferocious dog. After a lot of thought Akshoy Mondol finally hit upon a plan.

'He sent a woman who posed as his wife and a man posing as his elder brother to see Kamal Babu. The house had to be vacated and delivered to the wife. Akshoy Mondol might be an absconding murderer, but his wife had not committed any crime. However Kamal Babu did not pay any heed to them. He threw them out. Akshoy Mondol then threatened Kamal Babu by sending him an anonymous letter, but even that proved to be fruitless. Kamal Babu refused to budge.

'Akshoy Mondol then resorted to another ploy.

'I think that the colleague in the bank, who had been coaxing Kamal Babu to accompany him on the pilgrimage, had some link with Akshoy Mondol. If Kamal Babu and his family could be removed from the house even for a few days, Akshoy Mondol's task could be accomplished. He had the situation more or less under control, but Kamal Babu had his misgivings on one issue. He was apprehensive of losing possession of the house. He came to me for advice.

'I went to inspect the house. There was a strong sun, so I had carried an umbrella. As I climbed up to the first floor I noticed a horseshoe, hung loosely between three nails on the top of the door. But it wasn't actually a horseshoe, although it looked like one. I stretched my umbrella towards it and the metal tip of the umbrella instantly got stuck to the horseshoe.

'I realized that my suspicions were correct. It was a powerful magnet shaped like a horseshoe, which had attracted the iron tip of my umbrella with ease. I learnt on enquiry that the article had belonged to Akshoy Mondol. Then I started thinking.

What could Akshoy Mondol have to do with the magnet? And why had he hung it above the door, so that it just appeared to be a horseshoe? Then I remembered that a few iron cartons had been found during the police search. Slowly the mystery started to clear up.

'After that when I found the water-tank on the roof and had a close look at the iron-framework, covering the roof-top, I had no further difficulty in understanding what Akshoy Mondol had been doing. A magnet, however powerful, is incapable of attracting gold. Which is why he used to pack the gold biscuits in iron cartons and throw them into the water-tank. Thereafter he picked them up as and when needed by fishing them out with the magnet attached at the end of a thread. He could not remove the entire gold when he made his escape after murdering Harihar Singh. Now he wanted to collect the rest. But he had never thought that the situation could become so complicated.

'I had been able to trace the gold. Just as pearls are found in oysters at the bottom of the sea, so was gold, inside tin cartons, held at the bottom of the water tank. But just retrieving the gold would not have served the purpose; we had to nab the murderer as well. I advised Kamal Babu to proceed on pilgrimage with his family and then plotted with Rakhal for setting up a trap.

'Kamal Babu and his family left on their pilgrimage yesterday morning. Akshoy Mondol had kept the house under surveillance. He came to know that his path was clear.

'Rakhal and I set up our meeting at the empty house after dusk. We had not expected that Akshoy Mondol would arrive yesterday itself, but we had to remain on guard nevertheless. One could never tell. The prey set foot in the trap at two in the morning. Then — he was floored by a single strike of the torch.'

Satyabati asked in a subdued voice, 'How much gold was found?'

Byomkesh lit up a cigarette and said, 'Fifty-seven iron cartons, two gold biscuits in each carton, each biscuit weighing fifty grams. Now work out the worth yourself.'

Sayabati let out a deep sigh.

The Crooked Circle

'You have to come, Byomkesh Babu,' said Dr. Suresh Raksit, 'The patient is in a critical condition and a few words of assurance from you might save his life.'

Dr. Suresh Rakshit was around forty with a lean and dry appearance, which made him look somewhat ill at ease in his new and expensive European clothes. But his attitude and bearing were quick and sharp. He had come to see Byomkesh that morning with a strange request.

Needless to say Byomkesh was not keen to call on the patient. He looked at Dr. Rakshit with half-closed eyes and asked, 'What is he ailing from?'

The doctor said, 'Paralysis. He had an attack about three months back. He has been able to tide over the initial impact, but his blood pressure is very high, although his brain seems to be clear. He sent me to request you to please pay him a visit. A little mental support from you may perhaps help him to survive.'

Byomkesh asked, 'Is he under your treatment?'

Dr. Rakshit replied, 'Yes, sir. I am his tenant, occupying the ground floor of his house and also his family physician. The gentleman is very rich, — engaged in money lending business. You might have heard the name of Bishu Pal.'

Byomkesh asked, 'What was the name you mentioned, *Shishupal?'

**Shishupal* – a king of the *Chhedi* Dynasty in the Mahabharata, who was granted a boon by Lord Krishna that he would go unpunished if he committed one hundred crimes, but he committed one more than a hundred crimes and was then killed at the hands of Krishna.

The doctor smiled and said, 'Bishu Pal; although some call him *Shishupal* as well. I do not know why, — because the man is no doubt a moneylender and makes money on interest, but he is not one of those people who are driven to unscrupulousness by their greed for money. And after being bedridden for the past three months, he has now become totally helpless.'

Byomkesh said, 'But what can I do for him? I am not a doctor.'

The doctor said, 'Then let me tell you what the real situation is like. Bishu Pal has a debtor by the name of Abhoy Ghoshal, who is a downright scoundrel. He had borrowed a lot of money from Bishu Pal when he was in trouble, but now he is not bothering to repay the loan. Bishu Pal had sent him strong reminders and in response Abhoy Ghoshal is said to have threatened Bishu Pal that if he pressed for the money he would kill him. Shortly after receiving the threat Bishu Pal sustained a stroke and is bedridden since then for the last three months. There is of course no immediate fear of death. With proper medication and treatment, he may even be able to get up and walk some day. But that is not his real problem. He has developed a deep fear in his mind that Abhoy Ghoshal shall murder him in any event even if he agrees to waive the loan. – You do not have to treat him Byomkesh Babu, all Bishu Pal wants is to unburden his worries to you. If you choose to give him any advice after hearing him that might help him as well.'

Byomkesh seemed to be lost in his thoughts for a while. He then said, 'If any one is determined to kill *Shishupal* it is even beyond the powers of Lord Shiva to save him. However, as the gentleman is so anxious for my company, I shall go. Be it in this world or the next it is always handy to have a rich moneylender on your side. What do you say, Ajit?'

I said, 'Very true.'

Dr. Rakshit stood up smiling and said, 'Thank you. Here is our address. When would you come?' He took out a card and handed it over to Byomkesh.

Byomkesh read the card and gave it to me. I noticed that Bishu Pal's residence was not very far from our place; it was located in a lane off Amherst Street. Byomkesh said, 'We shall be there at around five this evening.'

After the doctor had left, Byomkesh smiled and said, 'This would be my first attempt at consoling a paralyzed invalid.'

It was a long, winding lane, twisting and turning like a rivulet descending from the mountain. I have seen that however narrow a lane may be, the houses built on it are never small in size; unable to expand in width, they tend to rise in height.

Noticing Dr. Suresh Rakshit's nameplate on the door of a three-storeyed house, we knew that we had arrived at Bishu Pal's house. Observing us from a window, Dr. Rakshit came out to greet us.

It was an old-style house. A narrow verandah, looking like a tunnel, had made it's way towards the interior, with a door at one end and two windows at the other end. The doctor's chamber was visible through the door; it was a bright and tidy room, but there were no patients. A middle-aged assistant was standing at the door. Dr. Rakshit did not take us to his chamber as he said, 'I am afraid you'll have to climb the staircase. Bishu Babu lives on the second floor.'

Byomkesh said, 'That's all right. Do you live in this building as well or you only have your chamber here?'

The doctor said, 'There are three rooms on the ground floor. I have converted two of them into my chamber and use the third as my living accommodation. I am single, so there is no problem.'

There were three rooms on the first floor as well, which were used as an office. It was not an office set up with tables and chairs, but more like a business shop of *Marwari* style with mattresses laid on the floor. Several clerks were sitting there and doing their work.

Byomkesh asked, 'What is this?'

The doctor replied, 'This is Bishu Babu's office. He has a huge business; many important people of high status have their holdings mortgaged to him.'

Byomkesh did not say anything.

A *Gurkha* guard, seemingly dressed for battle with a loaded rifle on his arm, was sitting on a stool at the second floor landing. He stood up on hearing the sound of footsteps and cast an oblique glance at us. The doctor said, 'It is all right.' The guard saluted and stood aside.

After walking a few steps along the verandah we came across a closed door. The doctor knocked on the door. A woman's voice enquired from inside, 'Who is it?'

The doctor said, 'This is Dr. Rakshit. Please open the door.'

The door was opened by a few inches and we could see the emaciated face and apprehensive eyes of a middle-aged married lady. She seemed to be reassured after studying our faces one by one and finally opened the door. We entered into a semi-dark room.

We heard a male voice, saying, 'Switch on the light, dear.'

The lady switched on the light and then covered her head with her sari before going to an adjoining room.

We could now see the room distinctly. It was a medium-sized room, with a bed placed in the middle. A man, looking almost like a ghost, was lying on the bed, covered by a linen sheet. Beside the bed there was a small table, which held several medicine bottles, a glass of water and some other items. The remaining furniture in the room gave the impression of a patient's cabin in a nursing home.

The ghost-like man was of course Bishu Pal. He was staring at us with lusterless eyes set on a sunken, emaciated face. His hair was pale grey. Due to absence of teeth both his upper and lower lips had sunk inside. His age could be fifty or sixty or even as high as seventy. In a mumbling voice he said, 'Is it Byomkesh Babu? Oh, I am so very obliged that you have come. Please come in.'

We advanced and stood close to the bed. Bishu Babu folded his shaking hands to greet us and said, 'I have put you to so much trouble. I should have gone to you myself. But you can see my condition.'

The doctor said, 'You should not talk too much.'

Bishu Pal said in a distressed tone, 'But, doctor, how can I stop talking? I have to tell Byomkesh Babu every thing.'

'Then say whatever you have to say, —quickly.' The doctor picked up a bottle from the table, poured a little medicine from it into a glass, added a little water and extended it to Bishu Pal. He said, 'Here, take this first.'

Bishu Pal drank the medicine with the irritated expression of a sick man.

Then, he spoke in a comparatively normal voice, 'Doctor, please get some chairs for these gentlemen.'

The doctor fetched two chairs and set them close to the bed. After we were seated, Bishu Pal looked at Byomkesh's face and started talking.

'I won't talk much, because the doctor shall be displeased. I shall speak briefly. You must have heard that I have a money-lending business. I started this business about twenty-five years back and now my investment in the market is to the tune of twenty lakh rupees. I have many important people among my clients.

'I never lend money without security. But about two years back I had acted foolishly for which I am paying the price today. I had given a loan of thirty thousand rupees without any security.

'You wouldn't know Abhoy Ghoshal. I used to know his father Adhar Ghoshal, who was a man of high principles. He had amassed a lot of wealth. I had had a few business dealings with him, so I knew him. He was a truly upright person.

'Adhar Ghoshal died about ten years back. His only son, Abhoy Ghoshal inherited all his wealth.

'I had not seen Abhoy till then. I heard some rumours about him after his father's death. I thought that all young men become a little wayward after inheriting their father's wealth, but they get over their fickleness in course of time. This is seen to happen quite frequently.

'About two years back, when I had almost forgotten about Abhoy Ghoshal, he suddenly came to me one day. I was charmed when I saw him and heard him speak. He was as handsome as he was sweet-tongued. After introducing himself, he said that his late father was my friend, which is why he had come to me as he was in trouble. He had been placed in grave danger by his enemies, who had falsely implicated him in a murder case. With great difficulty he had been able to secure bail and had come running to me. He needed thirty thousand rupees to fight the case.

'You wouldn't believe me, — I, Bishu Pal, went so far as to hand over thirty thousand rupees to him without any security save for a signed hand-note. The fellow had cast a spell on me; he had mesmerized me.

'The hearing of the murder case was commenced at the court in due course. The reports started appearing in the newspapers. It was a long drawn affair. It seemed that there was hardly any misdeed, which Abhoy Ghoshal had not committed. He had practically squandered away all his inherited assets. There was no end to the number of women whom he had ruined. He had enticed a young married girl away from her home and murdered her after a year or so by poisoning her. This was the cause of the criminal suit. I had gone to the court one day to hear the proceedings. Abhoy Ghoshal was seated on the dock like a cornered cougar. It felt scary to see him. Good God, was this the same man whom I had lent money!

'But the suit was dismissed. Abhoy Ghoshal was acquitted of all charges through the loopholes of law. The murder-charge could not be established.

'A year or so passed after this incident. I had kept an eye on Abhoy Ghoshal and came to learn that he was about to sell off his house. This was the last immovable property that he owned and once he disposed of it, there would be no way of getting access to him. My money would be lost.

'I started issuing reminders. First I sent him a letter from my office, to which there was no reply. When there was no response even after I had written three successive letters, I went to see him personally one day. We, moneylenders know very well how to prick a man's weak points. I had decided that before filing a lawsuit I would give him a piece of my mind, just in case it served the purpose. All this happened about three months back. I took a *Gurkha* guard with me when I went to his house. Abhoy Ghoshal was sitting all by himself in the front room. On seeing me, he neither got up from his chair, nor spoke a word. He just went on staring at my face. Ingratitude is an ingrained trait of human nature.

'Any way, I had gone there with the intention of abusing him and I soon lost my temper. For about half an hour I abused him in the filthiest language that I could think of. Then all of a sudden I happened to look at his eyes. Oh God, they were such terrible eyes! The fellow was not speaking, but I could clearly read from his eyes that he would kill me. A man who had escaped scot-free after committing one murder was bound to have grown bolder. I was struck with a deadly fear, which reached the very depth of my heart.

'Without lingering there any further I came back in a rush. But on reaching home my body started shaking from head to foot. When the shaking wouldn't stop I sent for the doctor. The doctor gave me some medicines and somehow managed to stop the shaking for the time being, but it returned with severe intensity in the late hours of night. Then a senior physician was called. He examined me and found that I had sustained a stroke, — both my legs had become stiff and devoid of sensation.

'I have been bedridden since then. And I have also lost my peace of mind all together. The doctors have assured me that I wouldn't die of this illness, but I still can't get over my fear of death. I am certain that Abhoy Ghoshal would not spare me. I do not go out of this house, I have posted *Gurkha* guards at my entrance, but still I can't seem to find any confidence. – Now please tell me, Byomkesh Babu what is my remedy?'

After concluding his narrative, Bishu Pal remained lying on the bed as if he was half-dead. The doctor checked his pulse once, but did not seem to find it necessary to give him any medicine. With a deep frown on his face Byomkesh remained seated with his head lowered.

Bishu Pal's wife entered the room, her head half-covered by her sari, carrying two cups of tea in her hands. Byomkesh and I rose to our feet and she handed over the cups to us. She left the room after casting an anxious look at her husband. She seemed to be one of those silent women, who spoke very little.

As we sat down again, I noticed that Bishu Pal was staring at Byomkesh's face with questioning eyes.

Byomkesh took a sip of tea and said, 'You have taken all possible precautions, what else is there to do? Who cooks your meals?'

Bishu Pal replied, 'There was a male cook, whom I have got rid off. My wife does the cooking. No food comes from outside.'

'What about domestic servants?'

'There was a servant and a maidservant. I sacked both of them and posted a *Gurkha* guard on the staircase landing. Tell me what more can I do.'

'How is your business being managed?'

'A head clerk manages the business. If unavoidably necessary, he comes up to consult me. But I don't allow him to enter this room; he stands near the door and talks with me. The only outsider who is allowed to enter this room is the doctor.'

Emptying his teacup, Byomkesh stood up and said with a smile, 'You seem to have done every thing that had to be done, I can't think of any thing else that you need to do. But does Abhoy Ghoshal really intend to kill you?'

Bishu Pal tried to get up excitedly, but failing to do so, he sank back on the bed again and said in an anxious voice, 'Yes, Byomkesh Babu, I know in my heart of hearts that he is determined to kill me. Tell me, why otherwise should I feel so scared? After all Calcutta is not a lawless city.'

Byomkesh said, 'That is true. But how long can this continue?'

Bishu Pal said, 'That is what I am worried about, — how long can this continue? That is why I sought your help. Byomkesh Babu, you must do some thing.'

Byomkesh said, 'I shall think over the matter and let you know if any thing comes to mind. I'll take your leave now. Goodbye.'

Bishu Pal said, 'Doctor!'

Immediately Dr. Rakshit tock out a hundred rupees note from his pocket and held it before Byomkesh.

Byomkesh raised his eyebrows in surprise and asked, 'What is this?'

From his bed Bishu Pal said, 'A token of my regard for you. I have troubled you a lot and wasted a lot of your time.'

'But I had not come here with any such understanding.'

'Whatever it may be, you have to accept this.'

Byomkesh took the note with obvious reluctance. The doctor then escorted us out of the room.

The *Gurkha* guard stood up and saluted us at the staircase landing. While going down the staircase, Byomkesh asked Dr. Rakshit, 'Does this guard remain on duty all the time?'

The doctor said, 'No, there are two guards. Both are old employees and they used to guard the first floor earlier. Now one of them remains on duty from ten in the morning to eight at night and the other stays from ten at night to eight in the morning.'

Byomkesh said, 'Then there is no guard for two hours in the morning and two hours at night.'

The doctor said, 'No, I remain here during those hours.'

On reaching the first floor we found that the office had been closed. The clerks had locked up the place and left.

Descending to the ground floor, Byomkesh said, 'Dr. Rakshit, I would like to ask you a few questions.'

'Certainly. Let us talk in my dispensary.'

We entered the front room. It was a waiting room for patients, nicely set up with a new table, chairs and benches etcetera. The assistant was dozing with his knees lifted on a bench at one side. On seeing us he got up hurriedly and went to an adjoining room.

Byomkesh cast his eyes all around the room and said, 'You have set up your chamber quite nicely.'

The doctor spoke in a dry tone, 'I had to. As you know, when there is no show there is no dough.'

'How long have you been in practice?'

'I have been here for about three years; before that I was in the suburbs.'

'Your practice seems to be going on quite well.'

'Not bad – getting on – making slow progress, you know. I have a few fixed families among my patients. Lately the practice has grown a bit. If I can get Bishu Babu back to his feet—'

Byomkesh nodded his head and said, 'Yes, of course. Now tell me Doctor, this fear of death that Bishu Pal is seized with, is it just a mental sickness or are there any genuine reasons for such fear?'

The doctor remained quiet for a while and then said, 'He has reasons to feel scared. Of course those who have a lot of wealth are more prone to suffer from the fear of death. But Bishu Pal's fears are not entirely groundless. This fellow Abhoy Ghoshal is a vicious killer. I have heard that he has committed at least three murders. It is even suspected that he had a hand in poisoning his own father.'

Byomkesh exclaimed, 'Really! Then he must be a remarkable rogue. Now I recall that I had read a report on his murder charge in the newspapers about two years back. Do you know where he lives?'

The doctor said, 'I do. In fact he lives quite close by, — about a mile from here. I can give you his address, if you wish to see him.'

The doctor wrote down the address on a chit of paper and gave it to Byomkesh. While putting the folded chit in his pocket, Byomkesh said, 'I have one more question. Does Bishu Babu's wife suffer from any illness?'

The doctor replied, 'Nervous disorder. She is a nervous type, on top of which she is childless, you know.'

'I understand. All right, I'll make a move now. Bishu Babu has placed me under an obligation by paying me a hundred rupees. Now I shall have to apply my mind to his problem.'

The street-lights were on when we came out. Byomkesh looked at his watch and said, 'Half past six. Come, let us have a look at the seasoned murderer. Since Bishu Pal has given me money, I should at least try to do some thing for him.'

We hired a rickshaw at the street crossing and proceeded in a northerly direction. I have observed that comparatively fewer pedestrians choose to use Amherst Street. Even during peak hours when there is a stream of people flowing like an ocean in full tide along the many roads all around, Amherst Street remains comparatively free from any crowd of pedestrians. It seems as if running parallel to a turbulent sea Amherst Street remains tranquil as a shallow canal.

The rickshaw stopped at an address at the northern end of the street. We alighted from the rickshaw. Byomkesh checked the address and said, 'This is the house.'

The house did not stand on the footpath, but was set back by a small piece of open land, on which stood a cluster of *champak* trees, concealing the house from the street. The upper floor of the two-storeyed house was dark, but through the tree-leaves we could see a glimmer of light emerging from a room on the ground floor.

We entered the compound through a small gate.

The front room was set up with a table and chairs, giving the impression of an office. A man seated on a chair was lazily scrawling some thing on a notepad. He raised his eyes when we reached the door.

He was really handsome. Aged around thirty-five, with a very fair complexion, curly hair parted in the middle, deep-set eyes and a sharp nose, which looked as if they had been drawn with an artist's brush. Like Bishu Pal I too was simply charmed by his appearance at first sight.

Standing by the door, Byomkesh enquired, 'May we come in?' My name is Byomkesh Bakshi and this is Ajit Bandyo.'

Abhoy Ghoshal's eyes became alert. Then very slowly his face broke into a smile, as he said, 'Byomkesh Bakshi, the seeker of truth! I am honoured. Please come.'

We went in and sat down facing him. Putting down the pencil, he said, 'Now tell me what is the matter. I don't recall having committed any crime lately.'

Byomkesh smiled and said, 'We have come to see you.'

Abhoy Ghoshal said, 'Thank you. I must then be a creature worth-seeing . Have you come here on your own or has any one sent you to see me?'

Byomkesh said, 'Nobody sent me. But Bishu Pal, the money-lender, narrated his tale of woe to me, so I thought of paying you a visit.'

'Oh—*Shishupal.*' Abhoy Ghoshal paused for a while and then said, 'I had guessed that some one had sent you, but I had not thought that it could be *Shishupal.*'

Byomkesh said, 'You are probably aware that Bishu Pal has become paralyzed.'

Abhoy seemed quite surprised as he said, 'Really? No, I was not aware. *Shishupal* had called on me here about three months back and abused me in filthy language. God is great!' There was no trace of anger in his voice or face. He picked up the pencil and started scribbling on the paper.

Byomkesh said, 'He sustained a stroke immediately after returning home from here. Since then he is confined to his bed. But then, paralysis is not the only reason why he is staying confined in the house. He cannot step out of the house because he is scared of you.'

'Scared of me! – What are you saying? I am the borrower and he is the lender. It is I who should lie in constant fear of him.' Abhoy Ghoshal raised his eyebrows while saying this, with the hint of a smile on his lips.

Byomkesh said, 'He is scared that you shall murder him.'

'There you are. A branded man is blamed for every thing that goes wrong under the sun. I got entangled in a murder case just once and so every one started thinking of me as a seasoned criminal. Nobody bothered to consider that I was acquitted because I was found not guilty of any charge.' Abhoy Ghoshal took a pause and then said in a comparatively soft voice, 'But there is one thing which is true. It is written in my horoscope—those who antagonize me do not live very long. – Are you leaving?'

Byomkesh was already on his feet, as he said, 'Yes. I had come to see you and that job is done. Now I shall take leave of you, but let me tell you some thing before I go. If Bishu Pal meets with an unnatural death, I shall be very sorry. And in the end you too shall be sorry.'

There was a sudden change in Abhoy Ghoshal's expression. The smile was wiped off from his face and a cruel viciousness appeared in his eyes. He glared at Byomkesh, fixing unflinching eyes, deadly as a snake's stare, on his face.

My heart lost a beat and then started beating again at a fast pace. This was the same glare, which must have petrified Bishu Pal with mortal fear for his life. I had not seen such a clearcut promise of certain death in any one's eyes ever before.

Byomkesh cast a contemptuous glance at him and said, 'Come Ajit. Let us go.'

As we reached the pavement I saw a taxi standing on the opposite side of the road. I raised my hand to beckon the driver, but the taxi started moving and vanished after picking up speed.

I looked at Byomkesh, who stared at the disappearing taxi and asked, 'Was there any one in the taxi?'

'I could not see. But the driver had been looking towards us, which is why I thought that it was empty. But there could have been someone in the rear seat.'

'Hmmm,' – Byomkesh started walking. 'Somebody was probably following us.'

'Who could be following us?'

'Barring Dr. Rakshit no one knew that we were coming here.'

'But why? With what purpose?'

'That I don't know. But then, it could also be a pure coincidence. There was probably a passenger in the taxi, —a total stranger, the driver had stopped the car for some reason and then gone off.'

It was half past seven. We started walking in the direction of our residence. But I could not rid my mind of a confusing feeling.

Opening the newspaper next morning, I exclaimed excitedly, 'Hey, listen –'

Byomkesh turned around in a trice and enquired, 'What is it? Bishu Pal has been murdered?'

I said, 'No, not Bishu Pal—Abhoy Ghoshal.'

Byomkesh looked blankly at me for a while and then snatched the newspaper from my hand and started reading.

The newspaper report was very brief. Abhoy Ghoshal, a rich man, residing at Amherst Street, had been murdered on the previous night while he was asleep. The police had visited the crime-scene. It was not yet known who committed the murder. Two years back

Abhoy Ghoshal had been charged of murder, but was acquitted, as he was found not guilty.

As my mind had been prepared for other possibilities, I sat, stunned in bewilderment for some time. We had been with Abhoy Ghoshal till seven-thirty the previous evening and he had engaged in a verbal duel with Byomkesh, smiling with ease all the time. But what could have happened after that? He had tauntingly told us that he had many 'friends.' Then was one of his 'friends' lying in wait for him in the taxi and returned to murder him after we had left? Was the man in the taxi Dr.Rakshit? But why should Dr. Rakshit murder him?

All these speculations whirling in my mind were interrupted by the unexpected arrival of Inspector Romapati Babu.

We did not know him closely, but had been slightly acquainted with him in connection with one of our previous cases. He had a growing reputation in the police department as an efficient officer. He was of our age, with a well-built physique, amicable manners and sharp, penetrating eyes.

Greeting him cordially, Byomkesh invited him to sit down and then said, 'I just read in the newspaper that a resident of this locality by the name of Abhoy Ghoshal was murdered last night.'

Romapati Babu narrowed his eyes and asked, 'Did you know Abhoy Ghoshal?'

Byomkesh said, 'I did not know him, but I met him for the first time last evening. We had gone to his house to meet him.'

'Really? Why did you go to see him?'

Byomkesh shook his head with a disarming smile and said, 'You must give me all your news first; then I'll tell you what I know.'

After a brief hesitation, Romapati Babu said, 'All right, I'll talk first. The police had their eyes on Abhoy Ghoshal for a long time. The man went round wearing a mask of civility, but such a dastardly rogue is rarely seen. There is no count of the number of women of good families whom he had ruined. He had a wife, who suddenly died of unnatural causes. Then he eloped with the wife of a gentleman; the husband divorced her. The woman might thereafter have pressed Abhoy Ghoshal to marry her; he killed her by poisoning.

'Abhoy Ghoshal was arrested by the police and a case was brought up for trial. But the case was dismissed by the court as the criminal charges filed against Abhoy could not be fully established. The suit had been filed under Section 302; the order could go either way. Abhoy Ghoshal was acquitted.

'This is the past history of Abhoy Ghoshal. There are at least ten people in this city, who would have gladly murdered him.

'At about twelve last night the maidservant, who worked for Abhoy, came and reported to the police station that Abhoy had been murdered. I was not at the police station at that time, but I went to investigate when I received the information. Abhoy Ghoshal's financial standing was on the decline. He used to live all by himself in his house and there was only a young maidservant who attended to the household work. It was she who had come to report the matter to the police station.

'On reaching the house I observed that Abhoy Ghoshal was lying on his bed on the first floor, with his face turned to one side. A long metal pin, like a packing needle was sticking out from his left shoulder. On questioning the maidservant it was learnt that Abhoy had gone to bed at around nine last night after finishing his meal. The maidservant had then completed her chores, taken her meal, closed the doors and windows of the house and gone up to Abhoy's room to find that somebody had meanwhile murdered him and gone.

'We have held the maidservant in police custody for the time being, but it does not look like she had committed the murder. I have meanwhile checked the alibis of all those who had enmity with Abhoy, — and those who had given evidence against him at the hearing, but it does not seem that any of them were involved.

This is the up to date situation. Now please tell me what you know.'

Byomkesh asked, 'How did you come to know that I knew some thing?'

Romapati Babu took out a piece of paper from his pocket and extended it towards Byomkesh, saying, 'This piece of paper was found on the table in the sitting room on the ground floor of Abhoy Ghoshal's house.'

Stretching my neck I saw that the chit carried a lot of scribbling in pencil, at the end of which it was written—*Byomkesh Bakshi – Shishupal.* I then remembered that on the previous night Abhoy Ghoshal had been scribbling some thing on a sheet of paper while we sat before him.

Romapati Babu said, 'When I saw your name on this chit I thought that you might know some thing about the case and so I am here.'

Byomkesh said, 'You did the right thing. Now let me tell you what I know.'

Byomkesh recounted in detail every thing that had happened on the previous day from beginning to end, starting with the visit of Dr.Rakshit in the morning. Romapati Babu listened to him with close attention. After Byomkesh had completed his narration, Romapati Babu looked a little dubious as he said, 'It does seem suspicious. But I can find no motive for Bishu Pal, on top of which the man is an invalid. — What do you think?'

Byomkesh said, 'I can't make out anything yet. Have you been able to determine the time of death?'

'The police surgeon says between nine and twelve last night.'

'Hmm'— Byomkesh thought for a while and said, 'I think we have to get Bishu Pal checked very thoroughly to determine whether he is actually an invalid.'

Romapati Babu said, 'That's true. Since no one else is available let us try to shake down Bishu Pal and see what happens. Do you have a phone? Can I make a call from here?'

'Certainly. Come.' Byomkesh took him to the adjoining room.

Romapati Babu came out after some time and said, 'I asked the police surgeon to proceed to Bishu Pal's house. I am also going there now. Would you like to come with me?'

'Good idea. Let's go.'

We got ready within five minutes and left with Romapati Babu.

There was a stir in front of Bishu Pal's house. The surgeon was seated in a police van in front of the entrance. Dr. Rakshit was standing anxiously near the door. On our arrival the surgeon, Sushil Babu alighted from the van. Dr. Rakshit advanced towards us and asked, 'Byomkesh Babu, what is the matter?'

After Byomkesh had completed the introductions, Romapati Babu said to Dr. Rakshit, 'The police surgeon wants to examine Bishu Pal. Do you have any objection?'

Dr. Rakshit stood looking utterly surprised for a while and then said, 'Objection? Not the least. But why? What has happened?'

Romapati Babu said, 'A man called Abhoy Ghoshal was murdered by some one last night.'

Dr. Rakshit repeated the statement, 'Somebody has murdered Abhoy Ghoshal! Oh, now I understand; you suspect that Bishu Pal has murdered Abhoy Ghoshal.' A dry smile appeared on his face. 'In other words Bishu Babu's paralysis is not real, it is just a pretence. Very well, come and examine him yourself.'

We climbed up the staircase.

The office was functioning as usual on the first floor. The *Gurkha* guard was seated on the staircase landing on the second floor. After speaking to him Dr. Rakshit led us inside and knocked on the closed door. Opening the door by a few inches, Bishu Pal's wife looked at us with apprehensive eyes. It was a repetition of what had happened in the previous evening.

All five of us entered as soon as Bishu Pal's wife had gone to the adjoining room. Dr. Rakshit switched on the light.

Bishu Pal was lying on his bed, his lower body covered by a linen sheet. He spoke out in an aggrieved tone, weakened by illness, 'What do you want? Doctor, why are all these men here?'

Dr. Rakshit bent down towards the bed and spoke to him, 'A doctor from the police department is here. He wants to examine you.'

Bishu Pal's tone became sharper, 'Why? Why does the police doctor want to examine me?'

Dr. Rakshit spoke calmly, 'Abhoy Ghoshal has been murdered, that is why –'

The upper portion of Bishu Pal's body became restless. 'Who has been murdered? What did you just say, doctor?'

Dr. Rakshit said once again, 'Abhoy Ghoshal has been murdered.'

A glimmer of relief appeared for a moment on Bishu Pal's face to be immediately replaced by an expression of distress. He spoke in a mumbling voice, 'Abhoy Ghoshal has been murdered! But I had lent him thirty thousand rupees, which now amounts to thirty-three thousand with interest. What would happen to my money?'

The doctor spoke dryly, 'You can think of the money later. These people have come here to examine if you are actually paralyzed.'

'What does that mean?' Bishu Pal turned his eyes towards us.

Advancing towards the bed, Romapati Babu spoke in a soothing voice, 'Look, we have not come here with any evil design. All we want is that our doctor may examine you. Do you have any objection?'

'Objection? Why should I have any objection? Can the police doctor cure me?'

Sushil Babu said, 'Well, I can certainly try.'

After some more questions and replies, Bishu Pal finally gave his consent. Sushil Babu then removed the linen sheet from his body and started examining him. Bishu Pal's legs had become numb through paralysis, but he still had control over his upper body.

Sushil Babu pricked a needle on the legs, but found no response. Then he conducted several other tests; he checked Bishu Pal's pulse and blood pressure and put several questions to Dr. Rakshit. In the end Sushil Babu let out a deep sigh and placed the linen sheet back on Bishu Pal's body.

While the doctor was conducting his examination, my eyes had once strayed towards the door of the adjoining room. I had noticed that Bishu Babu's wife had opened the door by a few inches and was looking intently at her husband. Her anxiety did not seem to be entirely natural, but more like a strained and panic-stricken tension.

Sushil Babu said, 'My examination is over. Let us go.'

We turned towards the door. Bishu Babu spoke out from his bed, 'What did you find? Shall I be cured of my ailment?'

Sushil Babu said in a somewhat embarrassed voice, 'You may be cured. Your doctor is treating you well. Goodbye, sir.'

On our way home in the police van, Byomkesh asked, 'The ailment is genuine then,— not play acting.'

Sushil Babu said, 'No, not play acting.'

Byomkesh spent the whole afternoon, stretched on bed, staring at the ceiling with distracted eyes and smoking countless cigarettes. When he did not get up even when tea was served in the late afternoon, I said to him, 'Look, the police did not invite you to investigate the murder of Abhoy Ghoshal. Then why are you so worked up?'

Byomkesh said, 'Not worked up, Ajit, conscience-stricken.'

Then he abruptly walked into the next room. I could hear that he was speaking to some one on the telephone. When he came out after a while, I observed that he had a happy look on his face.

'Whom did you telephone?'

'Dr. Ashim Sen.'

We had become acquainted with Dr. Ashim Sen in connection with a previous investigation.

Byomkesh drank up the lukewarm tea in one gulp and then said, 'Let us go.'

'Where?'

'To Bishu Pal's house.'

When we reached Bishu Pal's house the clerks were coming down the staircase after finishing their day's work. Dr. Rakshit was smoking in the dispensary with his feet raised on the table. He quickly brought down his feet on seeing us.

Byomkesh told him, 'I notice that you are not occupied with any patient at the moment. Let us go up. I want to say some thing to Bishu Babu in your presence.'

The doctor looked at Byomkesh with a complacent expression and then led us upstairs without speaking.

The *Gurkha* guard had disappeared. The door to Bishu Babu's room was wide open. Today it was not necessary to switch on the light. Plenty of light was pouring into the room through the open windows. Bishu Pal had overcome his fear of unnatural death. He was lying half-reclined on the bed with a few pillows placed under his back, but he turned sharply on hearing the sound of our footsteps.

Drawing close to the bed, Byomkesh stared at Bishu Pal's face for some time and then said very softly 'You have played a nice game!'

Bishu Pal went on looking steadily at Byomkesh's face with the fixed expression of an owl's stare. Byomkesh continued speaking in a firm voice, 'You had included the doctor in your plot, because your scheme would not have succeeded without him. But why did you involve me? So that I could provide evidence on your behalf?'

Dr. Rakshit had been standing behind us, now he rushed up and exclaimed in an angry voice, 'What's all this rubbish? How dare you defame me!'

Byomkesh turned to him like a wounded tiger and asked, 'Doctor, have you heard of a drug called *procaine*?'

The doctor became deflated like a pricked balloon. Byomkesh went on staring at him with angry eyes for some time and then turned towards Bishu Pal. Taking out a hundred rupee note from his pocket, he threw it down on the bed and said, 'Here, pick up your money. Do not forget that I can send both of you to the gallows. If you are held in police custody for two days the real nature of your paralysis shall be exposed.'

Bishu Pal almost broke down in tears, 'Byomkesh Babu, please have mercy on me. Believe me, whatever I have done is only to save my own life.'

Byomkesh went on staring hard at Bishu Pal for some time and then said, 'I can show you mercy only on one condition. You shall have to donate one lakh rupees to the Defence Fund. Are you ready?'

Bishu Pal asked in a thin voice, 'One lakh rupees!'

'Yes, one lakh rupees, not a paise less. You shall deposit one lakh rupees with the Reserve Bank tomorrow morning and send me the receipt. If you don't —'

'All right. I shall donate one lakh.'

"Remember, I shall wait till twelve noon to see the receipt from the Reserve Bank. —Come Ajit, let us go.'

While sipping a second cup of tea after returning home I was thinking,— a donation of a lakh of rupees to the Defence Fund was no doubt a noble gesture, but why did Byomkesh let off two confirmed murderers from his grasp? Byomkesh must have read these thoughts on my face. He explained, 'There was no other option but to let Bishu Pal off the hook. Even if the case was brought up for trial Bishu Pal would have been acquitted, because nobody would have believed his motive of murder.'

I said, 'But the motive was real.'

'From Bishu Pal's view, — yes. He had murdered Abhoy Ghoshal really to save his own life. But the jury wouldn't have believed that, they would have laughed at the suggestion.'

'Well, tell me some thing. The law says that killing in self-defence is not an offence, right? Then what offence had Bishu Pal committed by murdering Abhoy Ghoshal?'

'A man has a right to kill another man in self-defence, but killing a man after plotting in advance for three months cannot be condoned by law. Bishu Pal was aware of this, which is why he took all possible safeguards with meticulous care before embarking on his plan.'

'I can understand that. But I still want you to explain the whole thing to me.'

Byomkesh then started talking –

'We saw Abhoy Ghoshal yesterday. He had an ever-smiling face, but his eyes held the vicious cruelty of a ruthless murderer. He was a real killer. Not one word of all that we had heard about him yesterday was untrue.

'Bishu Pal had been carried away by Abhoy Ghoshal's sweet talk and loaned him thirty thousand rupees. But when the time came for repaying the money there was no response from Abhoy Ghoshal. He did not even bother to acknowledge the loan.

'Till then Bishu Pal was not familiar with Abhoy Ghoshal's real character, which is why he went over to Abhoy's house one day and abused him in filthy terms. Abhoy Ghoshal did not utter a word; he only went on staring at Bishu Pal with those deadly, vicious eyes. Bishu Pal was thoroughly shaken up by that stare. He then realized what Abhoy Ghoshal really was; — he had committed murders before and he would most certainly murder Bishu Pal now.

'But Bishu Pal did not lack shrewdness. When he was convinced that Abhoy Ghoshal would not rest till he had murdered him, he decided that he would murder Abhoy Goshal first. He had no fear of losing his money, because Abhoy Ghoshal still owned a house property, which could be seized through a court decree and the loan then recovered with full interest.

'Bishu Pal had one advantage. He knew that Abhoy Ghoshal wanted to kill him, but Abhoy Ghoshal had no inkling that Bishu Pal was intent on killing him. Which is why Abhoy had taken no precautions.

'Bishu Pal stopped going out from his house. A *Gurkha* guard was posted at the staircase landing. Then Bishu Pal sat down to chalk out his plan.

'Dr. Suresh Rakshit was occupying the ground floor as a tenant. It was quite obvious that he did not have much of a practice. He was even unable to pay his rent and soon became Bishu Pal's debtor. Bishu Pal told him about his plan. Deeply in debt to Bishu Pal, Dr. Rakshit consented to lend a hand in the plot.

'Bishu Pal bought new items of furniture and fixtures to set up the doctor's chamber, so as to give the impression that Dr.Rakshit was not just a run-of-the-mill physician but had a good practice. Then Bishu Pal had paralysis.

'Medical science has made a lot of advancement lately. Earlier a patient had to be given chloroform to make him unconscious before a surgery, but that is no longer necessary these days. A new drug of the *procaine* group has been invented, which, if injected into a particular spot of the spine, causes a certain area of the body to become numb, allowing a surgery to be conducted on that area without the patient feeling any pain.

'Dr. Rakshit did just that. Bishu Pal's legs became numb. Then a renowned physician was called; he diagnosed the ailment as paralysis and prescribed accordingly.

'The effect of *procaine* lasts for about five to six hours, after which it passes off. But outsiders were not aware of this, it was only known to Bishu Pal's wife and the doctor. The clerks worked on the first floor, they knew that their boss had been paralyzed. The head clerk was not allowed to enter the room; he stood outside the door and saw that the boss was bedridden. No body had any doubt, nor was there any reason to raise doubts.

'But Bishu Pal was a shrewd man; he would not do a bungling job. He needed impartial and disinterested eyewitnesses,— witnesses, whose testimony would not be disbelieved by others. He sent Dr. Rakshit to me yesterday morning, requesting me to see him. I agreed to call on him in the evening. The doctor went back and injected *procaine* in Bishu Pal's spine at around one in the afternoon.

'On reaching at five in the evening we observed that Bishu Pal was bedridden and powerless to get up. He narrated his sad story to us and then got rid of us after paying me a hundred rupees. He had planned to murder Abhoy Ghoshal last night itself.

'The doctor informed Bishu Pal that I had collected Abhoy Ghoshal's address. Bishu Pal was worried that his plans might be upset if we stayed late at Abhoy Ghoshal's house. So he sent the doctor to keep an eye on us. The doctor came in a taxi and waited in front of Abhoy Ghoshal's house. He left as soon as he saw us coming out of the house. He was relieved, because the line was clear.

'By around seven in the evening the numbness passed from Bishu Pal's legs; he was restored to his normal strength.

'One *Gurkha* guard went off at eight and the other reported at ten 'o clock at night. Bishu Pal left the house at around nine, probably covering his face with a wrapper. He was carrying some weapon like a packing needle in his hand. During the past three months he had gathered detailed information about Abhoy Ghoshal's routine and movements. He knew that barring a maidservant there was nobody else in the house, that Abhoy Ghoshal usually went to bed by nine after finishing his meals and that the front door was closed well after ten by the maid-servant when she had eaten her meals and finished all her chores.

'So Bishu Pal had no problem. After murdering Abhoy Ghoshal he returned home well before ten. Nobody came to know. Even if anyone had seen him, it would have been difficult to crack his alibi. How could a man, bedridden with paralysis for three months, go round and commit a murder? And what could be the motive of his murder?

'Bishu Pal had another injection early this morning. There was no harm in being cautious. Then we went to his house with the police doctor, who examined him and confirmed that he was indeed paralyzed.

'I had a faint suspicion from the very outset. Why should a moneylender, who thrived by squeezing his borrowers for interest, spend a hundred rupees for just making me listen to his tale of woe? That was where Bishu Pal had made a small error in judgement. And then when I read about the murder of Abhoy Ghoshal in the newspaper this morning, I was left with no doubt that Bishu Pal had caused the murder. But how?

'There were three people,—. Bishu Pal himself, his wife and Dr.Rakshit. Dr.Rakshit was in deep waters; he might have helped Bishu Pal indirectly, but would he commit a murder with his own hands? It was unlikely. Bishu Pal's wife was a woman; for saving her husband she might feed poison to Abhoy Pal if he happened to be nearby, but it was not possible for her to travel all that distance and use a knife. A knife was not a woman's weapon. That left me with Bishu Pal. But he was laid down by paralysis –

'I had taken out the two *Gurkha* guards from the list of suspects at the outset. *Gurkha*s are not averse to killing and they are also skilled in using their *kookri*. But Bishu Pal was not such an inept plotter that he would get his own guards to commit the murder. *Gurkhas* by nature are not used to complicated ways of thinking, they are simple and headstrong. The moment they were caught they would have revealed everything.

'Then who committed the murder?

Suddenly the entire deception was exposed before my eyes. I could have perhaps guessed the truth much earlier if I had possessed some knowledge in medical science. Bishu Pal's paralysis was not a real paralysis; it was a temporary substitute for paralysis – anaesthesia created through a medical reaction.

'I telephoned Dr. Ashim Sen. He is an experienced doctor and he explained the matter to me straight away.

'My only regret is that along with Bishu Pal, Dr. Rakshit too managed to get off scot-free. Being a professional doctor, there is no way that he can be forgiven for what he did.

'Any way, a donation of one lakh rupees to the Defence Fund is not such a bad bargain either.'

Thus Spoke Kavi Kalidasa*

The town where Byomkesh and I had gone on a short visit could well be termed as a 'coal town'. There were about four coalmines within a periphery of three to four miles and the town seemed to have spread it's webs like a spider drawing coal from every direction to its railway station, from where it was transported to various destinations by goods trains. It was a prosperous town, bustling with activity. Many rich businessmen had set up their offices; there were quite a few banks and no end of advocates, doctors, engineers, brokers and moneylenders. There was a heavy rush of motorcars, taxis, buses and trucks in the streets. Raw material extracted from the mines was constantly changing hands for cash. The town was literally controlled by a single commodity – coal. All around there was only the talk of coal and the bustle of coal business. It was by no means an old town and yet some invisible coat of coal-dust seemed to have cast a shade of premature agedness all over it's facade.

We were there at the invitation of a gentleman named Manish Chakraborty, who owned a coalmine called *Phuljhuri*. During the past few months there had been a series of mysterious disturbances in the coalmine. Sporadic fires in the mine-pits, breakdown of costly machinery damaged beyond redemption and similar freak accidents

*'*Thus spoke Kavi Kalidasa, phrasing a riddle in a whimsical tone: the room fled through the window, the house-holder is left all alone.*' [An oft-used limerick in Bengali, cited by the author in his introduction of this story when it first appeared in 1963.]

were occurring with increasing frequency. There were also signs of growing discontent among the labour gangs for no tenable reasons. Manish Babu was quite convinced that certain people were trying to cause him harm. In the circumstances he did what seemed to be appropriate; he sought the help of the police and also sacked several newly recruited employees, but neither of these steps helped to mitigate the problem. In the end he sent out a secret invitation to Byomkesh requesting him to pay him a visit.

We arrived at Manish Chakraborty's residence on an early spring evening. It was a two-storeyed house surrounded by expansive gardens in an aristocratic area of the town. We were greeted warmly by Manish Babu, who had just returned from the mine. He was around fifty, fair, handsome and still quite able-bodied. The firmness of his jaw indicated that he was a man of strict principles.

After we were seated comfortably in the drawing room and had exchanged pleasantries, Manish Babu said, 'Byomkesh Babu, I am afraid both of you shall have to stay here under assumed names. You shall be known as Gagan Babu and Ajit Babu as Sujit Babu. If your real names are disclosed everyone is bound to know why you are here, which would defeat our purpose.'

Byomkesh smiled and said, 'That's all right. As long as I am here I shall be content to stay as Gagan Babu and Ajit would have no objection to assuming the disguise of Sujit Babu.'

I had already noticed a young man, who stood by the door, fidgeting in an uncomfortable manner, obviously waiting to be introduced to us. Manish Babu called out, 'Phani.'

The youth came in eagerly. Manish Babu looked at us and said, 'This is my son Phanish. Phani, you know who these gentlemen are, but none outside this house must know their identity.'

Phani said, 'Yes, sir.'

'You may take them to the guest-room. See that they are settled comfortably. Byomkesh Babu, you may like to have a wash first. Tea shall be served shortly.'

The guest-room was right next to the drawing room. It was a large room, equipped with two beds, a table, a chair, a few other essential items of furniture and an attached toilet. Phanish took us to the room and then stood by the door.

He seemed to be a gentle and good-natured young man. He had inherited the good looks of his father, but his body and mind were yet to mature, which was evident from traces of juvenility in his attitude and bearing. He was in his early twenties.

We exchanged a few words with him while changing our clothes; Phanish shyly responded to Byomkesh's questions. He was his father's only child; he had been married a year back. He accompanied his father to the coalmine and attended to the duties assigned to him. I observed that while replying to Byomkesh's questions, he desperately wanted talk of some other matter, but was held back by hesitation.

There was no time then to find out what Phanish wanted to tell us. Returning to the sitting room, we found that tea and snacks had been served. We sat down at the table,— just the four of us. No lady appeared at the tea-session, although it was obvious to us that at least two ladies must have been present in the house. Manish Babu, I thought, had not boycotted our established traditions all together.

We had lit up cigarettes after finishing our tea when a huge car drove in and stood at the porch. A middle-aged man got down from the car. He had the appearance of a gorilla; his eyes, bearing the stigma of past misdeeds, were filled with calculated crookedness. If it was possible to read one's character from one's face I would have said that this man was a notorious rogue.

Manish Babu welcomed the visitor with warm courtesy and then introduced us. 'This gentleman is Gobinda Haldar, owner of a coalmine here. And these are my friends from Calcutta, Gagan Mitra and Sujit Bandyopadhyay; they have come here on a short visit.'

Gobinda Haldar went on appraising us with sceptical eyes as he spoke to Manish Babu, 'I came to enquire. Have you had any further trouble in the mine?'

Manish Babu's face became serious as he said, 'There is no end of trouble. Day before yesterday there was a mishap in the late evening. The pump in pit number five ceased functioning all of a sudden. Fortunately, the watchmen were alert, so there wasn't much damage. Otherwise...'

Gobinda Babu made clicking sounds with his tongue. Manish Babu said, 'All you people are getting on without any problem. It is only in my mine that all these troubles have to crop up. Why should these wretched rascals have their eyes set on me alone is something I cannot understand.'

Gobinda Babu said, 'You know, about six months back there was trouble in my mine as well. I knew that the police would be of no use, so I straightaway engaged my own spies. I had employed eight of them and within a week or so they gave me the names of the mischief-makers. Five of those men were the ringleaders; I had them beaten up severely one day. After that I didn't even have to sack them; they ran away on their own. Since then every thing is quiet and peaceful.' After saying this he smiled toothily like a grinning gorilla.

Manish Babu said, 'I too had employed spies, but it didn't work. Anyway...' He started talking of other matters. The conversation flowed in a normal course. Tea and snacks were served to Gobinda Babu. Even as he sipped his tea, his eyes hovered around us. Perhaps he had found it difficult to believe that we had arrived there on a visit without any purpose.

Gobinda Haldar got up after an hour or so. Manish Babu escorted him to the covered porch; we followed him. The driver opened the door for Gobinda Babu; as he was about to get into the car, he turned his face towards Byomkesh, smiled and said, 'Try and see what you can do.'

He got into the car and the car drove off.

We exchanged glances with Manish Babu, who said in a morose tone, 'This man, Gobinda Haldar is a very shrewd person. It is not easy to hoodwink him.'

It was almost eleven by the time we went to bed after finishing our dinner. We were tired after the train journey and fell asleep almost immediately.

It was well past eight when we woke up next morning.

A servant informed us that both Manish Babu and his son had left for the colliery in the early hours. We washed quickly and walked out to the sitting room to find that tea and breakfast had been laid out for us and a young woman was standing by the table.

Not having met any of the ladies of the house during the previous night we were a little surprised at first. As Byomkesh looked at her with a smile on his face, the girl lowered her eyes and said in a somewhat hesitant voice, 'I am Indira, the daughter-in-law. Please sit down and have your breakfast.'

She was Phanish's wife. Of a mild dark complexion, she was tall and slim and her face was pretty and impressive. Around eighteen years old, she was evidently of a shy nature and not accustomed to talking with strange men who were older than her. I thought that she had perhaps felt obliged to attend to the guests due to the absence of the male members of the family.

We sat down to eat. Byomkesh said, 'Why don't you sit down?'

Indira sat down shyly in a corner of a sofa.

Taking a sip of tea, Byomkesh picked up some food on a plate and said, 'We were late in getting up today. Does your father-in-law leave for work very early in the morning?'

'Yes, he leaves at seven.'

'And your husband?'

Indira's face was instantly lowered. Without raising her eyes, she said in an undertone, 'He too.' Then, she forcefully overcame her shyness and said, 'They come home at twelve, have their lunch and go back to the mine at three.'

Byomkesh looked at her and smiled but did not say any thing more. I was observing Indira while I ate. She was sitting quietly, but at times she was casting sudden, sidelong glances at Byomkesh. It seemed that besides attending to the guests she had some other design. She was aware of Byomkesh's identity; Phanish must have disclosed it to her, which was why she wanted to tell him some thing. But having resolved to speak out, she was held back by hesitation. We had seen almost the same sort of hesitation on Phanish's face during the previous night.

Byomkesh finished his breakfast, took a last sip of tea from his cup and then while wiping his face on a napkin, he said in a pleasant voice, 'Now tell me what you have in mind.'

All this time I had been observing a conflict between resolve and hesitation on Indira's face. Now taken totally by surprise, she got to her feet unconsciously. Then all her anxiety was released in a single breath as she said, 'Byomkesh Babu, please save my husband. He is in great danger.'

Byomkesh got up from his chair and sat down on the sofa. He invited Indira to sit down beside him and said, 'Tell me what danger your husband is facing.'

Indira sat down at an angle on the edge of the sofa and said in a broken voce, ' I – I won't be able to tell you every thing properly. If you kindly agree to help him he shall speak to you himself.'

Byomkesh asked, 'Does it have any thing to do with the mine?'

Indira replied, 'No, no, it is some thing else. But please don't talk about this to my father-in-law. He knows nothing about the matter.'

Byomkesh spoke in a calm and reassuring voice, 'Don't worry, I won't speak to any one.'

'Would you help him?'

'I still don't know any thing about the problem. But if your husband is innocent I shall certainly help him.'

'My husband is innocent.'

'Then you can stop worrying.'

There was a row of rooms in the compound along one side of the property. After relieving Indira's anxiety, we lit up cigarettes and started walking in that direction.

A middle-aged gentleman came out from the first room. He looked somewhat foppish in an extra-fine dhoti and kurta and he had apparently dyed his hair as well, because grey roots were visible under the black hair.

Byomkesh said, 'My name is Gagan Mitra and this is Sujit Bandyopadhyay. We are Manish Babu's guests.'

The gentleman became somewhat flurried as he greeted us, saying, 'Come sir, please come. I had heard from the boss that he was expecting you. My name is Surapati Ghatak. I am the supervisor here.'

Surapati Babu was obviously unaware of our real names. Byomkesh said, 'So this is the office of the coalmine and you are in charge of the office.'

Surapati Babu said, 'That is right. There is a small office at the coalmine, but this is the main office. Would you like to come in and have a look?'

We went round the rooms. Several clerks were working with books and ledgers and we could hear the clatter of a typewriter from somewhere. After completing the round we eventually came back and sat down in Surapati Babu's office.

We talked on general topics for a while. Then Byomkesh said a little hesitantly, 'Let me tell you some thing in strict confidence; the two of us have planned to buy a small coalmine. Not here, it's somewhere else and available at a moderately cheap price. But neither of us has any knowledge about how to run a coalmine. This is why we have come to see Manish Babu's mine. We want to gather some experience both about the work at the office and at the mine.'

Surapati Babu became most enthusiastic as he said, 'Of course, of course. There is nothing to worry. I'll teach you all that you have to know about the work of this office in two days and the work at the mine is also not very difficult to pick up. And if you wish I can recommend a very good man whom you may employ for running your coalmine.'

Byomkesh asked, 'What sort of a man?'

Surapati Babu said, 'Some one who knows both the office work and the work which has to be done at the colliery. A man whom I have trained myself.'

Byomkesh showed eagerness and exclaimed, 'Is that so? Well, if we can find a good man who knows his work we shall gladly employ him. I'll talk with you on this matter later. We'll also try to pick up the work done at this office. We shall be here for a few days.'

From the office we came back to Manish Babu's residence. Manish Babu and Phanish returned at around twelve. It was well past one when we finished our lunch. After resting for some time the four of us set out for the mine in a motorcar.

It was a large car. Phanish drove, while the three of us sat in the back seat. Leaving the town, we took an isolated road. The coalmine was about three miles away.

Byomkesh said, 'We met Surapati Babu this morning. How long has he been with you?'

Manish Babu said, 'Nearly twenty years. He is a well-experienced person.'

Byomkesh said, 'We told him that we were planning to buy a coalmine. We did not reveal our true identities to him.'

Manish Babu nodded and said, 'You did the right thing. Surapati, of course, is a trustworthy man. If he could be said to have a single fault — it is that he got married for a second time about two years back.'

Now the cause of Surapati's dyed hair and stylish clothes was clear to us. It was only natural that in his middle age he should try to put up an illusion of youth to impress his second wife, who must be much younger than him.

After a brief silence, Byomkesh asked, 'Has anyone offered to buy your mine recently?'

Manish Babu said, 'Not recently, I received an offer a few years back from a *marwari* businessman. He had offered a good price, but I did not sell.'

Byomkesh raised his second question, 'Are you on good terms with the owners of the other mines here?'

Manish Babu said, 'I can't claim to have close intimacy with them, but I can say that I do not have any conflict with any one.'

'Can you think of any particular individual, who could be wearing a mask of courtesy but is intent on harming you all the time?'

'Even if there was some one like that how would I know him?'

'That's true. The person who visited last night – Gobinda Haldar—what sort of a man is he?'

Manish Babu said in a slow thoughtful tone, 'It is difficult to know Gobinda Haldar. His character is like that of a slimy eel, — quite impossible to touch or grasp. But his younger brother and partner, Arobinda is a really evil person. A drunkard, a gambler and a loose character. His wife found an escape from her miserable life about a year back by committing suicide. Since then Arobinda has become a reckless debauch.'

There was no further conversation, as we entered the compound of the coalmine.

I have no desire to provide any lengthy description of the coalmine. Those who have not seen a coalmine with their own eyes must have seen it in a movie or on a painter's canvas. It is by no means a pleasing sight. And moreover, the coalmine has very little to do with this anecdote, rather it can be said to serve merely as a background to the story. Without a background a story tends to become stark naked, hence the background has to be retained.

Coal! Extracted by machine from the interior of the earth, it then supplies energy to run the machine and thus runs the wheel of civilization. I salute thee, oh machine! Thy tool pierces the depth of the mine-pits, thy nail tears the soil to bits and behold how the bowels of the earth it slits! I salute thee, oh machine! The cycle starts and ends with thee.

We were introduced to Tarapada Babu, the manager of the mine. He was a middle aged man and we learnt that he lived in the company's quarters within the compound of the mine. He looked to be an imposing person with a strong personality. He took us around and explained the different activities of the mine. He also proposed to take us down into the mine-pit, but we declined the offer. *Sita had sufficient reasons to enter the netherworld but we had no such obligation.

In the evening we were served tea in Tarapada Babu's office. There we met the doctor attached to the mine, Dr. Jatindra Ghosh and other senior officers. The conversation was carried on general topics, nothing related to the real purpose of our visit. Needless to say we were introduced by our assumed names. I noticed at one time that Byomkesh had set up quite a lively discussion with Dr. Ghosh. Seated in a corner of the room the two seemed to be

*Sita in the Ramayana, passed through an ordeal by fire at the behest of her husband Ram and then Mother Earth opened up in response to her appeal; Sita stepped down and disappeared in the netherworld.

engrossed in a serious conversation, oblivious of others. Dr. Ghosh was of our age; he too lived in the compound of the mine, sharing his working hours between his dispensary and the hospital. He was wearing a coat and a pair of crumpled trousers and his appearance showed signs of fatigue from overwork.

We left the mine at dusk and proceeded towards Manish Babu's residence in his car.

Directly after dinner that night Manish Babu went up to his bedroom. We returned to the guest-room followed by Phanish.

Switching on the ceiling fan, Byomkesh stretched out on his bed, lit up a cigarette and then said to Phanish, 'Sit down. What have you been doing to get your wife so upset?'

Sitting down on a chair, Phanish went on wringing his hands for some time and then said in a diffident voice, 'I had persuaded Indira to speak to you, because I did not have the nerve to tell you myself...'

'But what is the problem? The way you are behaving gives me the impression that it is a serious matter.'

'Yes, sir, it is a serious matter. By chance I have become involved in a murder case. If my father comes to know...'

Byomkesh sat up on his bed, 'A murder case!'

Phanish spoke in a shrinking voice, 'Yes, sir, a very dirty business. The police have started their investigation, they have come to know that we...'

'Hang on, tell me every thing that happened from the very beginning.'

But Phanish was too nervous and agitated to recount every thing in a proper sequence. I have reproduced his tangled narrative below as clearly as I could.

There was a club in the town, which had been humorously given the name, 'Coal Club.' The subscription rate of the club was quite high; so barring the well-to-do people none others could become members. Phanish was a member of the club. There were other important and respectable members; notable among whom were Mrigendra Moulik, the owner of Uludanga Coalmine, Madhumoy Sur, the owner of Dhubipota mine and Arabinda and Gobinda Haldar, owners of Shimulia mine.

Tennis and badminton were played at the club in the afternoon. In the evening there were facilities for billiards, table tennis, cards and chess. Cards were played with small stakes fixed by the club, but this did not satisfy those who had a compulsive urge for gambling. Arobindo Haldar was one such dissatisfied member. But what could be done? There was no other place in the town where one could gamble in polite company.

About a year back an old gentleman became a member of the club. He was rich and had opened a money-lending business after arriving lately at the town. He had set up a small office in the market area, but he lived in a secluded street on the outskirts of the town. His appearance was like a vulture and his name was Pranhari Poddar.

Pranhari Poddar used to arrive and sit all by himself at the club. There were no senior members of his age group; barring a few middle-aged persons most of the members belonged to the younger generation. Gradually he got acquainted with a few members, but he could not become intimate with any one due to age-difference.

Phanish, Mrigen Moulik, Madhumoy Sur and Arobindo Haldar, — these four members had formed a group of their own in the club. Phanish was the youngest and Arobindo the oldest among the four. Arobindo was around thirty-five and it was he who assumed the leader's role in the group.

One evening these four members were sitting together and playing bridge, when Pranhari Poddar arrived and started watching the game. Going round the table he looked at the cards held by each player. Arobindo asked him casually, 'Can you play contract bridge?'

The old man smiled and said, 'I can.'

'Would you like to play?'

'Yes. What is the stake?'

'A rupee a point. Will that be okay?'

'Yes.'

When that rubber was over, a card was dealt to each player and the one who drew the lowest card sat out. Pranhari Poddar sat down to play in his place.

It was seen that Pranhari Babu was a skilled player. But that day fortune did not favour him; he did not receive good hands. At the end of the game it was found that he had lost twenty-one rupees. He promptly paid up the money.

Thereafter Pranhari Babu used to play bridge with Phanish's group almost every day. Some days he lost, some days he won, but he always seemed unruffled. Gradually he got himself included in the group.

A few months passed. Then while they were playing bridge at the club one evening, Pranhari Babu asked, 'Don't you people play any other games except bridge?'

Madhumoy Sur asked, 'What sort of games?'

Pranhari said, 'Say, poker or running flush?'

Mrigen Moulik said, 'We know every game. But it is against the rules of this club to gamble. *Bridge* is not a game of gamble, it is a *game of skill.*' He said this with a sneer.

Pranhari did not say any thing then. But after the game was over, he said, 'Why don't you people come to my residence one day and try your hand at some new games?'

Nobody had any objection to the suggestion. Arobindo said, 'That's not a bad idea. Where do you stay?'

Pranhari said, 'My residence is outside the town on the road to Uludanga mine. I live all by myself; it would be most enjoyable if you come. Why don't you come tomorrow?'

Everybody agreed. Pranhari boarded his taxi and left. He did not own a car. He had a fixed arrangement with a taxi in which he did all his movements.

The next evening all four of them boarded Arobindo's car and reached Pranhari's residence. It was a two-storeyed house, located on a secluded street at a distance of about one and a half miles from the border of the town. There was no other house within a range of two to three hundred yards.

Pranhari Babu greeted them warmly and then led them to a well-furnished sitting room on the ground floor. For some time the conversation moved on general topics. Pranhari Babu was a widower and had no children. Earlier he used to live in Cuttack in Orissa, but somehow he did not like the place, which is why he had moved out here. He had a maidservant, who cooked for him and attended to other chores.

Just then the maidservant entered, carrying cups of tea on a tray. Laying down the tray on the table she left the room, but came back again with a plate of cutlets. She was a very well-formed young woman of around twenty years. Her complexion was a little dark, but she had a most attractive face and her eyes bore the captivating magic of a restless doe. She did not at all look like a woman of the serving class and she caused a flutter in the hearts of some of the visitors.

While tasting the hot cutlets, Arobindo asked, 'This is your maidservant? I must say she has prepared excellent cutlets.'

Pranhari replied, 'Yes. I brought Mohini from Orissa. She cooks very well.'

After the tea and cutlets had been consumed they sat down to play. With common consent they started playing 'running flush' with three cards. Everybody had brought good amounts of money. Pranhari started playing with five hundred rupees.

They played for two hours. There was no big win or loss; some won fifty rupees, some lost a hundred rupees. Pranhari Babu had been on the losing side. It was decided that they would meet and play cards at the same place after three days.

Phanish was not feeling at all comfortable. He was no doubt fond of playing cards, but he was not a gambler. Moreover he had a strict father on whom he was largely dependent in financial matters. He had got involved in this gambling affair just because he happened to be a member of the group, but if he tried to opt out at that time he would have become a laughing stock. So he had to remain attached to the gambling group despite his reluctance.

The second day's game was very exciting. Mohini had made chicken fries. They had it with tea and started playing. Midway in the game Pranhari Babu brought out a bottle of imported whiskey. Phanish couldn't stand alcohol, he felt like vomiting whenever he tried to drink whiskey. So he refrained from drinking. But the others drank, Arobindo the most. The stakes were raised progressively. Everybody was very excited, only Pranhari Babu remained unruffled.

The winnings were worked out after the game was over. Arobindo had won around a thousand rupees, the others had all lost money. Pranhari Babu had won two hundred rupees.

Thereafter they used to meet and play cards at Pranhari Babu's house once or twice a week. One of them would lose on a particular day, someone else would lose on another day, but the rest would all win. Pranhari Babu never lost much; he seemed to be a winner in the long run.

Simultaneously with the card-games another side-show had begun; this involved Mohini. Madhumoy and Mridanga might have been attracted towards Mohini, but Arobindo pursued her in a most shameless manner. On the days when the card-games were to be held he used to reach Pranhari Babu's house before anybody else and stand by the kitchen door, holding amorous conversation with Mohini. He probably visited Pranhari Babu's house even in the daytime during his absence. It could not be said how far his relationship with Mohini had progressed, but she belonged to a class of women who would not normally shun the attention of a rich patron.

About five to six weeks passed in this manner. Phanish was not at peace with himself, he tried to avoid his friends, but couldn't; Arobindo dragged him to the place almost by force. Then one day their eyes were opened. They found out that Pranhari Babu was a seasoned gambler and that he resorted to sleight of hand at every given opportunity. There was a lot of argument that night, after which the guests got up from the game and left in a huff.

In the ultimate reckoning it was found that each of the visitors had lost around three to four thousand rupees and the entire sum had gone to Pranhari's pockets. Arobindo had lost the most — nearly five thousand rupees.

At the club Arobindo started chafing, 'Let the old bag of bones come here, I shall beat the daylights out of him.' Madhumoy and Mridanga did not make any comments, but their attitude seemed to indicate that they would not spare Pranhari if they could lay their hands on him.

But Pranhari Babu was a cautious person, he never showed up at the club.

After about a week Arobindo said, 'The bugger has gone into hiding. Let's go to his house and beat him up.'

Phanish tried to object, saying, 'What is the point? When the money is already lost...'

But Arobindo cut him off and said, 'The money is immaterial. Why should we let the bugger cheat us and get off scot-free? What do you think, Mrigen?'

Mrigen said, 'The fellow should be a taught a lesson.'

Madhumoy said, 'Barring the maidservant no one else lives in his house, so there is nothing to fear.'

The four of them set out around eight that night. They hired a taxi from a taxistand close to the club and proceeded towards Pranhari's house. They thought that it was not advisable to take their own cars. Although the road was secluded, plenty of vehicles travelled by that road from Uludanga Colliery during the night. Someone could have noticed and recognized one of their cars if it was parked near Pranhari's house. Moreover, the drivers employed by them were not deaf and dumb; they were bound to gossip. While beating up a man it was desirable to avoid eyewitnesses as far as possible.

Stopping the taxi at about a hundred yards away from Pranhari's house they got off from the vehicle. The road was unlit. Madhumoy was carrying a big electric torch in his hand, which he flicked on from time to time as they proceeded towards Pranhari's house. They had asked the taxi driver to reverse his vehicle and wait.

A light was on in the first floor. The entrance door to the ground floor was open. Sound of cooking could be heard from the kitchen; Mohini must be at work. They entered quietly, treading softly like hunters.

The sitting room was at the front and next to it was the staircase leading to the first floor. The four friends stood there and talked in low voices. Then Arobindo took the torchlight from Madhumoy and tiptoed up the staircase. Coming down a little later, he said in a soft whisper, 'There is a door at the staircase landing, which is quite strong and fitted with a Yale lock. But it is closed; I couldn't find out if it is locked from inside or outside.'

After some further discussions it was decided that the ground floor should be searched more thoroughly. The old man was very shrewd; he might have switched on a light upstairs and then hidden somewhere in the ground floor. Arobindo walked down softly and peeked into the kitchen. With her back to the door Mohini was cooking all by herself, there was nobody with her.

Then the four friends went off in different directions to search every room in the ground floor as well as the open compound in the rear.

They returned to the foot of the staircase after about fifteen minutes. None of them had been able to find Pranhari. So the old man must be upstairs. Arobindo said, 'Come, let us try to push the door and see if it opens.'

This time all four of them climbed up the staircase. As soon as they pressed the door it opened easily. The light was on. Pranhari Poddar was stretched in the middle of the floor, his face turned to one side. There was a long bleeding bruise on the right side of his head, as if he had parted his sparse hair and smeared vermilion on the parting. His face was distorted, his teeth were exposed and it seemed as if even while lying on his back for the last time Pranhari was making faces at the spectators.

The four friends stood stunned near the door for a while and then they rushed down the staircase, running straight out to the road.

Approaching the taxi they found that the driver was sleeping with his head resting on the steering wheel. Each man placed a finger on his lips to warn the others. Then they got into the taxi. The driver woke up and started driving.

When they returned to the club they found that it was only nine. They sat together, away from others and discussed the situation. There was no need to inform any one. The news of Pranhari's unnatural death would, of course, come to be known in due course, but there was no proof that the four of them had gone to his house. The taxi driver was a hundred yards away, he had not seen them entering Pranhari's house. So it would be wise to remain silent about the misadventure.

They played cards at the club till around ten thirty that night and then went home as if nothing had happened.

The news of Pranhari's death was heard all over the town on the following day, but the names of the four friends were not linked with the murder. On the third day however the police visited Arobindo's house, obviously on the basis of information received from some sources.

But all these four men were influential businessmen, wielding a lot of power, so none of them had yet been arrested, nor had any news trickled outside. The police had been conducting the investigation in all earnestness; they had contacted each of the four friends once so far. It was difficult to say what the outcome of the investigation was going to be. Phanish's plight was by far the most precarious. On one hand there was a murder charge and on the other hand if his father, who was a man of strong-principles came to know that he had been gambling and had become involved in a murder case, drastic action would follow.

It was almost midnight when Phanish finished recounting the narrative. Byomkesh told him by way of assurance, 'Tell your wife that there is nothing to worry. I am taking the responsibility of finding out the truth. Tomorrow we shall go on a visit to the town, we shall need a car.'

Phanish said, 'I shall instruct the driver. The small car shall remain at your disposal.'

Phanish left shortly thereafter. We switched off the light and went to bed.

I asked, 'What did you think of the whole thing?'

Byomkesh said, 'Of the five suspects I have met only one. I can't say any thing till I meet the others.'

'Five suspects?'

'Yes. The maidservant cannot be ruled out.'

There was no further conversation. I fell asleep thinking about the bizarre end of Pranhari Poddar's sordid life.

When I woke up next morning I saw Byomkesh seated at the table writing a letter with deep concentration. I sat up on the bed, stretched my arms and asked, 'To whom are you writing this early in the morning? To Satyabati? Have you started missing your wife in two days?'

Byomkesh went on writing and said, 'No, not her, — I am writing to Bikash.'

'Bikash?'

'Bikash Dutta.'

'Oh Bikash. Why are you writing to him?'

'I have secured a job for Bikash. An orderly's job at the dispensary of the coalmine. That's why I am asking him to come over.'

'Oh.'

Byomkesh went back to his writing. He wanted to install Bikash at the coalmine, so that while keeping his distance from the hub of activity, he could still gather information through his emissary. Standing on firm land himself he would send his spy to the deep waters.

During breakfast I noticed that Indira was looking much happier. Sunlight had broken through the cover of doubts and misgiving and was shining brightly. Phanish had obviously told her about Byomkesh's assurance.

Like the previous day both father and son had left for work long before we sat down for breakfast. While eating buttered toast Byomkesh cast a sidelong glance at Indira and said, 'Your husband is really immature.'

Indira lowered her face shyly. When she looked up again I could see that doubt and concern had returned to her eyes. In this girl's mind there was no end of worry about her husband. Byomkesh reassured her, saying, 'Do not worry. Every thing shall be all right. We shall be going out now.'

Indira looked at him and asked, 'Where would you be going?'

Byomkesh said, 'Oh, here and there. We might be back by late afternoon. If your father-in-law asks you, tell him that we have gone to visit the town.'

We got up from the table after breakfast. The driver came in and reported that the car was parked in the porch.

Getting into the car, Byomkesh asked the driver to take us to the post office first.

At the post office he posted his letter to Bikash under express delivery. Then, returning to the car, he said, 'Now take us to the police station, the head police station.'

A constable was standing on guard at the main gate of the police station. When Byomkesh sought an interview with the officer-in-charge, the constable produced a slip and said, 'Please write your name and business.'

Byomkesh wrote on the slip, 'Gagan Mitra. Regarding Manish Chakraborty's coalmine.'

The constable came back after a while and said, 'Please follow me.'

The officer-in-charge wearing full uniform was seated at a table in an inner room. He raised his face when we entered. The next moment he jumped up from his chair and caught hold of Byomkesh's hand, saying, 'What's this? Since when have you become Gagan Mitra?'

I could then recognize him. He was Pramod Barat. We had come in close contact with him a few years back in connection with an investigation at Golap Colony. A policeman's job was like a wanderer's mission. After moving from one assignment to another he had eventually arrived at this town as the officer-in-charge of the head police station. His complexion was pitch black; he had put on a little weight during the last few years, but his face was as sharp as before.

He greeted us with warm courtesy and invited us to sit down. Some time was spent in ruminating over the past. Then Byomkesh told him the real purpose of our visit to the town. After hearing him, Pramod Babu said, 'Hmm, the case related to the Phuljhuri coalmine is on our file, but we could do nothing. The police are not equipped to deal with such matters. We have to work with a lot of people, so confidentiality cannot be maintained. But you should be able to ...'

Byomkesh said, 'Do you remember Bikash Dutta? I have called him here; he would stay at the coalmine and conduct his investigation.'

Pramod Babu said, 'Of course I remember Bikash. He is a competent young man. But if I can be of any service...'

Byomkesh said, 'I have not come to you for that matter. Pramod Babu. Somebody was murdered here lately, an old man named Pranhari Poddar.'

'Oh, you have heard that too?'

'How could I remain without hearing? The son of the gentleman with whom we are putting up here happens to be one of your suspects.'

Pramod Barat had a woeful expression on his face as he said, 'I am in a real fix, Byomkesh Babu. All the four suspects are stalwarts of this town; they wield a lot of power. So I have been treading with great caution. There is no eyewitness, everything is based on circumstantial evidence; if I arrest any of these gentlemen by mistake I shall be in deep trouble.'

Byomkesh asked, 'Out of these four men whom do you suspect the most?'

Pramod Babu thought for a while and then said, 'Well, all four men had equal motives and equal opportunities. But if you ask for my personal opinion I would say that it could be the work of Arobindo Haldar.'

'You don't think that the four men had gone there to commit the murder collectively?'

'No.'

'There was a maidservant in the house; have you thought of her?'

'I did. She had ample opportunity, but I can't find any motive.'

'Hmm. Why don't you tell me every thing that you know. May be I can be of some help.'

'Oh, really! You'll help me! Thank you, Byomkesh Babu. Getting your help is a matter of rare good fortune.'

What Pramod Babu then told us is summed up below.

On the night that Pranhari Poddar died, a truck was coming from the direction of Uludanga colliery. The truck-driver stopped the car because a woman was standing on the road and waving her hands, asking him to halt. When the truck had halted the woman came running and told the driver, 'Some people have murdered the owner of this house. Please inform the police immediately.'

The truck-driver reported the matter at the police station. Within half an hour the inspector reached the spot. The woman was still standing anxiously by the road. Her name was Mohini. She was employed as a maidservant at Pranhari Poddar's house; there were no other servants.

Inspector Barat went up to the first floor and inspected the dead body. His subordinates searched the entire house. It was empty. On enquiring from Mohini it was learnt that she used to sleep in a small room on the ground floor beside the kitchen. Her master's bedroom was on the first floor. On his return from the town that evening he had taken his tea in the sitting room on the ground floor and then gone upstairs. Mohini had then started her cooking. Her master usually came down for dinner at nine. But when he did not come down till nine thirty that night, Mohini had gone up to call him and found him lying dead on the floor.

After sending the body for post-mortem Barat interrogated Mohini again. In response to his questions she said that usually nobody visited the house after dusk; but recently four gentlemen had been coming on some evenings for playing cards; on those days her master used to buy fish, chicken, minced meat or other delicacies from the market, which she was asked to cook and serve to the visitors. The gentlemen had not come that evening, so there was no extra cooking. All the four visitors were young men, not old like her master. They used to come in a motorcar; from their clothes and bearing they appeared to be rich people. Mohini did not know their names. She could not say if any one had come to the house while she was cooking. Pranhari used to meet his visitors on the ground floor; he did not take them upstairs. But the master had not come down that evening; Mohini would have heard him if he had come down.

After finishing his interrogation Barat had asked her, 'What are you going to do now? Do you have any acquaintances in this town?'

Mohini had replied, 'No, I do not know anyone here.'

Barat had then said, 'In that case you may come with me and spend the night at the police station. Tomorrow we shall make some arrangement for your stay somewhere else. It is not possible for a woman to stay all by herself in this house.'

But Mohini had said, 'I'll be all right here. I shall shut the door of my room on the ground floor and sleep. I shall not feel scared.'

Barat agreed to her suggestion, deputed a constable for guarding the house and left.

While conducting his investigations about Pranhari, Barat had come to know that he was a member of the 'Coal Club.' On enquiring at the club he learnt that Pranhari used to play cards regularly with four members. The situation then became a little clear; it was quite likely that they were the same four men who used to visit Pranhari's house for playing cards.

Pramod Babu interrogated the four men separately. They admitted that they used to visit Pranhari's house occasionally for playing cards, but they strongly denied that they had gone to his house on the night he was murdered.

Barat interrogated the four personal drivers employed by the gentlemen. Three of the drivers said that their masters had not gone by car to Pranhari's house that night, while the fourth stated that the four gentlemen had come out of the club at around eight, but instead of going by car they had travelled on foot and come back in about an hour. He had no idea where they had gone.

Barat then started interrogating the taxi drivers. There were around fifty taxis in the town. Ultimately one of the taxi drivers pointed at another and said, 'That man had gone out with passengers that night. You may ask him.' The second driver when questioned said that on the particular night he had taken four passengers to the road leading to Uludanga coalmine. Barat fetched the taxi driver to the Coal Club and let him see the four men without their knowledge. The driver positively identified the four men.

Thereafter Barat had interrogated the four men again, but they had resolutely denied every thing. The situation had thus been reduced to a stage where there was no other witness except a taxi driver and based on his statement it was not possible to arrest four important residents of the town on a murder charge.

After completing his narration Barat said, 'I have told you every thing that I have come to know till now. Oh yes, there is one not very relevant matter, which I might as well inform you. Gobinda Haldar, the elder brother of the prime suspect had offered me a bribe of five thousand rupees.'

'Really?'

'Yes. He is a very crafty person. He took me aside and hinted to me that if I drop the case I shall receive a reward of five thousand rupees.'

Byomkesh looked at his watch. It was half past nine.

He asked Barat, 'Are you very busy at this time? I have a mind to see the murder site.'

Barat said, 'Certainly. Let's go.'

Byomkesh asked, 'Is the young woman still there?'

Barat said, 'Yes, of course, she is there. She has nowhere to go. So she is living there.'

The three of us came out of the police station. Pramod Babu got into our car. As the car started moving Byomkesh instructed the driver, 'Take us to the house where your young master and his friends used to go for playing cards.'

There was no change in the stoical expression on the driver's face as he went on driving.

The car stopped in front of Pranhari Poddar's house after ten minutes. There was no one at the entrance. The house looked somewhat bare; there were no compound walls on any side; set back by a few yards from the road, the house seemed to stand immodestly exposed. The front door was wide open.

Barat frowned, casting his eyes in all directions and said, 'Where has the wretched constable disappeared?'

Barat entered the house first; we fell in behind him. A loud croaking voice could be heard from the kitchen. Proceeding in that direction we found that the constable in full uniform was twirling his moustache as he stood by the door of the kitchen, having amorous exchanges with a young female who was inside. He stiffened to attention on seeing us.

Barat looked at him angrily and said, 'Go and stand outside. What the hell are you doing here, leaving the door wide open?'

Barat's question was entirely superfluous. Even the dumbest fool could realise what the guard was doing. What does a fly do when it is near a pot of honey?

The guard saluted and left. Barat then cast a suspicious look inside the kitchen. Mohini was seated on the floor, chopping vegetables. She hurriedly got to her feet and looked searchingly at Barat.

Her complexion was dark, but her body, face, eyes and every single movement of her limbs carried a mysterious magic, — filled with an irresistible attraction of voluptuous youth. She could have been called an exquisite beauty if she was fair, but even her dark complexion had the intoxicating power of a seductive midnight, which captivated the mind.

But Pramod Barat was not a romantic man; he asked, 'Where did you get all this fresh vegetable?'

Mohini said, 'Guard *sahib* has got them. He brings vegetables of his choice and gives them to me, I cook them for him. I get my meals as well.'

Barat cleared his throat and said, 'Yes, the guard *sahib* seems to be kindness personified.'

It was not clear if Mohini had understood the sarcastic comment. She asked, 'Do you need me for any thing, Inspector *sahib*?'

Pramod Babu said, 'Stay here. I shall call you after a while.'

'All right.'

As we walked away from the kitchen, Byomkesh smiled and said, 'You have made an error of judgement, Inspector Barat. You should have posted an old guard here.'

Barat said, 'Byomkesh Babu, you don't know these men. The older a guard gets the more amorous he becomes.'

Byomkesh started laughing and asked, 'And what about old money-lenders?'

Barat cast a startled glance at Byomkesh and said, 'That I have still not been able to decide, but the circumstances are suspicious. Why don't you interrogate the girl and find out if she was involved in any hanky panky with the old man.'

'I shall do so.'

We took the staircase adjoining the sitting room and went to the first floor. There was a strong, heavy door fitted with a Yale lock at the landing. This door seemed to be of a more recent installation as compared to the other doors of the house. Pranhari Poddar might have installed this door after hiring the house.

Barat took out keys from his pocket and opened the door. The room was dark, but then Barat opened the windows and it became flooded with sunlight.

The room had two doors and two windows. One door was at the staircase landing through which we had entered and the other door was installed in the rear wall. The room was about fifteen feet square with hardly any furniture. A bed was laid out on a plain cot; facing the bed and almost grazing the wall stood a gigantic iron safe. Pranhari's used garments were hanging on a clothes' stand fixed to the wall. Presumably he had no dearth of money, but his style of living was most ordinary. With the iron safe close to his head and the door secured with a Yale lock, he used to sleep on a shabby bed laid on a plain cot.

Casting inquisitive looks all around the room, Byomkesh enquired, 'Where was the body found?'

Barat pointed to a spot about four feet away from the door leading from the staircase landing and said, 'Here.'

Byomkesh stooped down and inspected the spot, saying, 'I can't see much signs of blood, just a drop or two.'

Barat said, 'The old man hardly had any blood in his body. He was like a dried up piece of bamboo.'

Byomkesh said, 'But then there isn't much bleeding if the skull is cracked. Has the murder weapon been found?'

'No. There was no weapon in the room. And we found nothing in the house, which could have served as the murder weapon.'

'You must have opened the safe. What did you find?'

'Yes, the key to the safe was in a bunch of keys tied to Poddar's waist. When I opened the safe I found a book of accounts tied up with a string and ten thousand rupees in cash.'

'Ten thousand rupees!'

'Yes. The old man had a money lending business, which could be why he kept all that cash at home.'

'Hmm. Did he have money in the bank?'

'Yes. And it is still there. I do not know who would inherit it. It's not a small amount, nearly one and a half lakhs.'

'Really! Have his relatives heard of his death?'

'Probably there is nobody. Otherwise they would have gathered here by now like a pack of vultures.'

'I heard that the old man had an office in town. Did you find any thing when you searched that place?'

'The office was just a tiny room, like a secret cubbyhole. There were a few books of accounts, from which it seems that the money lending business was not doing too well.'

Byomkesh became thoughtful and spoke almost to himself, 'The money lending business was not doing well, but still there was one and a half lakh in the bank and ten thousand in the safe.' Waking up from his reflections, he asked, 'What is there on the other side of that door?'

Barat said, 'A bathroom.'

This door too was new and strong. Pranhari Poddar had converted his bedroom into a well-protected fortress, maybe because he used to keep cash in the safe.

Byomkesh opened the door. It was a narrow bathroom. A little light was emerging through a ventilator on the opposite wall and below the ventilator there was a narrow door. Barring an empty bucket and a mug, there was nothing else in the bathroom.

The narrow door on the opposite wall was bolted at the top and bottom. Byomkesh unfastened the bolts and threw open the door. I peeped out and saw a rickety iron ladder stretching down from the door to the ground. It was presumably for the use of the sweeper, — a second entry to Pranhari's fortress.

Byomkesh asked Barat, 'When you came here for the first time that night were both these doors closed?'

Barat said, 'Yes, they were both closed. Only the front door accessible from the staircase landing was open.'

Byomkesh said, 'Let's go down. I'll ask the girl a few questions and see how she responds.'

We sat down in a well-furnished sitting room on the ground floor. Mohini stood in front of us, her hands resting on the back of a chair. There was no sign of fear or concern on her face, rather her attitude and bearing were quite controlled and restrained.

In my own mind I was comparing Pranhari's bare bedroom with this well-decorated sitting room, when Byomkesh started interrogating Mohini.

'How long have you been working for Pranhari Babu?'

Mohini said, 'A little more than two years.'

'Have you been with Pranhari Babu since he was in Cuttack?'

'Yes sir,'

'Does Pranhari Babu have any close relatives?'

'I do not know.'

'What is your present salary?'

'In Cuttack I used to get a salary of ten rupees per month with food and clothing. After coming here my salary was raised by five rupees.'

'What sort of a man was Pranhari Babu?'

After remaining silent for a while, Mohini said, 'He was my master, he must have been a good man.' In other words, he was my employer, I shall not talk ill of him, but you are free to form your own opinion.

Byomkesh asked, 'Was he a miser?'

Mohini remained silent. Byomkesh went on looking intently at her and then asked, 'What sort of relations did you have with him?'

Mohini raised her eyes towards Byomkesh with a look of surprise and a brief flicker of emotion seemed to flash past the corner of her lips. Then she replied quietly, 'Good relations. He had affection for me.'

Byomkesh said, 'Hmm. Did he have any weakness for women?'

'No sir. He was an old man, he didn't have any such flaws. His only addiction was for playing cards. He used to sit all by himself and play cards.'

'All right. Now tell me some thing about yourself. Pranhari Babu has been murdered, but you are continuing to live in this house all by yourself. Why?'

'Where shall I go? I know nobody else in this town.'

'Why don't you go back to your family?'

'Yes, that is what I shall do. But the Inspector *Sahib* has ordered that I shouldn't move from here till the investigation is over.'

'Who are there in your family?'

'My old parents.'

'And your husband?'

Mohini raised her eyes and then lowered them without replying.

'You must have been married?'

Mohini nodded her head silently.

'Where is your husband?'

Mohini raised her face and replied quietly, 'My husband deserted me; he hasn't come back again.'

Byomkesh kept his eyes fixed on her face while lighting a cigarette and asked, 'How long has your husband been away from home?'

'Three years.'

'What was his occupation?'

'He used to work in mills and workshops.'

'Why did he desert you?'

Mohini's lower lip distended a fraction; casting a quick, sidelong glance at Byomkesh, she said, 'I do not know.'

While I listened to these questions and answers and observed Mohini very closely, I could not stop wondering about her character. Was she a chaste woman or a wayward character? Among the class that she belonged to devotion and loyalty to a husband were not counted as top priorities. Material needs often drove them to immoral and evil ways. And yet from this woman's appearance she did not seem to belong to that category of ordinary maidservants. There seemed to be a significant difference somewhere. Side by side with her youthful liveliness she possessed both strength of character and courage. If this girl became loose or depraved she would do so knowingly and at her own free will, not under the demands of external needs.

Byomkesh pulled at his cigarette and asked, 'The four gentlemen who came here to play cards, you had seen them a few times, hadn't you?'

Mohini's eyes flicked from right to left and her lips parted for a moment as if she was about to break into a smile, but then she checked herself and said, 'Yes, I had seen them a few times.' She had obviously guessed the direction in which Byomkesh's interrogation was about to proceed.

Byomkesh asked, 'Can you tell me what sort of person each of them was like?'

The suppressed smile now found expression. Shaking her head a little, Mohini said, 'Is it possible to find out what sort of person a man is by looking at his face? But one of them was the youngest and the most innocent. The remaining three ...', she stopped speaking.

Byomkesh asked, 'Yes, how were the remaining three men?'

Mohini put out the tip of her tongue and pressed it between her teeth, saying, 'Sir, I do not know.'

Mohini possessed a strange quality; even while saying, 'I do not know,' she seemed to imply that she knew a lot.

Byomkesh crushed his cigarette butt on an ashtray and asked, 'Apart from the occasions when they visited this house for playing cards, did they come here at any other time?'

Mohini raised her eyes towards the ceiling and said, 'One of them did. He used to come here after the master had left for office.'

'Who was he?'

'I do not know his name. He was dark and heavily built and he could talk in a very oblique manner.'

Barat said in an undertone, 'Arobindo Haldar.'

Byomkesh addressed Mohini, 'Then he used to come only to see you.'

Mohini merely nodded her head.

Byomkesh asked, 'Did he propose any thing to you?'

Mohini's look became hard all of a sudden; she said in a sharp voice, 'He offered to give me a gold ring and a silk *sari*.'

'Did you accept them?'

'No. I am not that cheap.'

Byomkesh went on looking at her intently for some time and then said, 'All right, let us stop here today. I might ask you a few more questions later if necessary. But you are from Orissa and yet I notice that you can speak Bengali very fluently.'

Mohini's tone softened as she said, 'Sir, I have been working for Bengali families from my childhood.'

On our way back I was thinking that the young and innocent looking man described by Mohini was, of course, Phanish. Of the remaining three men Arobindo Haldar seemed to be a shameless debauch. And the other two? Probably they were not so shameless, although in their heart of hearts they were lusty and accustomed to practice their vices in secret. Mohini had claimed that she was not that cheap. But what was the price of her honour? Did the price of one's honour increase or decrease in proportion to one's youth and physical charm? Or was it measured by any other unit? Only someone with a specialised knowledge on this subject could answer these questions.

Barat alighted from the car at the police station.

Byomkesh told him, 'We shall be back this afternoon. I would like to meet the Civil Surgeon, who conducted the autopsy.'

Barat said, 'You are most welcome. I shall fix up your appointment with the Civil Surgeon. The post-mortem report is, of course, ready.'

Byomkesh said, 'I would like to see that too.'

Barat said, 'Fine. I'll fix up your appointment between four and four thirty.'

It was well past twelve when we reached Manish Babu's residence. He and his son returned a little later. When Manish Babu raised his eyebrows enquiringly, Byomkesh told him, 'Rest assured that I am doing all that is necessary. I have met the police and some steps have been initiated. I shall tell you everything in due course.'

Manish Babu seemed content with this response and he went for his bath. Phanish continued hovering round us anxiously. Byomkesh smiled and told him, 'You too can stop worrying. There has been some progress. We shall go out again in the afternoon.'

The father and son went out at three in the afternoon. We walked over to Surapati Ghatak's office. He made us sit down and went on expounding many facts and theories about coalmining to us. Then two young men appeared together at the door. Clad in clothes of handloom cotton, they appeared to be both gentle and polite, with an expression of intelligence mixed with humility on their faces.

Surapati said, 'Ah, here they are. Byomkesh Babu, these are the young men I was talking about. They are brothers, Bishwanath and Jagannath. I have taught them everything myself. Although they are still quite young, they are thoroughly conversant in their work.'

Byomkesh responded by saying, 'That's good.' He then looked at the young men and asked, 'I hope you have no objection to leaving this place and going to work somewhere else?'

Bishwanath and Jagannath shook their heads to indicate that they had no objections. Surapati Babu said, 'But I wouldn't be able to release both of them at the same time, that would seriously hamper my work here. You may have your pick of any one of them.'

Byomkesh said 'That's fine.' Taking out a notebook from his pocket, he wrote down the names and addresses of the two men and told them, 'You shall be notified in writing at the proper time.'

Bishwanath and Jagannath folded their hands in *namaskar* and left.

Byomkesh told Surapati Babu, 'I liked both of them. And I'll be happy to engage whichever of the two you are willing to release.'

Surapati Babu looked pleased as he said, 'Both brothers are equally efficient. You shall not be a loser if you engage either of them.'

It was almost four o'clock and time for us to leave for the police station.

Barat was in his office. He said, 'The Civil Surgeon would see you at four thirty. Here is the post-mortem report.'

Byomkesh scanned through the report and handed it back to Barat. We then proceeded towards the hospital. The Civil Surgeon's office was housed within the hospital building.

The Civil Surgeon, Birajmohan Ghoshal was seated in his office, smoking from a hubble-bubble. He was a middle-aged man, a little bulky, but fair and good looking. He burst out laughing as soon as he saw us and said, 'I have found out your real name, Byomkesh Babu. Inspector Barat tried to bluff me, but he didn't succeed.' He laughed loudly once again.

Byomkesh responded in a humble voice, 'When driven to a tight corner even the five *Pandavas* had to resort to disguises. I am but a mere mortal. I am here on a confidential assignment, which is why I had to conceal my identity.'

'Don't worry. Your secret shall remain safe with me. Please sit down.'

The conversation proceeded on general topics for some time with light humour and laughter. Doctor Ghoshal was a jolly character. Despite dealing with dead bodies all his life his sense of humour had not been subdued.

Eventually the conversation was led to the business, which had brought us there. Byomkesh said, 'I have seen Pranhari Poddar's post-mortem report. But I want to know some thing more from you. The man was old, lean and frail. Did he have no physical energy left in him at all?'

Biraj Babu said, 'Physical energy?'

'What I mean is – virility. A man's virility can last till an advanced age. There are instances of a man fathering a son even at the age of a hundred years. Was Pranhari Poddar's body-machine active in that respect?'

Biraj Babu broke into loud laughter again and said, 'Oh, that is what you want to know? But why should you have any embarrassment to discuss this topic with a doctor? No, there was no juice left in Pranhari Poddar's body, it was just like a piece of dry wood.' He had two pulls on the hubble-bubble and then continued, 'I have noticed that those who spend all their time thinking of money, cannot retain that strength too long. And Pranhari Poddar, as you know, was a usurious moneylender.'

It seemed that Byomkesh became a little disappointed on hearing this. He sat frowning for some time and then said, 'Well, let's talk of some thing else. Tell me about the murder weapon. Barring a single blow on the skull was there any other sign of injury?'

'No.'

'Death occurred as a result of that single blow?'

'Yes.'

'What was the type of the weapon?'

Biraj Babu went on pulling at the hubble-bubble for some time and then said, 'It is difficult to identify the type of the murder weapon. It must have been longish, — yes, —long and heavy. Not sharp as a chopper, nor blunt as a police baton.'

Byomkesh asked, 'Could it have been an electric torch?'

'Electric torch?' Biraj Babu shook his head, 'No, that wouldn't have left such a clear-cut crack on the skull. Suppose for instance, — if the reverse side of a chopper's blade, in other words the chopper's spine, was struck very hard on the head, — then the skull-bone could have cracked in that manner.'

'A kitchen ladle, tongs or a cooking spud?'

'No, it had to be some thing much heavier.'

Byomkesh sat quietly for a while with a hand on his cheek and then said, 'It is the murder weapon which has got me worried. It is hard to believe that any of those under suspicion had gone down to commit the murder armed with some weapon similar to a chopper. But it's not totally impossible either. Now tell me something else. Did the murderer strike from the front or from behind?'

Biraj Babu replied without hesitation, 'From the front. The bone had cracked from the forehead to the centre of the skull, there was no crack on any bone on the back side.'

'You think that there is no possibility that Poddar was struck from behind?'

Biraj Babu thought for a while and said, 'If Poddar was seated on a chair he could have been struck in that manner, but not if he was standing — unless the murderer was ten feet tall.'

Byomkesh got up smiling and said, 'If there was a man of ten feet height here we wouldn't have missed him. We'll take leave of you now. Thank you for sparing your time.'

When we returned to the police station, Barat asked, 'What next? Do you wish to meet the other three suspects?'

Byomkesh said, 'Of course. Would I find them at their homes now?'

Barat said, 'No, this is the time when they go to the club for relaxation.'

'Then let's not try it now. If you accompany me to the club the quarry is bound to get scared. Oh yes, there is something else. Can you let me see Poddar's account book? I want to go through it and see if I can find anything.'

'Of course, it's here in the office. Anything else?'

'And – it would be most helpful if you can do something. We have no information regarding Pranhari Poddar's past life. The old man was in Cuttack about a year and a half back. Can you find out anything about him from the police authorities of Cuttack?'

Barat said, 'I had enquired from Cuttack police. Poddar does not have any police record there. But if you want to know about him in general, I could write to one of the police officers there, with whom I am acquainted, Inspector Pattanaik.'

'Please do so. Send a telegram to Inspector Pattanaik, so that we can get the information as soon as possible. I'll take your leave now. We shall see you again tomorrow morning.'

After dinner that night Manish Babu went upstairs to his bedroom. We came back to our room. Switching on the overhead fan I made preparations for going to bed, but Byomkesh sat down on the table with Pranhari Poddar's account book in front of him. Bounded in a coarse, dyed cloth of red colour, it was a long notebook folded in the middle on which accounts were written in traditional Bengali style.

Byomkesh was slowly turning over the pages of the account book and I had almost finished my cigarette, when Phanish came and stood by the door. Byomkesh raised his face to glance at him and then did some thing very strange. There was a round paper-weight of glass on the table, which he suddenly picked up and hurled at Phanish.

Phanish caught it in mid-air, otherwise it would have hit the floor and got broken. Byomkesh smiled and said, 'Come Phanish.'

As Phanish drew near with a bewildered expression on his face, Byomkesh took the paperweight from his hand and said, 'I see that you are surprised. That was nothing; I was simply testing your reflexes. Sit down. I want to ask you a few questions.'

Phanish sat down on a chair facing him. Byomkesh asked, 'Don't you go the club these days?'

Phanish said, 'No, I haven't been there after that incident.'

Byomkesh said, 'Why? If you stop going there all of a sudden it might draw the attention of other people.'

Phanish said, 'All right, I'll go tomorrow.'

'We would like to go with you. I hope there would be no problem in taking us as your guests?'

'No. But –is there any reason why you have to go to the club?'

'I want to observe your three friends without their knowledge. Now, tell me something. That evening when you people went to beat up Pranhari Babu, did any of you carry any sort of weapon with you?'

'No, we had no weapons, but Madhumoy Babu had a long torch in his hand, a torch with a heavy head. And Mriganga Babu was carrying a cane stick.'

'What sort of stick? Heavy or light?'

'Light. The type which is called a swagger cane.'

'Hmm. And you? You had nothing in your hand?'

'No.'

'Was Arabindo Haldar carrying anything?'

'No.'

'Was it possible to carry anything like an iron rod or something of that sort hidden under the clothes?'

'No. It was summer. We were all wearing light clothes, *dhoti* and *kurta*. If we carried any such stuff, it was bound to have been noticed.'

'Hmm,' Byomkesh lit up a cigarette and smoked for a while before saying, 'I don't seem to get anywhere. Any way, go to bed. – Can you recite poems? Recite to your wife – *Keep faith night and day, dear mind, there is bound to be a way.*'

Phanish left with a somewhat abashed expression on his face. I lay down on the bed. Byomkesh went on examining the account book for some more time. Then he switched off the light and went to his bed.

In the darkness I enquired, 'I notice that you have taken to recite poems with a lot of flourish, but have you found out anything during the whole day?'

In reply Byomkesh said, 'I have uncovered three facts. One – the person who murdered Pranhari Poddar was not greedy for money, two – the person was ambidextrous, and three—anyone could commit murder for a woman like Mohini. Now go to sleep.'

When I got up next morning I saw that Byomkesh was again seated at the table with the account book.

We finished our breakfast at the usual time and left for the town. Byomkesh carried the account book in his hand.

When we reached the police station Inspector Barat smiled and asked, 'Oh, you have finished with the account book so soon?'

Byomkesh said, 'This book only contains the accounts of one and a half years, which would indicate that Pranhari had started entering his accounts in this book after arriving here.'

Barat enquired, 'Did you find anything?'

Byomkesh said, 'I haven't found anything that could throw light on the murder. But there is one particular issue on which I am having some misgiving.'

'What is it?'

'Pranhari had engaged a taxi driver, who used to fetch him from his house every day and take him back. There must have been some arrangement for paying his charges. But this account book shows just the reverse. Here, take a look yourself.' Byomkesh opened the account book and showed it to us.

There were two separate columns, showing debit and credit entries on each page. The debit column showed expenses even to the tune of one or two paise on some days, but the credit column was mostly vacant. Occasionally the interest deposited by some borrower was noted in the credit side.

'And here,' Byomkesh pointed his finger and showed us, 'you can see that on the third day of the month there is an entry in the credit column stating: taxidriver thirty-five rupees. You shall find a similar entry every month. But there is no mention of any expenses towards taxi charges in the debit column.'

'Perhaps the expense was written in the credit column by mistake?'

'Could there be the same mistake every month?'

'Hmm, what do you think?'

'I can't understand. The book does not even show the gambling losses and gains. Doesn't all this strike you as a little mysterious?'

'Yes it does. But what do you think we can do to solve the mystery?'

Byomkesh pondered for a while and then said, 'I would have liked to interrogate the man in whose taxi Pranhari used to do his movements. Do you happen to know him?'

Barat said, 'No, I didn't think it necessary to find out about him. But I can do something. I can send for Bhuban Das, he may be able to provide us with the necessary information.'

'Bhuban Das?'

'The taxidriver who took those four men to Pranhari's house that night. His name is Bhubaneswar Das.'

'Oh—would he be available?'

'The taxistand is close by. I'll send for him.'

Bhuban Das arrived fifteen minutes later, saluted and stood before us. He had a well-proportioned body; clad in khaki shirt and trousers, he wore a cap like those worn by train-guards. In his early thirties, he had blood-shot eyes and a solemn face, which gave us the impression that he was probably addicted to drugs or alcohol.

Barat inclined his head and pointed at Byomkesh.

Byomkesh cast a good look at Bhuban Das from head to toe and then started his interrogation: 'Your name is Bhuban Das. You were in the army?'

'Yes, sir.'

'Were you a soldier?'

'No sir. A truck driver.'

'How long have you been driving a taxi?'

'Three to four years.'

'Have you been driving a taxi here for three to four years?'

'No sir, I am here for about a year and a half. Before that I was in Calcutta.'

"Where is your place of domicile?'

'Bhagabanpur village in Midnapore District.'

'You took those four gentlemen to Pranhari Poddar's house that night?'

'Not to the house, sir, up to some distance away from the house.'

'Quite. Did they talk among themselves while travelling in your taxi?'

Bhuban Das remained quiet for some time and then said, 'They did, but I did not pay heed to all that they said.'

Byomkesh said, 'Do you remember anything?'

Bhuban Das again kept silent for some time, before saying, 'They were probably talking about some woman. Their voices were lowered; I could not hear properly.'

Byomkesh said, 'Let it be. Now tell me, did any of the four men have any weapon in his hand?'

'One of them wore a wrist watch.'

'None of the others had anything?'

'I did not take notice.'

'Do you have any addiction?'

'No sir', Bhuban Das cast a sidelong glance at Barat as he said this.

'What is your home address in this town?'

'I have no home. I sleep in my taxi at night.'

'Is this taxi your own?'

'Yes sir.'

'You must be acquainted with the other taxi-drivers of this town?'

'Acquainted, yes, not intimate with anyone.'

'Can you tell me the name of the person in whose taxi Pranhari Poddar used to make his up and down trips to the town?'

A quick flash of humour seemed to pass through Bhuban Das's blood-shot eyes. But he said in a grave voice, 'In my taxi sir.'

We looked at him in surprise. Then Barat asked in a stern voice, 'Why didn't you tell this to me before?'

Bhuban replied smoothly, 'But you never asked me, sir.'

Byomkesh suppressed his laughter as he took out his cigarette packet. My experience about taxidrivers as a class was not very extensive, but I had observed that they talked very little and did not waste words without reason. Unless of course there was any dispute regarding fares, which was a different matter altogether.

Byomkesh asked, 'Then you knew Pranhari Poddar from before?'

Bhuban said, 'Yes sir.'

'What sort of a man was he?'

'He was a good man, sir. He never let his hire-charges fall in arrears.' To Bhuban this was the highest proof of integrity.

'Did he pay up the hire charges every day?'

'No sir, there was a monthly arrangement.'

'What was the monthly charge?'

'Thirty-five rupees.'

Byomkesh had a quick exchange of glances with Barat and then he spoke to Bhuban, 'Tell me every thing that you know about Pranhari Poddar.'

Bhuban said, 'I don't know much, sir. He has an office in the town. He summoned me about a year back and proposed to hire my taxi on a monthly basis, to which I agreed. Since then I used to fetch him from his house in the morning and drop him there in the evening. Towards the beginning of each month he used to call me to his office and settle my charges. Apart from this I do not know anything about him.'

'You had agreed to charge just thirty-five rupees per month? Did that leave you with any margin of profit?'

'A small profit. But he was a fixed client, which is why I had agreed to his terms.'

Byomkesh sat with his eyes closed for some time and then asked, 'Do you know if Pranhari Babu had any business transactions with any other taxidriver?'

Bhuban said, 'No, sir, I do not know.'

Byomkesh let out a sigh and then said, 'All right you may go now. But if you happen to remember any thing about Pranhari Poddar make sure that you report the matter to the Inspector sahib.'

'Yes sir,' Bhuban Das saluted and left.

The three of us sat in silence for some time. Then Barat broke the silence and said, 'We couldn't find a single thing. It would seem that the expenditures have been shown in the credit column of the book by mistake.'

Byomkesh said, 'Or it could be a coded statement of debit and credit.'

Barat asked, 'What sort of coded statement?'

Byomkesh said, 'Suppose Pranhari Poddar was blackmailing someone. Bhuban Das might think of him as a good person but my conclusion is that Pranhari was a crooked character. Suppose he was collecting seventy rupees per month as blackmail. But of course he could not show this income in his account book. Then on the other hand he had to pay thirty-five rupees per month as taxi-hire. So in his code system he deducted thirty-five from seventy rupees and showed the net sum of thirty-five rupees in the credit column. He could not write the name of the person whom he was blackmailing, so he wrote the name of the taxidriver. Do you understand?'

Barat said, 'Yes, I understand now. Not impossible. Pranhari's mind was very twisted, but your mind seems to be even more complicated.'

Byomkesh got up smiling and said, 'All right. I'll make a move now. We could have perhaps traced some clue to the murder if we knew who were being blackmailed by Pranhari, but I don't think that any such indication was available from his documents?'

'No. The few documents which were found carry no hint of any illegal activities. Would you be coming here this afternoon?'

Byomkesh said, 'No, I won't bother you today. We shall be going to the Coal Club with Phanish.'

The building of the Coal Club was surrounded by a sprawling compound. There was a garden and a car-parking space on the front, while tennis and badminton courts had been laid out on the two sides. The building was single-storeyed and contained several rooms of large sizes. The central hall held a billiard table; there was a table tennis board in another room and four or five card tables had been neatly set up in a third room. Then we found a room on which a thick carpet had been laid on the floor; it was used for chess and dice games. There were two rooms of comparatively smaller sizes in the rear side, one of which was the manager's office and the other was used for serving snacks and assorted hot and cold drinks to the members.

There was still enough daylight when we reached the club. Many members were present and a game of tennis was in progress. Four members were playing a doubles match, while others were watching the game sitting on garden chairs set up by the court. Phanish led us in that direction.

After watching the game for some time, Byomkesh drew close to Phanish and whispered to his ears,'Are any of your friends present here?'

Phanish said, 'That gentleman there, who is playing, the one with a blue towel shirt and white trousers, — he is Mrigen Moulik.'

Although a little on the slim side, Mrigen Moulik had a sportsmanlike figure. He had a tendency to show off a bit, but he was a good tennis player. He had a strong backhand and was also quite good at the net.

While watching the game, Byomkesh asked, 'The other two aren't here?'

Phanish said, 'No. Let us go inside.'

Just then we heard a voice from behind, 'Byomkesh Babu, sorry – Gagan Babu, isn't it?'

Turning back we saw Gobinda Haldar looking at Byomkesh and grinning like a gorilla.

But Byomkesh did not smile. Looking steadily at Gobinda Babu, he said, 'You seem to have found out my real name. How did you do it?'

Gobinda Babu said, 'I became suspicious at our first meeting. Then I added two and two and reached a perfect solution. Gagan – Byomkesh, Sujit – Ajit.'

Byomkesh commented, 'Our names were not chosen with adequate care, — it was a bungling effort. But is it necessary to give wide publicity to our real names?'

Gobinda Babu said, 'I am not about to publicize the matter. Your name just slipped off my tongue accidentally. Any way, it is indeed a matter of great pleasure that you have set foot at our club. Are you here for any particular purpose?'

Byomkesh asked, 'What do you think?'

Gobinda Babu's eyes moved slowly towards Phanish and then turned to Byomkesh as he said, 'You are a busy person, it is unlikely that you would wander around merely for amusing yourself without any reason. You must have come here on some work. But what work? Unravelling the mystery of the coalmine?'

Byomkesh again asked, 'What do you think?'

Gobinda Babu's eyes contracted and turned into slits. He said, 'Then my guess was correct. Look, you are a careful man, but I would still like to warn you. Don't try to dig too hard for unearthing some unexpected results.' He cast a single glance at Phanish through his contracted eyes, then walked off towards the tennis court and sat down on a chair.

Phanish's face was filled with anxiety. He said in a faltering voice, 'Gobinda Babu is Arobindo Babu's elder brother. If he tells everything to my father...'

Byomkesh said, 'You have nothing to worry. Gobinda Babu shall not tell anything to anyone. He is far too fond of his depraved brother. Let us go inside.'

Various daily newspapers and weekly magazines had been kept neatly arranged on a table in the front verandah. We sat down on chairs set around the table. Phanish hailed a liveried waiter and ordered three glasses of *lassi.*

As we sipped our ice-cold drinks I noticed that dusk was about to set in and it was becoming dark. The tennis game was soon over. The members started coming in. Scraps of their conversation floated to our ears. Bright lights had been switched on in the inner rooms. The rhythmic sound of the ping-pong ball hitting the table and the bats could be heard from the table-tennis room, broken by the abrupt voice of some member — 'Hey, waiter!'

We were witnessing a passing picture from the life of an elite and opulent set.

We finished our drinks and strolled inside. In the central hall two members were playing billiards in unhurried silence; it seemed as if the three balls were engaged in a game of hide and seek on the large table like three lively kids. None of those whom we wanted to see were present there. We then walked down to the table-tennis room where a game was in progress. The ball was flying about with a rapping sound from one side of the table to the other like a bustling white bubble. Here too there was none of the three men whom we had come to see.

Loud shouts were emerging sporadically from the adjoining room, where a game of dice was in progress. Four players were sitting around the board. One of them was rubbing the bones vigorously in his hands and addressing the dice in a fond voice, 'Dice! Twelve-five- seventeen! Show this to me just once, - twelve –five-seventeen!' He threw the dice. A loud cheer was raised by his opponents – 'Three singles! Three singles!'

We moved away from the door and arrived at the card room.

Not all the card tables had been filled up yet. One man was playing 'patience' all by himself at a table. At another table three members were playing 'cut-throat' bridge owing to the absence of a fourth player. Four men were engaged in a game at a separate table; they were staring at the cards in their hands with deep concentration. One called out, 'Three hearts.' They were playing contract bridge.

Phanish whispered to Byomkesh, 'The gentleman who just gave the call is Madhumoy Sur and his partner is Arobindo Haldar.'

Byomkesh did not approach the table; he went on looking at the players from a distance. Arobindo Haldar needed no introduction to be identified as Gobindo Haldar's brother. He bore the same gorilla-like appearance, — but was younger. Madhumoy was a well-dressed dandy; his appearance showed a distinct lack of personality, which he had tried to make up by wearing a fashionable *kurta* with diamond buttons.

The game was on; none of the players had any time to notice anything beyond their cards.

After watching the game for about five minutes Byomkesh made a signal and we left the card room. It seemed that he was not satisfied after observing the suspects, but he said in a dry voice, 'We have seen what we had come to see, let's go home now.'

While being driven home in the car, I asked,'What did you see?'

Byomkesh replied, 'I saw three men, their environment, the movement of their hands and feet. Phanish, we shall visit their homes tomorrow morning. It is necessary to have some direct interaction. It is unlikely that I'll get anything more than what I gathered today, but still ...'

'Then you did gather some thing today?'

'Yes, although it was a negative response.'

Phanish did not accompany his father to the coalmine next morning. Manish Babu went out all by himself. Phanish had dispensed with the services of the driver, saying that he would drive the car himself. After starting the car, he asked, 'Where would you like to go first?'

Byomkesh said, 'We have no preferences. Take us first to whichever person's house is nearest.'

'Then let us go to Mrigen Babu's house.'

Mrigen Moulik's house was very decently built, indicating the excellent taste of its owner. When our car crossed the garden and reached the porch I saw Mrigen Moulik reclining on an easy chair and reading the newspaper. He was wearing a pair of loose pyjamas and a silk dressing gown. As we got down from the car he folded the newspaper and looked at us. There was no welcoming smile on his face, rather his face darkened in a frown and as we drew near, he asked in a rude voice, 'What do you want?'

Taken by sheer surprise we stopped where we stood. Phanish said, 'Mrigen Babu, these gentlemen are my father's friends, they have come from Calcutta ...'

Casting a look of deep loathing at Phanish, Mrigen said, 'I know. Which of you is Byomkesh Bakshi?'

Phanish was flabbergasted. Byomkesh said, 'My name is Byomkesh Bakshi. I wanted to have a few words with you.'

Mrigen turned up his lips in a gesture of disdain and said, 'You'll not get any thing here. You may go.' He wrapped the newspaper under his arm and went inside the house.

We looked at each other. Phanish's face had turned crimson in humiliation; there was an embarrassed smile on Byomkesh' lips, as he said, 'Gobinda Haldar has obviously forewarned the suspects.'

Phanish said, 'Let's go home.'

Byomkesh shook his head and said, 'No, when we have set out with a purpose we shall go home only after we finish our job. Phanish, you have no reason to feel ashamed. Those whose mission is to search for truth have to overcome shame, hatred and fear at the outset. Come, let us now go to Madhumoy Sur's house.'

While travelling in the car, I asked, 'But why? What could be the reason for such rude behaviour? If Mrigen Moulik is innocent what is there for him to be afraid of?'

Byomkesh explained, 'They have come to the conclusion that I am on Phanish's side and that I am intent on saving Phanish and get them implicated.'

Madhumoy Sur's house was of old design, devoid of the adornment of any garden. Madhumoy was lying on a mat in the entrance verandah of the house, with a towel wrapped around his torso, while a strong, well-built servant was massaging him with oil. Madhumoy's body was not very fleshy, but he had grown a small but solid paunch. He sat up on seeing us.

Phanish started speaking in a thin voice, 'Forgive me, Madhumoy Babu. I know this is an awkward time for calling on you ...'

Without paying any heed to Phanish, Madhumoy blinked his eyes a few times at us and then said in a rehearsed, singsong tone, 'Why have you come to me? I know nothing about Pranhari Poddar's death. If anybody has said that I had visited his house on the night of his death he has lied. I am not aware if anybody else called on him, but I didn't.'

After saying this Madhumoy Sur was about to lie down again.

Byomkesh said, 'But the taxidriver has identified you.'

Madhumoy said, 'The taxidriver is a liar. You may leave now. Goodbye.'

Byomkesh asked all of a sudden, 'Do you own a torch?'

Madhumoy said, 'I have five torches. Goodbye.'

Madhumoy lay down; the servant resumed massaging oil on his body. We left the place.

As we proceeded towards Arobindo Haldar's house Byomkesh said, 'Madhumoy knew that we were going to call on him. He had learnt by heart whatever he was going to tell us. But say what you may, Madhumoy Sur is a model of courtesy as compared to Mrigen Moulik. Did you notice how sweetly he told us, you may leave now, goodbye. I must say — the young man does not lack etiquette.'

Arobindo Haldar and Gobindo Haldar lived in the same building but in different wings. Arobindo was lying on a divan in his carpeted drawing room, his head resting on a thick cushion and smoking a cigarette. On seeing us he got up by resting his weight on an elbow. His eyes were blood rimmed and his dark face was unshaven and rough. After inspecting us one by one, he eventually said, 'Come Phanish.'

With his face gone pale, Phanish started saying, 'These gentlemen ...'

Arobindo said, 'I know. Please sit down' and extended his cigarette tin towards us.

We were a little taken aback, as we were not prepared to be treated with such courtesy. Byomkesh sat down on the edge of the divan; Phanish and I took our seats beside him. Arobindo said in an easy tone, 'Had a little too much to drink last night, the hangover is there still. Hey, Gadadhar!'

A servant entered carrying some drink in a glass, which Arobindo drained in one gulp and then asked, 'What should I get for you? Tea? Soft drinks? Beer?'

Byomkesh responded in a humble voice, 'Thank you. We don't need any thing. I shall be grateful if you grant me an opportunity to have a few words with you.'

Arobindo said, 'Certainly. But let me inform you some thing at the outset. I don't know what Phanish has told you, but I did not visit Pranhari Poddar's house on the night of his death.'

After remaining silent for a while, Byomkesh said, 'Arobindo Babu, I have not come here with any evil intentions. It is not my practice to implicate any innocent person in a murder charge. I am a seeker of truth. But, of course, if you are guilty ...'

Arobindo said, 'I am innocent. I had not been anywhere near Pranhari's house on the night of his death. Bearing that in mind, you may ask me what you want.'

Byomkesh said, 'All right, let us dispense with that topic. But before Pranhari's death you had gone to his house quite a few times.'

Arobindo said, 'Yes, I did. The four of us used to go there for gambling.'

Byomkesh said, 'Besides the visits for gambling there were a few occasions when you visited that house all by yourself.'

A lewd smile flashed on Arobindo's face. He said, 'That I did.'

'What was the purpose of your visits?'

'To see Mohini. To get to know her closely.'

Byomkesh asked in a cynical voice, 'But it didn't work out?'

The smile disappeared from Arobindo's face. He looked at Byomkesh with wide eyes and asked, 'Didn't work out—what do you mean?'

Byomkesh said, 'You can well understand what I mean. Are you trying to tell me that —.'

Abruptly Arobindo broke out in loud laughter. Then he stopped laughing and said, 'Byomkesh Babu, you may be a great detective, but you are a novice in worldly matters. There is nothing that you can't get if you are prepared to spend money. And Mohini is just a woman, a mere maidservant.'

Byomkesh asked, 'How much did you spend?'

Arobindo raised two fingers and said, 'Two thousand rupees.'

'You paid two thousand rupees to Mohini. Wasn't it a bit too much for a mere maidservant?'

'I did not pay Mohini. I paid the money to her pimp, Pranhari Poddar.' Arobindo spat out these words with venom.

Byomkesh remained quiet for a while and then said, 'Anyway, let us talk of something else. What sort of a man was Pranhari Poddar?'

'He was a skinflint, he was unscrupulous and he was excessively greedy for money. He was no better than any man from the streets.'

It was obvious that Arobindo did not have a high opinion about a man from the streets. Byomkesh asked, 'Were you people cheated by Pranhari Poddar for a considerable amount during your gambling sessions at his house?'

Arobindo spoke in a contemptuous tone, 'He won and we lost. I can't say if he had cheated us.'

'Then why did you go to beat him up?'

Arobindo had opened his mouth to respond, but he stopped at the last moment and looked hard at Byomkesh, before saying, 'Who told you that I had gone to beat him up? Let those who had gone to him speak for themselves. I didn't go to beat up anyone.'

I cast a sidelong glance at Phanish. He had been listening with his head bowed all this time, now he raised his eyes to look at Arobindo for a moment and then lowered his face once again.

Byomkesh sighed and got to his feet. He then spoke very slowly, 'There are discrepancies even in the brief statement that you have just made. Your statements are inconsistent with what Mohini has told us. Maybe your statement is true. Any way, thank you and goodbye. You may tell your elder brother that it is not safe to offer bribes to policemen; it raises suspicion. And not all policemen accept bribes.'

The next three days passed in listless inactivity. The mystery of Pranhari Poddar's death remained suspended in uncertainty. No new information was forthcoming. We had to rely on what little evidence had been gathered till then. The letter received from Inspector Pattanayak of Cuttack regarding Pranhari's past life hardly threw any light on the murder. Pranhari Poddar was a professional gambler, but he was never implicated in any police case. He lived in Cuttack for about two years, but it was not known from where he had come to Cuttack. He had no dependents, nor any business of any sort. He had got hold of a few foolish young men of rich families and set up a gambling den at his home. But gradually these young men came to realize that Pranhari was cheating them and they resolved to give him a good beating. But before their resolution could be converted to action Pranhari disappeared. A young maidservant had been employed by him. She too disappeared at the same time. It is possible that old Pranhari had some illicit relationship with the maidservant.

The only conclusion that we could draw from Pattanayak's letter was that Pranhari's style of conducting business followed a routine pattern.

Byomkesh was not in a happy mood. Indira's face was again clouded with dismay and apprehension. Phanish was becoming restless. Manish Babu was a man of reserved temperament, but even he seemed to be displaying some signs of impatience. The unknown miscreants at the coalmine had not yet been nabbed.

Bikash Dutta had arrived and started working at the hospital of the coalmine. We had gone to the coalmine one day along with Manish Babu. With the pretext of inspecting the hospital Byomkesh had met Bikash and suitably instructed him.

Only one particular incident occurred during these three days, which is worth mentioning here. Byomkesh had become weary after spending all his time lying in bed or pacing up and down in the room. So after dusk on the third day, he said, 'Come, let us take a stroll on the road.'

The road was lonely, the lights were not very bright and a cool breeze was blowing. We met one or two pedestrians from time to time and a few motorcars passed by. Byomkesh suddenly blurted out, 'Is there any point in investigating the murder of a third-rate person like Pranhari Poddar? Whosoever had killed him had done the right thing and should be awarded a gold medal.'

I said, 'Even if we have to hand out a gold medal, we have to know the identity of the person.'

After strolling for some more time Byomkesh said, 'I have to pay another visit to Mohini. There is some thing which I have omitted to ask her.'

It was then that I noticed a bicycle. We had been walking along the edge of the road. Now we observed a bicycle about fifty yards away coming towards us from the opposite direction. The cycle did not have a lamp; the rider was indistinctly visible in the streetlight. He had a *sola* hat on his head, which covered most of his face. Soon the bicycle drew close to us and then the cyclist dropped some white object near our feet and pedalled past us very quickly.

Byomkesh grabbed my arm and drew me back in a flash. Moving away to a distance of about ten yards he went on staring closely at the white object. But nothing happened. The object, which looked like a tennis ball lay inert on the road. It had not struck me at first that it could be a bomb. But now seeing Byomkesh's reaction and the way he was behaving my heart started beating very fast.

Byomkesh told me, 'Ajit, go and fetch a torch from the house very quickly.'

He kept standing there while I walked back and went to the house. On hearing the news both Phanish and Manish Babu came out with me.

'What is the matter?'

Byomkesh said, 'Don't go close. It may be nothing, but still it is better to take precautions. Ajit, give me the torch.'

After taking the torch from me he focussed the light on the object lying on the ground. I stretched my neck and saw that a white paper covering the object was fluttering in the wind. Byomkesh went close to it and after inspecting the object for some time he picked it up with his hand. Then he laughed and said, 'A piece of coal wrapped in paper.'

Manish Babu exclaimed, 'Coal —!'

Byomkesh said, 'The coal is not important, the paper is the real thing. Let's get back to the house.'

Byomkesh carefully opened out the paper as he stood under the bright lights of the drawing room. Laying down the piece of coal on the table he held the two ends of the wrinkled paper with his fingers and stretched it against the light. The paper was of the size of an ordinary note-sheet and it carried two lines of bold letters written with ink —

Byomkesh Bakshi, if you do not leave this town immediately, you shall never return from here.

'This is terrible! They have come to know your identity,' Manish Babu extended his hand, saying. 'Let me have a look.'

Byomkesh shook his head and said, 'No, it's better that you don't touch it. The paper might have some fingerprints.'

Holding the two ends of the paper with great care Byomkesh walked down to our room. There was an illustrated foreign magazine on the table, which he opened and softly placed the paper between two pages.

I asked, 'Who could have sent this letter? Of course, the piece of coal would seem to indicate that the culprits at the coalmine have come to know about you.'

Byomkesh said, 'That could be a bluff. Gobinda Haldar is aware that I have come here in connection with the coalmine.'

On returning to the drawing room we found that the head clerk Surapati Ghatak had arrived in the meantime and was engaged in discussing some office matters with his boss. On seeing us he humbly folded his hands in respect.

After he had finished his conversation and left Byomkesh asked Manish Babu, 'I hope you did not tell any thing to Surapati Babu?'

Manish Babu said, 'No. – But the crooked rascals are now scared.'

Byomkesh replied, 'If they were not scared they wouln't have tried to scare me.'

Manish Babu became pleased and said, 'I have no idea what you have been doing in secret, but you must have been doing some thing which has scared the rascals. Any way, I hope you yourself are not scared after receiving the note?'

Byomkesh had a dry smile on his face as he said, 'I am not too scared, but I would still like to bolt the door of our bedroom before I go to sleep.'

After dropping us at the police station next morning Phanish told Byomkesh, 'I have to make a trip to the market for getting some things which Indira has asked for. I shall return in an hour or so. I hope that wouldn't be inconvenient.'

'No, we shall be here for about an hour.'

As Phanish drove off with the car we entered the police station.

Pramod Babu was seated at his table surrounded by files and papers. Byomkesh placed the illustrated magazine on the table and said, 'There is a piece of paper in this, which might have some fingerprints. Do you have any fingerprint expert?'

Opening the magazine Barat glanced at the paper and then said, 'Of course I have an expert. But what is the matter?'

Byomkesh narrated the previous night's incident. After hearing him, Barat said, 'Seems to be related to the coalmine. I shall make necessary arrangements right now. You shall receive the report by this evening.'

Barat called a subordinate and sent the magazine alongwith the paper inside it to his fingerprint expert with necessary instructions. He then turned to Byomkesh and said, 'You haven't been here for the last three days. Is there any news from your end?'

'Things are just as they were before. There is no news. But there is one point on which I am having a little misgiving.'

'What misgiving?'

'Pranhari used to pay Mohini a salary of fifteen rupees per month. But there is no mention of this in the account book.'

Barat pondered for a while and then said, 'Hm. Pranhari's account book seems to be full of errors. Well, what would you like to do?'

Byomkesh said, 'I was thinking of interrogating Mohini. She is still there, I hope?'

Barat replied, 'She is there all right, not showing any inclination to move out. I too am unable to release her till the case is solved.'

'Then let us pay her a visit.'

'Let's go.'

'No, no, I can see that you have a lot of other work. You don't have to come. Ajit and I shall go. Shall we find your young constable there?'

Barat smiled and said, 'Most certainly.'

We came out of the police station. It was still not time for Phanish to return. We started walking towards the taxi stand.

The taxi stand was close to the police station and located under an enormous fig tree. While walking in that direction I asked, 'Byomkesh, is there any link between Pranhari and the affairs of the coalmine?'

He said, 'None at all. I am the only link.'

On nearing the taxistand I saw that there was only a single taxi under the shaded tree and a large, black car was parked by the edge of the road with its rear end towards us. The taxidriver Bhuban Das was standing by the window of the black car and talking with the driver. As we drew a little closer the black car drove off and Bhuban Das started walking back towards his taxi.

Byomkesh asked me with a deep frown, 'Do you know who owns the big car? It belongs to Gobinda Haldar. I had taken note of the registration number on the first day.'

'What did Gobinda Haldar have to do with the taxidriver?'

'He could be trying to corrupt his evidence. Come, let's see.'

By the time we had reached the taxi Bhuban had taken out a jack from the boot and was about to set it up under the car. On seeing us he stood up, saluted and asked, 'Do you need a taxi, sir?'

Byomkesh said, 'Yes, we have to pay a visit to Pranhari Poddar's house as I have some business with a woman who lives there.'

Bhuban cast a sidelong glance at Byomkesh and scratched his head, saying, 'But, I would need a little time, sir. There is a puncture in one of the tyres, I have got to change it first.'

Abruptly Byomkesh enquired, 'What was Gobinda Haldar telling you just now?'

Bhuban was startled, 'Sir? He – he knows me and so he stopped his car to have a few words. He is a very good man.' After saying this, he started moving the jack very fast till the tyre was raised from the ground.

Just then I happened to look at Byomkesh and saw that he seemed to have been gripped by a sudden spell. His eyes were fixed on Bhuban, but he appeared to be observing some thing else in his mind's eye. I said softly, 'Byomkesh.'

Moving his head towards me, he said in a mumbling voice, 'Ajit, what is the sum total of thirtyfive and fifteen?'

I said, 'Fifty. But what are you babbling about?'

He said, 'Come' and started walking back rapidly towards the police station. Walking behind him, I turned back after going a few yards. Bhuban was looking fixedly at us.

When we entered the police station Barat looked up in surprise from his files and said, 'What's the matter? You didn't go there?'

Byomkesh said, 'Pramod Babu, is there any quiet place in your police station where I can sit and think for a while.'

A jeweller can read the glitter of a gem at a single glance. Barat got up instantly and said, 'Please come with me.'

There was a covered verandah on the rear side of the police station; there was nobody there, only a few chairs were lying scattered. Byomkesh laid himself down on an easy chair and lit up a cigarette. Barat smiled and left.

After smoking around five cigarettes within half an hour, Byomkesh said, 'Let's go. I have got it.'

I asked, 'What have you got?'

'Supernal vision. A vision of truth. Come.'

When we reached Barat's office room and stood by his table, he looked up at us eagerly.

Byomkesh asked, 'Pramod Babu, in which bank did Pranhari maintain his account?'

Barat said, 'Central Bank. Why?'

Byomkesh asked, 'Do you know if he had a safe deposit vault there?'

'He might have.'

Looking at his watch Byomkesh said, 'The bank must have opened by now. Let's go.'

Barat got up without asking any further questions. As we came out of the police station we found Phanish had just arrived and was about to get down from his car. Byomkesh called out to him, 'Phanish, don't get down. You'll have to take us to the Central Bank.'

The bank's office was located in the centre of the town. An armed guard was standing at the gate. While getting down from the car Byomkesh told Phanish, 'You can return home from here. We might be a little late in coming back. By the way, where is your wife's hometown?'

Phanish turned around in surprise and said, 'Nabadwip.'

Byomkesh said, 'Hmm. Then she must know how to make **malpoas*. Tell her that we would like to eat *malpoas* this evening.'

We got off from the car. Phanish looked a little disappointed as he drove off. He had realized that the mystery of Pranhari Poddar's murder was about to be solved.

Barat took us directly to the chamber of the bank manager, with whom he was already acquainted. He said, 'We have come in connection with the affairs of Pranhari Poddar. Do you have safe deposit vaults in this bank?'

'Yes, we do.'

**Malpoa* a delicious Bengali sweet made of flour pancakes, fried in oil and dipped in sugar syrup.

Barat turned to Byomkesh, who asked the manager, 'Did Pranhari Poddar hire a vault here?'

The manager called up an assistant and asked him the same question. The assistant replied, 'Yes, he had hired a vault.'

Byomkesh said, 'We want to inspect the contents of his vault.'

The manager seemed a little embarrassed as he said, 'But that is against the rules of the bank. Unless of course there is a search warrant.'

Barat said, "Pranhari Poddar has been murdered. The police has a warrant to inspect all his deeds, documents and papers.'

The manager pondered for a while and then said, 'All right. Have you brought the key?'

'Key?'

'Every locker of the safe deposit vault has two keys. One is held by the person who has hired the locker and the other is held in the bank's custody. The locker cannot be opened unless both keys are available.'

Byomkesh exchanged glances with Barat. Barat then asked, 'Surely there is a duplicate key?'

'Yes, but I cannot deliver it to you without the permission of the bank's directors. Obtaining such permission would take about four to five days.'

Byomkesh spoke to Barat, 'Come, let us search Pranhari's safe once more. The key must be somewhere there.'

Barat got up and told the manager, 'We shall come back again. If we can't find the key I shall make out an official application.'

We returned to the police station; from there we picked up two more men and reached Pranhari Poddar's house in a police car.

The young constable was sitting on a stool outside the entrance door. On seeing us he got up and saluted smartly.

On entering the house Byomkesk told Barat, 'I would like to ask Mohini a few questions. Meanwhile you and your men can conduct your search upstairs. I don't think you would have much problem in finding the key. It should be in the safe; you didn't find it earlier because you were not looking for any hidden items. And of course you didn't know then that Pranhari had hired a safe deposit vault.'

The police party took the staircase and went upstairs. Byomkesh and I went and stood in front of the kitchen.

Mohini was cooking with her back towards the door. She turned around on hearing the sound of our footsteps. As she saw us her eyes widened in a quick flash of apprehension; then she took down the pot from the oven and came and stood before us, wiping her hands on the edge of her sari.

'Do you need me for any thing, sir?' She had got over her initial nervousness.

Byomkesh said, 'You are still here! Why aren't you going back to your hometown?'

'How can I go, sir, unless I am released by the police?'

Byomkesh asked, 'Have you informed your parents and your husband?'

Mohini kept her eyes lowered for a while and then said, 'I do not know where my husband is now. But I did not inform my parents. They are old people, what would be the point in informing them?'

Byomkesh said, 'That is true. Now, tell me something. On the night that Pranhari Babu was murdered, did you go to his room when he did not come down for dinner?'

Mohini nodded her head and said, 'Yes, sir.'

'Was the light in the room switched on?'

'Yes sir.'

'And you had noticed that the door to the bathroom was open?'

'No sir.' Mohini's face became clouded with anxiety.

'Was that door closed then?'

Mohini seemed to have a moment's uncertainty, then she said, 'Sir, I saw nothing. When I saw the master lying dead I came down running.'

'You did not close the bathroom door?'

'No sir.'

'Hm.' Byomkesh had a slight frown on his face as he asked, 'Pranhari Babu used to pay you a salary of fifteen rupees per month?'

'Yes sir.'

'Did he pay your salary in due time each month?'

When a person is pre-occupied with certain thoughts while talking of some thing else, there is a distinct indication of the mental state in the facial expression. It was with just such absentmindedness that Mohini now said, 'My salary used to be held with the master. I used to ask for a rupee or two from him when I needed any money.'

Looking sideways at Byomkesh I could see that he was smiling. He said, 'I think all your accumulated salary is now lost. Well, here is my last question: are you acquainted with any left-handed person?'

'Left-handed person! What does that mean?'

Byomkesh said, 'You don't know? Someone who uses the left hand more frequently than the right hand is called a left-handed person.'

Abruptly Mohini placed a hand on her chest and then after a moment's pause, she said, 'No sir, I do not know any such person.'

She remained standing at the same spot as we went up to Pranhari's bedroom.

The key had been found. It had been fixed with wax to the back of the safe and could be reached through the narrow space between the safe and the wall. Barat handed the key to Byomkesh and said, 'Here you are.'

It was a long key with a number engraved on it. Byomkesh examined it and then said, 'Let's go to the bank again.'

On reaching the bank the key was shown to the manager. He raised no further objections, but got up and escorted us himself to the vault. It was an underground room, with steel lockers neatly arranged in long rows along three walls.

Pranhari's locker was opened with the help of two keys. There was no money or ornaments in the locker, it only held some old letters and a bundle of mortgage deeds and handnotes.

The letters were not written by Pranhari, nor were they written to him. They were written by various unknown men and women to other unknown persons. These letters were probably the instruments used by Pranhari for blackmailing the people who had written them.

Byomkesh was not interested in the letters; he gathered the mortgage deeds and came upstairs. Sitting in the manager's room he went on scanning the deeds one by one. Then he picked up one of the documents and said to Barat, 'Here is your murderer.'

The deed stated in legal terms that Pranhari Poddar by profession a moneylender had loaned a sum of two thousand five hundred rupees to Bhubaneswar Das, resident of Bhagabanpur, against the mortgage of a taxi vehicle, which the latter wanted to purchase. The mode of repayment of the loan by Bhubanewar Das was also mentioned in the deed: fifty rupees in cash plus thirtyfive rupees per month towards hire charges for Pranhari's use of the car. Thus the loan was to be repaid at an aggregate rate of eightyfive rupees per month.

Barat looked at Pranhari with raised eyebrows. Byomkesh told him, 'My job is over, now you may do what remains to be done.'

Barat said, 'But what about the evidence of the murder?'

Byomkesh said, 'There is proof, but I cannot say if it would stand up in court. Now we have to return home. It is half past one already.'

'Let me drop you home.'

There was not much conversation in the police car. Barat spoke out only once, asking, 'Shall I arrest Bhuban?'

Byomkesh said, 'You may. If you can get him to confess, your problem shall be solved.'

The car dropped us at the gate of the house and drove off. Before leaving Barat said, 'I'll call on you this evening.'

It was five in the evening and we had just sat down to eat delicious *malpoas*, when Pramad Barat arrived.

Manish Babu had gone to the coalmine; Phanish was at home. Indira had been sitting with us all this time, but she had gone inside on Barat's arrival. My mind had been in a whirl ever since I had heard about the identity of the murderer; now I had regained my composure to some extent.

Inspector Barat's face was pale. He looked visibly disturbed and seemed to be wearing the same uniform, which he had put on that morning. He came in with an unsmiling face and taking out an envelope from his pocket he handed it over to Byomkesh, saying, 'These are the photographs of the fingerprints and a report. The fingerprints of three separate persons have been found.'

Byomkesh put the envelope in his pocket without opening it. Then he looked at Barat's face and said, 'It seems that you haven't had any lunch today.'

Barat shook his head and said, 'How could I? The man you identified as the murderer has escaped!'

Byomkesh nodded his head as if to indicate that he had expected this development. Then he looked meaningfully at Phanish, who nodded and went inside. Barat leaned back on his chair and said in a tired voice, 'Not the murderer alone, even Mohini has fled. Both of them disappeared in the taxi. The constable was posted to guard Pranhari's house, but he was not given any orders to detain Mohini. Bhuban Das arrived in his taxi and blew the horn from the road; Mohini went out and got into the taxi and they drove off.'

Phanish brought a plate loaded with food and placed it before Barat. Barat started eating mechanically with a morose expression on his face. We too applied ourselves to the *malpoas*.

After finishing our scrumptious repast we were about to light up cigarettes when a man in an orderly's uniform entered the room from outside. He had a *Gandhi* cap on his head and was clad in a loose handloom *kurta* and pyjamas. I had not been able to recognize him at first. Taking off his cap he threw it down with some force on the ground and then said in a strong voice, 'I have nabbed both the brothers-in-law, sir!'

It was Bikas Dutta. His identity was revealed only when he had taken off the cap. Byomkesh greeted him warmly and said, 'Come, come Bikas. You have finished your job then?'

'Yes sir, I have finished the job. They had planned to beat me up and that is how they got caught.' Bikas stretched himself on a sofa and said firmly, 'They were the two brothers-in-law.'

'Two brothers-in-law? Who are you talking about?'

Before Bikas could reply Surapati Ghatak entered the room. Despite his fancy clothes he seemed to look somewhat like a disguised wolf and his eyes were very alert. After taking in the situation in the room with a swift glance, he asked in a humble voice, 'Is the master at home? I had some ...'

Byomkesh said, 'Please come in, Surapati Babu.'

Bikas suddenly sat up straight. Staring very hard at Surapati Babu, he aked, 'This gentleman is Surapati Ghatak? He is the head clerk of the main office?'

Byomkesh said, 'Yes. Now tell me, what is the matter?'

Bikas pointed his forefinger at Surapati Babu and said, 'Sir, I was talking about the two brothers-in-law of this gentleman, Biswanath and Jagannath Roy. They are the ones who are creating all the trouble at the coalmine.'

Surapati's eyes were filled with fear. He said in a weak voice, 'What? What is it? But I do not –'

Very slowly Barat turned his eyes towards him and went on looking steadily at his face.

Byomkesh asked, 'Surapati Babu, the two young fellows whom you tried to dump on us are your brothers-in-law?'

Surapati Babu said, 'Why? Why should it matter?'

Byomkesh said, 'Nothing. Last night I received a note, which bears the fingerprints of three persons. We want to verify if you are one of those three. Inspector Barat, would you please take Surapati Babu's fingerprints. If they tally we can determine how deeply he is involved in this conspiracy. Phanish, do you have an ink pad for using rubberstamps?'

Surapati Babu had been receding step by step. Nearing the door he turned round and tried to escape. By chance Manish Babu was about to enter the room just then. They collided and both were about to fall but managed to regain control. Then Surapati Ghatak ran away at a fast speed.

Manish Babu had just returned from the coalmine. Entering the room he looked around, bewildered and anxious. As we all got to our feet, he asked, 'What's happening here? – Inspector Barat—why did Surapati run away like that?'

Barat said, 'Please sit down, sir. The people who were creating trouble at your coalmine have been caught.'

Manish Babu said, 'They have been caught?'

Byomkesh said, 'Yes. This young man is Bikas Dutta; he is my assistant. After consulting Inspector Barat I had sent Bikas to the coalmine in the guise of an orderly at the hospital. It is he who has caught them.'

Manish Babu asked, 'Who – who were they?'

Byomkesh said, 'Surapati Ghatak and his two brothers-in-law.'

'What! Surapati!' Manish Babu slumped into a chair.'But – Surapati! He has been working for me for the last twenty years. How could he do this!'

All of us took our seats again. Then Byomkesh said, 'Manish Babu, after a second marriage most men are controlled by their wives, Surapati Babu was controlled by his brothers-in-law. There is not much difference.'

Manish Babu asked, 'But why? Why did they want to harm me?'

Byomkesh said, 'That hasn't been found out yet. But it shouldn't be difficult to find. I have a feeling that the *Marwari* gentleman who wanted to buy your coalmine has been pulling strings from the background. Or it could be somebody else. The truth shall be revealed when a little pressure is applied on Surapati Babu.'

'But, have you been able to find any direct evidence against Surapati?'

'Not yet. But the way he ran off when I mentioned about taking his fingerprints clearly indicates that he has a guilty mind.'

Manish Babu emitted a deep sigh and got to his feet. It seemed that he had been affected more by sadness than surprise. He said, 'Would you gentlemen kindly excuse me for a while? Phani, come with me, we have to make some arrangements for running the office. And Surapati ...' he looked enquiringly at Barat.

Barat said, 'I shall make necessary arrangements for Surapati.'

Manish Babu walked off in the direction of the office with his son.

The four of us sat quietly for some time. Then Byomkesh asked in a casual voice, 'You must have procured an arrest warrant in Bhuban's name?'

Barat said, 'That is what took the whole day.'

Byomkesh enquired, 'There is no hopeful news?'

Barat said, 'I have received a report from a railway station about forty miles from here that an abandoned taxi without number-plates has been found. I have sent my men to inspect the vehicle. It could be Bhuban's taxi, he could have dumped it there and caught a train.'

'He could have gone to Bombay or Madras, who knows?'

'Hmm. Byomkesh Babu, I have to make a move now. There is still a lot of work to do at the office.'

'All right. It is your duty to catch the guilty persons and I know that you would do your best. But, personally I shall feel happy if you are not able to catch them.'

There was a wry smile on Inspector Barat's face as he left.

Manish Babu went to bed directly after dinner. Arrangements had been made for the three of us to sleep in the same room that night; a camp cot had been set up for Bikas. We were lying on our beds and smoking while Bikas was recounting how he had caught the two brothers-in-law. Just then Phanish entered our room very quietly. On seeing Phanish Byomkesh sat up on his bed and said, 'Come Phanish.'

Phanish pulled up a chair close to Byomkesh's bed and sat down, saying in an aggrieved tone, 'Do you have to leave tomorrow?'

Byomkesh said, 'Yes, the way the two brothers-in-law have threatened me, it is better to get away from here as soon as possible. If you ever happen to visit Calcutta with your wife you must come and see us. My wife would certainly like Indira.' Saying this he broke into a smile as if remembering the days of his own courtship.

Phanish nodded his head and then said very softly, 'I want to hear the story.'

Byomkesh pulled a pillow on his lap, saying, 'You want to hear the story – Pranhari's story? All right. But it would be just a story, not an entirely true episode from beginning to end. Somewhat like a historical novel.'

Phanish raised his eyebrows in confusion. Byomkesh said, 'You didn't understand me? Those who write historical novels do not adhere strictly to actual facts. They pick up some characters and some incidents from history and with those as a framework they build up their story. The story that I am about to tell you would be some thing like that. I do not know the whole incident, but from what little I do know I have been able to compose a whole story. Truth and imagination have equal roles in this story. Do you want to hear it?'

Phanish said, 'Please.'

Byomkesh lit up a fresh cigarette and started talking.

'Let me start the story with Bhubaneswar Das. Even after hearing his name it had not struck me that he was not a native of Bengal but belonged to Orissa.Those who reside at the border of Bengal and Orissa can talk fluently in the dialect of both states, it is difficult to trace their origin. If I had realised this, the mystery could have been solved much earlier because Mohini was from Orissa as well. Two and two make four.

'Mohini was Bhubaneswar's wife. They belonged to the class where both husband and wife go out for manual labour and earn their livelihood. Bhuban used to work in a motor-reparing workshop at Cuttack and Mohini worked as a maidservant with Bengali families. And they were very much in love with each other. It is on their love that this story is based.

'Bhuban had high ambitions, he did not like that Mohini should work as a maidservant. While working in the motor workshop he got a truck-driver's job in the army and left; before going away he told Mohini that he would save money and buy a taxi and then she wouldn't have to work anymore.

'There was no news of Bhuban for about two years. Meanwhile, Mohini had started working at Pranhari Poddar's house; she worked there during the day and went back to her parents at night.

'Pranhari had an inordinate lust for money. He was as miserly as he was greedy. Even though he had grown old while chasing money all his life and amassed considerable wealth through cheating, deception and blackmail, his lust for money had not abated. He did not have any weakness for women or may be such weakness had faded with age. But when Mohini came to work for him, he was struck with an evil design as he saw her, thinking up a new way of earning money. Many wayward sons of rich men came to his house for gambling, if only he could dangle Mohini before their eyes ...'

'The strong sexual attraction of Mohini's body had led Pranhari to form a wrong impression about her character. He started collecting money in Mohini's name from the sons of rich men by bluffing and misleading them. But Mohini did not yield to their approaches. After this had gone on for some time the young men became annoyed with Pranhari; they had paid him money, why should they spare him? They decided to give him a good beating.

'Pranhari realized that unless he escaped from Cuttack he was bound to be assaulted. But he did need Mohini; where would he find such a succulent bait? He offered to take Mohini with him. Mohini did not object. Her husband was posted at a distant place; she had to earn her living as a maidservant; Cuttack or any other town was one and the same for her. So she agreed to go with Pranhari at one and a half times higher salary.

'But Bhuban returned to Cuttack before they had left the town. He had saved some money from his wages, but it was not enough for buying a taxi. The husband and wife discussed the matter among themselves after which Bhuban went to see Pranhari.

'Bhuban mentioned about the money to Pranhari. He said that he had some money, but if he could get another two and a half thousand rupees he could buy a taxi. Pranhari thought that if he loaned money to Bhuban he would have both him and his wife in his clutch; Mohini would then have to comply with his orders. So he agreed.

'A registered deed was prepared, which stated that the loan shall be recovered by adjusting Mohini's salary of fifteen rupees per month, in addition to which Bhuban shall pay thirty-five rupees per month from his income from the taxi and a further thirty-five rupees per month shall be paid by Pranhari for hiring the taxi as per his needs; thus an aggregate sum of eightyfive rupees per month shall be applied towards recovery of the loan.

'Everybody was happy. Bhuban bought the taxi. All three of them came to the coal town. Thereafter Pranhari took some time to pick up the trend of the town before commencing his activities.

'The Coal Club was the haunt of the rich men of the town. Pranhari arrived there and started fishing. He caught four large-sized fish. He took them to his home for gambling.

'In course of the gambling sessions they all saw Mohini. One of them in particular was strongly drawn to her; Arobindo Haldar was a licentious character; he became berserk in lust. Pranhari was stripping all four of them at cards; he started stripping Arobindo Haldar even more. He had intimated to Arobindo that for laying his hands on Mohini there was no way that he could bypass the proper channel.

'Once he received Pranhari's permission to make his move Arobindo started calling on Mohini at odd hours. But Mohini was a woman of strong character, she was not what she looked from outside. She had realized Arobindo's intentions, but she did not drive him away by speaking to him outright. Rather she treated him with courtesy while conversing with him, maybe even shared jokes and laughs with him, but she did not accept his gifts. Pranhari might have given some broad hints to Mohini; Mohini went only as far as those hints made it necessary. Pranhari was a shrewd character, he did not say anything clearly to Mohini; he had thought that his hints would serve the purpose. After all Mohini was a woman of a lower class.

'After pursuing Mohini vigorously for some days Arobindo realised that she was a hard nut to crack. On the other hand he had lost a considerable amount in gambling. Then one day Pranhari's cheating was exposed. The gambling sessions were stopped. It was only natural that all those who had lost money should be angry, but Arobindo's anger was the most intense. Because he had been cheated not only in gambling but also in another matter. He had been both cheated and humiliated, which his why he took his three companions with him one evening and went to beat up Pranhari.

'By sheer coincidence the taxi which they hired for calling on Pranhari belonged to Bhuban Das. While travelling in the taxi Arobindo had probably given voice to some of his chagrin about

Mohini. On hearing him Bhuban came to know that Pranhari had sold his wife for two thousand rupees.

'Bhuban had no home in the town. Pranhari had not allowed him to stay in his house. But I believe that whenever he had the opportunity Bhuban used to come in secret and spend the night with Mohini. The husband and wife used to share their confidences; possibly Mohini had hinted to her husband that the old fellow was not a good man. In his heart of hearts Bhuban detested Pranhari, which was only natural; there are hardly any instances of a cordial relationship between a moneylender and his debtor. Bhuban, however, was a careful person. He used to tell Mohini that once the loan was repaid, the taxi would be exclusively his own and they would then go away from this place ending their relationship with the old man once and for all.

'But Bhuban had never imagined that the old man was such a vile character. When he heard that Pranhari had accepted two thousand rupees and sold his wife his blood boiled. There were many wealthy debauches in this world, who eyed the wives of other men, Bhuban had no cause of anger against them; but Pranhari had sold his wife to a third person and Bhuban decided that he would kill the old rascal and settle the score.

'The opportunity arrived sooner than expected. The four passengers got off the taxi when they were close to Pranhari's house. Bhuban reversed the car and parked it facing towards the town; then he too got off carrying a spanner in his hand.

'Bhuban had been visiting that house twice or thrice every day both during the day hours and at night. He knew that there was a ladder placed at the rear end of the house for the sweeper's entry to the bathroom. Shrouded in darkness he walked down to the rear side of the house and then after climbing up the ladder he knocked on the door.

'Pranhari was then in his bedroom after locking up both the front and rear doors. He was probably unaware that four men had arrived to beat him up. But he was a careful person; on hearing the knock he went to the bathroom. Then when he heard Bhuban's voice on the other side he opened the door without hesitation, because he had no suspicions about Bhuban.

'They walked into the bedroom and stood facing each other.

'I do not know if there was any conversation between them. Bhuban had the spanner in his left hand; he raised it abruptly and struck it once very hard on Pranhari's head. Pranhari did not get an opportunity to open his mouth or make any sound. He fell down and died instantly.

'Bhuban then opened the front door very slowly. He had perhaps intended to make his escape by going down the front staircase if he heard no sound, so that the rear door could remain closed. But it was probably just then that the four men were holding their discussion at the foot of the staircase; so after lightly closing the front door from inside, Bhuban went down the way he had come, taking his spanner with him. Thus, to sum up the situation, both front and rear doors were open and it was difficult to determine as to which of the two doors had been used by Pranhari's murderer to enter the room.

'Arobindo had found the door to Pranhari's room closed on the first occasion. On the second occasion when all four of them went up they saw that the door was open and that Pranhari Poddar had concluded the role that he was destined to play in this world. They ran down the staircase and made their escape. Nearing the taxi they found that the taxi-driver was asleep with his head resting on the steering wheel. They woke him up and returned to the town.

'Mohini had been cooking all this time; she heard nothing. Any sound caused by the visitors must have been drowned by the sound of her cooking. When the old man did not come down for his dinner at the usual time she decided to go up. She saw that Pranhari was lying dead on the floor and that both the front and rear doors were open. The thought of Arobindo did not strike her then, the man who came to her mind was Bhuban. Where there is love there is apprehension. She had hinted to Bhuban that the old man was not a good person. Bhuban looked like a cool-headed person from outside but deep inside him there was a violent spirit born out of veiled pride. He would never tolerate any indignity shown to his wife.

'Mohini was a very intelligent girl. She did not lose her head even at the sight of the dead body, but quickly decided what she had to do: whosoever might have committed the murder the police should not be able to apprehend him. Mohini had no doubt in her mind that the murderer had entered through the rear door of the bathroom and gone out the same way. She closed the rear door from inside and then sent a message to the police through the truck driver. See what a daring woman she was! Never losing her head, she did just that much as was needed to misguide the police.

'Mohini had told us a lot of lies, but she never resorted to any unnecessary falsehood. Bhuban too did the same thing. I think that on the night of the murder Bhuban must have returned to the house at some time to report the whole incident to Mohini and that thereafter they used to meet off and on for sharing news on further developments. It was for this reason that Mohini did not wish to leave the house. She had to retain contact with Bhuban at any cost.

'Any way, when I made my entry to the stage the police had got their eyes focussed on the four suspects. They had both the motive and the opportunity to the fullest extent. Either all four of them had collectively committed the murder, or anyone of them could have committed the murder by befooling the remaining three. I had no reason to disagree with the views of the police. But it was difficult to accept the suggestion that the four men had joined hands for committing the murder. These suspects were not dacoits from the stories of the *Mahabharata*; they all held social status and were so-called civilized people. The suggestion that they would form a gang to commit a murder was preposterous.

'But if any one of them had committed the murder by hoodwinking the others, who could be that person? The man who was under the most suspicion was Arobindo Haldar. He was cheated not only at cards, but also in another affair, for which he felt extremely humiliated although he was unable to express his chagrin to anyone. The humiliation of a lecher is a peculiar phenomenon; he feels deeply mortified when he cannot lay his hands on the object of his lust for whom he has spent money.

'I had some misgivings after I started my investigation. The first question which cropped up in my mind was – where was the murder weapon? No weapon bearing the description provided by Dr. Ghosh had been found. If any of Arobindo's group had carried any weapon it would not have escaped the notice of Phanish or Bhuban. So none of those four men had brought or taken away any weapon to or from the site of murder. Then where did it come from and how did it disappear?

'The second conclusion that I arrived at from Dr. Ghosh's report was that the murderer was left-handed. Consider— there was not even a chair in Pranhari's bedroom. It was unbelievable that he could be sitting at the edge of the bed with his back towards the murderer. The murderer had struck him while he was on his foot facing him and the blow had been struck on the right side of the head, resulting in a livid bruise running down like a parting of the hair. So the murderer was left-handed; his left hand was more active.

'I started checking if any of the four suspects was left-handed. At the Coal Club I observed that Mrigen Moulik was playing tennis with his right hand, Madhumoy Sur and Arobindo Haldar were shuffling, dealing and playing cards with their right hands. Finally I threw a glass paperweight at Phanish, who caught it with his right hand. So none of them were left-handed.

'But if not left-handed, one of them could be ambidextrous. So I could not discard them all together. Barring them there were no other suspects. Mohini had not committed the murder. If she wanted to kill the old man she would probably have used poison, but she had no motive at all to kill him.

'I had been unable to make any headway anywhere when every thing became clear in a flash just like the strike of lightening across a cloudy sky in a dark night. I saw Bhuban turning the jack fitted under his taxi with his left hand.

'We all know that Bhuban Das was present at the site on the night of the murder, but strangely his name had not struck me at all. This is analogous to the phenomenon described by G. K. Chesterton in – *The Invisible Man.*

'The problem was then solved in a minute. Bhuban had struck Pranhari with a spanner, which tallied perfectly with Doctor Ghosh's description of the murder weapon.

'Bhuban has fled with his wife. He is a very intelligent person; he had realised that I had found him out. I do not know where they would set up their home. Could be Madras or Bombay, there are so many places. I very sincerely hope that Pramod Barat would not succeed in finding Bhuban. Because if he does find him, he would not award him a gold medal which he deserves.

'I have nothing more to say. If I have left out any thing you can fill up the gaps with your guesswork. If they are not apprehended Bhuban and Mohini shall remain as fugitives for the rest of their lives. Pranhari Poddar's relentless greed destroyed the lives of two persons; this is the biggest tragedy of this story.

The Mystery of the Fortress

PAST EPISODE

1

I had never thought that before the year was out Byomkesh and I would again be visiting the same town in the **Santhal Parganas* where we had gone earlier for a change of air. The second visit however was not in pursuit of health; rather we had set off on a hunt for a rare quarry on a tip-off provided by Purandar Pandey.

During our first visit we had become acquainted with a large section of the Bengali population of the town, but none had told us then about an affluent Bengali family, which lived just outside the town. This intriguing episode, which I am about to narrate, is centered round that particular family. So it is about the family that I shall speak first. I did not learn this entire story all at once; I heard it in bits and pieces from several sources. For the convenience of the readers, however, I have laid out the events in a proper sequence.

On the southern side of the town, in a direction opposite to the railway junction there was a road, which stretched out for about six miles. It was an ancient road, built during the reign of the Muslim rulers and it's surface was paved with cobblestones. Over the years grass and weeds had grown in the gaps between the stone slabs, but a motorcar could still be driven on the road without difficulty.

**Santhal Parganas:* Erstwile district of Bihar, where *Santhals*, an aboriginal tribe of India, were the principal inhabitants.

Bisecting the rocky roughness on either side, the road had maintained it's own rugged existence even to this day.

At the place where the winding progress of this road had come to an end there stood two small hills side by side with pointed peaks. They reminded the viewer of the description of Poet Kalidasa – a patch of green between twin breasts of the earth. The hills were not very high but a fold had developed between the two peaks. Even without taking the simile of Kalidasa into account, it was undeniably a pretty sight.

Neither of the peaks was bare. On the top of one there were the ruins of an ancient fortress, while on the other peak stood a white-painted house of modern construction. Shri Ramkishor Singh, owner of both the fortress and the house, lived there with his family.

A few words of introduction are required here about the ancient fortress and it's present owner. During the reign of Nawab Alibardi a man called Jankiram, belonging to the southern *Rarhi Kayastha* caste, had become a particular favourite of the ruler. Awarded the title of *Raja*, Jankiram had ruled the province of Bihar for some time and amassed enormous wealth. But the country was then going through a state of transition. After Aurangzeb's death the Mughal Empire was in a state of collapse; the irrepressible Maratha freebooters were devastating Bengal and Bihar through repeated raids; the British traders had cast off their guise of businessmen and were stretching their grasping hands towards the ruler's throne. There was acute unrest all over the country; be it a king or his subjects, the rich or the poor— there was no peace in any one's mind. Raja Jankiram was a man of keen intelligence; he built a small fortress in the middle of this impenetrable hilly gorge and it was there that he put up his family and stored the enormous wealth that he had amassed.

Therafter many lives were swept away under the strong waves of a nationwide revolution. But the solitary fortress of Jankiram remained safe and unscathed. His successors continued to live there for many generations.

A hundred years passed after the battle of Plassey.

Peace had been restored by and large in the country under the rule of the East India Company. Jankiram's fortress was then occupied by his fourth and fifth succeeding generations – Rajaram and his son Jairam. Rajaram was a man of mature age, his son Jairam was still in his youth. They lived comfortably with the income, which they earned from their ancestral wealth and the landed properties, which they had acquired in the neighbouring areas. Their accumulated wealth had not diminished but increased substantially at the hands of succeeding generations. Instead of spending their earnings Jankiram's successors had developed a habit of converting their savings into gold. And in the process they had come to own a large collection of gold coins, gold vessels and assorted items of gold. None of them had any bad habits. And where was the scope of indulgng in wanton luxury in the midst of the forest?

Then all of a sudden the country erupted under the mammoth explosion of the sepoy mutiny. The blaze of the mutiny was not restricted to the towns alone but spread like a forest on fire even to the remotest parts of the country.

As the head of his family, Rajaram became extremely concerned. Looting and rampage were taking place on a massive scale all over the country. In some areas the mutinous sepoys were engaged in plundering, while at other places the sepoys belonging to the British rulers were looting whatever they could lay their hands on. Rajaram received the news that a gang of sepoys was heading towards his fortress. He started making preparations for protecting his property.

But how could he protect it? The hundred years old fortress was incapable of resisting the assault of a well-trained enemy equipped with firearms. The dilapidated entrance gate of the fortress could have been blown off by a single canon-ball. No doubt a large canon was installed at the entrance to the fortress but it had become rusted and unserviceable through long disuse; the iron lid at its base was jammed and unopenable. There were a few muskets in the fortress, which could serve the purpose of shooting deer in the forests or scaring away thieves, but they were hardly adequate for resisting a gang of sepoys who were intent on looting the place.

After holding consultations with his son, Rajaram made arrangements for sending away the women and children of his family from the fortress. Several miles away, deep inside the forest there was a *santhal* village and it was there that Rajaram sent his wife, daughter-in-law and grandchildren, accompanied by a retinue of servants and attendants. Only Rajaram and his son Jairam remained at the fortress. Before his wife set off on the journey Rajaram tied up a few gold coins in a loose end of her *sari*. He was afraid to give her more gold, lest the servants were tempted to commit perfidy. After the family had departed, father and son set about to hide their gold.

Three days later a group of sepoys led by a British soldier arrived at the fortress. Rajaram had probably intended to make his escape with his son after hiding the gold. But they could not break out from the fortress as the sepoys appeared very suddenly and entered unresisted.

Nobody knew what happened at the fortress. The sepoys left in two days, but Rajaram and Jairam were not seen alive by anybody after that day. The fortress remained deserted and empty.

Peace was restored to the country in due course. Rajaram's family-members and their attendants returned after a few months to find that there was nothing left in the fortress barring the stones. Anything and everything that could be lifted had been taken away by the sepoys. At several places inside the fortress the sepoys had lifted the stones and dug up holes in the floor probably in search of any gold or jewels that might have been buried in the earth. It was not clear if they had found any thing. It could be that the sepoys had looted everything and gone away or it could be that they had found nothing and departed after killing both father and son.

For some time the two helpless women lived in the fortress with their children; but what was once a home had now become as bare as a crematorium. Gradually the servants and attendants deserted the family one by one, because just a roof above one's head was not enough for running a family, food and clothing were also needed. In the end the two widows were compelled to leave the fortress one day with their chidren. It is not known where they found shelter. Most probably they were given shelter at the home of some distant relatives in Bengal. The deserted fortress became a dwelling place for jackals.

There is no record of the next sixty years or so in the history of the lineage. It was in the second decade of the twentieth century that two young descendents of the family rose to prominence once again. They were two brothers, Rambinod and Ramkishor Singh. Although reared in poverty, they had not forgotten their family heritage. The two brothers launched into business and fortune smiled on them at long last. They made plenty of money by first trading in **ghee* and later in the iron business.

The elder brother Rambinod did not live very long. He died mysteriously in his youth. Ramkishor went on running the business single-handedly and earned even more wealth.

Time passed. Ramkishor got married and had children. Then towards the end of the third decade of the twentieth century Ramkishor bought back his old ancestral property and built a new house on the peak of the second hill on the other the side of the fortress. He also purchased extensive landed properties in the adjoining areas and started living with his family in the house on the top of the hill. A few repairs were undertaken at the fortress to preserve it as a memento of it's old glory, but it remained unoccupied as before.

2

The ancient, stone-paved road had not stopped at the foot of the hill, but had risen sharply up to some distance. At the point where the steep rise had commenced there was a large borewell by the side of the rocks. Nurtured by the moist ambience of the well a few trees had grown tall and wide over the years and formed a circle around it.

The steep rise had covered a distance of about fifty yards before terminating on a flat area, which served somewhat like a courtyard. Two separate flights of stone steps had ascended from this courtyard and stretched like a snake's forked tongue in two separate directions; one had ended up at the entrance gate to the old fortress and the other led to Ramkishor's dwelling house.

**ghee*: Clarrified butter made out of cow's or buffalo's milk.

There was a fairly long room on the courtyard for garaging a car and two small rooms to serve as living accommodation for the driver. It was in the long room that Ramkishor's vintage car was garaged, while his old driver Bulakilal lived in the adjoining rooms.

The steps rising from the courtyard towards Ramkishor's residence had not gone straight up but had followed a winding route embracing the body of the rocks. These steps were comparatively wider and had terminated at the entrance to the house.

The peak of the second hill had been levelled out and the house had been built in the middle of the area. All around the house there were fruit and flower gardens and the entire compound was enclosed by a cactus fence. The smoke-coloured fortress on the adjoining peak was clearly visible from the house at a distance of a hundred feet or so, while looking down towards the north the town could be seen indistinctly — about six miles away. On the southern side of the house the forest had started almost from the foot of the steep rocks and a dense growth of trees was visible as far as the eyes could be stretched. This forest was included in Ramkishor's property and he derived a substantial income from the timber of *sal*, teak and ebony trees, which had been grown there in large numbers.

When Ramkishor had moved into the house on the hill he was below forty and still quite robust; but he had sought this self-imposed exile at such an early age probably because he no longer had the need to do any running about for earning money. He was accompanied by his wife, two sons, a daughter, several servants and attendants and his old office-manager, Chandmohan Dutta.

In course of time Ramkishor had another son and a daughter and then his wife died. Ramkishor was thus obliged to bring up all his five children alone.

Ramkishor's family life was not happy. As the children grew up they started displaying some very odd traits. It could be that their nature had become warped because they were brought up in the midst of such wilderness, segregated from human society. The eldest son Bangshidhar was excessively hot-tempered; he had a habit of losing control of his senses when he was enraged. After passing the Matriculation examination from a local school he went to

Berhampore College. But just after a few months he was compelled to leave the college due to some grave offence. The college authorities did not disclose the actual nature of the offence. One of the professors happened to be Ramkishor's boyhood friend and it was he who was instrumental in getting the affair hushed up. Even Ramkishor had no knowledge of the actual incident; there could perhaps have been big trouble if he did.

Bangshidhar returned home and told his father that he wouldn't study any more, but would look after the family estates. Ramkishor was vexed and scolded him but in the end he did not impose his will on his son's wishes. Bangshidhar started looking after the family property; the manager Chandmohan Dutta took him in hand and started teaching him the work.

Ramkishor got Bangshidhar married in due course. But a few months after the marriage the bride met with an unnatural death. Bangshidhar was not at home at the time; he had gone out for inspecting some distant properties owned by the family. On the morning in question his wife was not found in the house. After extensive search her body was found in the chasm between the two peaks. She had probably gone out of her room for some reason during the night, drawn close to the ditch in the dark, lost her footing and fallen down. The death was shrouded in mystery. When Bangshidar heard of his wife's death after returning home he exploded in anger; in his blind rage he did not stop from blaming even his brothers or sisters. From then onwards his violent nature seemed to become even more vicious.

Ramkishor's second son was Muralidhar; he was about one and a half years younger than Bangshidhar. Bony and rickety in appearance; his pointed face was filled with mischief and he was so squint-eyed that it was impossible to tell in which direction he was looking. On top of this he was hunch-backed, which had made his lean body bent like a bow. Muralidhar was deformed since birth. His character was just the opposite of Bangshidhar; he was not ill tempered but he was a crafty rogue. As teenagers the two brothers had quarrelled one day and Bangshi had slapped his brother. Murali was not strong, so he had endured the slap in a show of tameness.

But a few days later Bangshi had a strong attack of diarrhea and vomiting, which almost cost him his life. There was nothing to prove that Murali had a hand in the matter. But nevertheless Bangshi had not dared raise his hand on Murali after that incident. He just restricted himself to cursing and threatening his brother when he was angry with him.

Muralidhar had had no education, on top of which his appearance was so repulsive that his father had never thought of getting him married. He lived on his own, chewing **pan* and **supari* all the time. He had a personal servant, whose name was Ganpat. Ganpat was of Muralidhar's age; he was short and stout with a round face and bulbous eyes and his eyebrows were curved like halfmoons. Looking at his face one would think that he was always struck with childish wonder, but in reality there were very few mischievous people like him. There was no misdeed which Ganpat was incapable of committing. Starting from abduction of women to burning down homes – Ganpat could undertake any job ordered by his master. There was an inseparable bond between the master and the servant and the two were heard to have jointly commited numerous crimes, but they had never been caught.

Ramkishore's third child was a daughter, whose name was Haripriya. She was four years younger than Muralidhar. She was moderately good-looking and had no physical deformity, but her eyes seemed to be tinged with venom and her mind filled with spite. Haripriya could not tolerate her siblings. It was her habit to constantly find fault with everyone, become extremely displeased at the slightest lapse on anyone's part and thereafter express her discontent in the strongest terms. When Bangshidhar's bride arrived, Haripriya's spite seemed to flare up even more. The bride was timid and good-natured. Haripriya humiliated her by finding fault with her all the time and made her miserable by her stinging remarks.

Then the bride died all of a sudden. A few months later when he could get over the shock of this mishap, Ramkishor got his daughter married. Knowing too well that his daughter would not be

**pan*: betel leaves.
**supari:* betel nuts.

able to live with her in-laws, he chose a poor youth for her husband. His name was Manilal. A good student, Manilal had a degree in Science. He possessed good health and a gentle nature and after his marriage he took up permanent residence at his father-in-law's home.

It was not known if Haripriya and Manilal had a happy married life. By nature Manilal was not a communicative person, on top of which he was poor and he was living at his father-in-law's home through the latter's benevolence; even if he had any genuine grounds for discontent he chose to remain silent on the subject. Haripriya never deneaned her husband before others; rather she used to snarl at her brothers if they tried to poke fun at him.

There was one issue, however, on which the husband and wife were in perfect accord. After his marriage Manilal had become deeply devoted to his father-in-law. Towards his brothers-in-law he was totally indifferent, having neither any affection nor any grudge against them. But that he held his father-in-law in much esteem and devotion was evident in all his words and actions. Haripriya too loved her father very dearly. There was perhaps no one else for whom she had any genuine feelings, but then the fact was that she was incapable of loving anyone deeply.

Haripriya had a brother and a sister who were younger to her; the brother, Gadadhar, was in his teens and the sister Tulsi was the youngest in the family. Gadadhar seemed to be a little dull-witted; his intelligence had not matured with age. He appeared to be at a loose end most of the time and had a habit of grinning vacantly without any reason. He was not attentive to his studies, preferring to spend time in the forest, hunting birds with a catapult.

His sister Tulsi was his constant companion in this pastime. Tulsi was not dull like Gadadhar; rather she was a little too intelligent for her age. She had a slim figure, a pretty face and an extremely restless nature. Her occupation was to roam about in the forest during the afternoon in search of birds' nests or rabbit-holes and acting as Gadadhar's guardian in all matters. What every single member of the family was doing at any point of time, — did not ever escape Tulsi's notice. On the other hand, it was impossible for any one to determine her whereabouts at any time. And yet among all the brothers and sisters Tulsi was the only one who could be said to be normal.

Apart from his children Ramkishor had another dependent young man, living at his home. His name was Romapati. Ramkishor had provided him shelter because he was a needy youth belonging to his own caste. As he had passed the Matriculation examination, Ramkishor had hoped that he might be able to tutor Gadadhar and Tulsi. There was no lack of effort on Romapati's part in this regard, but meetings between the tutor and the pupils occurred very seldom. Romapati was shy and diffident and his students simply ignored him, while the other inmates of the house hardly took notice of his insignificant existence. And thus Romapati lived unobtrusively in a corner of the house for two square meals a day and a roof above his head.

I have mentioned earlier about Chandmohan Dutta, the manager of the estate. He was Ramkishor's senior by about five or six years and had been with him from the beginning of his business career. Once Bangshidhar had taken over the responsibility of running the estate, Chandmohan was left with hardly any work, but he still kept a strict eye on every single activity; all incomes, expenditure and accounts were subject to his approval. He was a very careful man, well-conversant with property matters and having lived with Ramkishor for a long period he had become practically a member of his family.

It was true that Ramkishor had not enjoyed a happy family life, but as a man grows older his forbearance increases through the bonds of affection. By nature Ramkishor had been rough and intolerant in his youth, but he had mellowed down considerably with age. Previously he used to acknowledge self-help as the sole deciding element in one's life, but in later life he did not deny the role of destiny all together. Although not much drawn towards religious customs and practices he did not show any disrespect towards divine deities. His wife had belonged to a conservative **Vaishnava* family

**Vaishnava*: A worshipper of Vishnu, following the teachings of Shri Chaitanya.

and perhaps her influence on Ramkishor's life had not been wasted all together. It had at least left it's mark on the names chosen for his sons and daughters.

And yet, if for any reason he happened to lose his temper on some rare occasion, Ramkishor's vicious nature used to emerge from its shell and it was then that his towering, ruthless anger held in check like a genie in a closed bottle, found violent expression. None dared stand before him on such occasions; even Bangshidhar used to step back in apprehension. But Ramkishor's anger never lasted very long; it used to flare up in a moment and go off just as suddenly.

3

Towards the end of a winter season about eight to nine months after Haripriya's marriage a group of gypsies arrived and set up their tents close to the borewell. They were accompanied by a pack of donkeys, dogs, hens, snakes and assorted animals. At night they lit up bonfires and the men and women used to drink home-made liquor, dance and make merry and in the day time they used to gather wood from the forest, lay traps for catching wild fowl and rabbits and make use of the well-water as they pleased. Gypsies, as a tribe, never have much sense of morality.

Initially Ramkishor did not object when the gypsies set up their camp inside his property, but he became irritated after some time. The matter which worried him most was that Gadadhar and Tulsi had taken to roam around the gypsy-tents all the time forsaking food and sleep; even strong and repeated warnings did not help to relieve their intense curiosity in any way. The other residents of the house stayed away from the gypsy camp during the daytime, but it was quite possible that some of the servants and even a few members of the family visited the place in the darkness of night. What the gypsy girls lacked in beauty was more than compensated by the strong sexual attraction that they exuded.

A week or so passed in this manner, but then one morning a few male and female gypsies gathered at the doorstep of Ramkishor's house and laid out a large display of merchandise, comprising coloured stones, the navel of a *kasturi* deer, snake poison, sulphurous soap and other assorted stuff. Bangshidhar was present in the house at that time; he threatened to beat up the gypsies and drove them away. Ramkishor ordered the gypsies to get off from his property that very day.

The gypsies complied with the order but not in entirety. That evening they lifted their tents and equipment and moved away to a distance of two to three hundred yards away, where they set up their camp once again at the edge of the forest. When Bangshidhar saw this on the following morning he was livid with rage. Carrying his rifle he reached the gypsy camp accompanied by a few servants. At Bangshidhar's order the servants started beating up the gypsies. Bangshidhar fired a blank shot in the air. Then the gypsies took fright and fled from the area.

The nuisance was no doubt got rid off, but the manager Chandmohan shook his head and said, 'I do not think that what was done was right. These people are very mischievous, they might try to do us some harm.'

Bangshidhar asked in a truculent voice, 'What harm could they do to us?'

Chanadmohan said, 'How can I say? They could throw poison in the well or set the forest on fire.'

Everybody remained on guard for a few days, but no calamity of any sort occurred. The gypsies had not tried to do any harm or even if they had done so they had not succeeded.

After a month or so Ramkishor took out his entire family to the forest on a picnic. This was one of the annual events on his calendar. A suitable spot was to be chosen in the forest, where a canopy would be hung and the master would sit and relax under the canopy and play a game or two of chess with Chandmohan. The servants would meanwhile kill a lamb and cook it; the young men would roam around with their guns looking for birds or prey. After a sumptuous lunch and a brief rest they would all return home in the evening.

That morning Ramkishor and his party reached the appointed place. In the midst of dense *sal* wood trees, an area had been cleaned up in advance. A *durrie* had been laid on the ground and an awning fixed above the area. The cook was lighting up a logfire; the servants were making preparations for the cooking. The driver Bulakilal had gathered a whole bunch of **bhang* leaves and was grinding them with a pestle in an iron mortar for concocting a sherbet, which was to be served in the evening. The sky was lit up with golden sunlight; a cool breeze was blowing gently through the leaves of the *sal* leaves. There was no trace of any impending calamity anywhere.

The two old men laid their chessboard under the awning; the others disappeared into the forest in various directions. Carrying a gun on his shoulder Bangshidhar went in one direction, Muralidhar accompanied by his constant companion Ganpat, went in another direction; they were both expert shots.

Gangadhar and Tulsi left together; their tutor Romapati followed them at some distance. It was not impossible for children to lose their way in the forest and he had been told by Ramkishor to 'keep an eye on those two.'

The son-in-law, Manilal sat down with a book under the cover of a tree at some distance from the awning. Ramkishor had given him an English book on *tantras*, which he was reading and underlining with close attention. He had no interest in hunting.

That left only Haripriya. She spent some time strolling around the place where the preparations for cooking were in progress, then she walked over to the tree where her husband was sitting; finally she entered the forest all by herself. On this one day everybody had been granted freedom. It seemed as if so many people staying under the same roof had become stifled in each other's close proximity and being now released in the open environment of the forest they were relishing the pleasure of being alone by themselves.

The day rolled on. The two old men had become engrossed in their game; the sound of distant gunshots floated in from time to time from the forests; gradually the air became filled with the pleasant aroma of cooking. Between the leaves of the surrounding trees the dilapidated fortress and the white-painted dwelling house could be

**bhang:* leaves and shoots of hemp.

seen on adjoining peaks. They were not very far off, half a mile at the most. The shadow of the old fortress had overlapped the chasm and spread across the white walls of the house.

Suddenly a shrill and continued scream shattered the rustling murmur of leaves. The two chess-players looked up, startled. Manilal stood up under the tree, throwing his book on the ground. Tulsi was seen running back breathlessly through the light and shade of the *sal* trees and screaming at the top of her voice.

Before Tulsi could reach the awning, Manilal grabbed her and shook her firmly by the shoulders, saying, 'Here, Tulsi! What's wrong? Why are you screaming?'

Tulsi stared for a while, raising her eyes which looked blank as if she had lost her senses and then screamed loudly, 'It's sister! She is lying under a tree, she is probably dead! Please come with me right now. Father, uncle, please come right now!'

Tulsi ran back in the direction that she had come from. Manilal ran alongside her. The two old men followed, their clothes tousled.

There was a thick bush about two hundred yards away. Drawing close to the bush Tulsi pointed her finger towards the foot of a tree. Haripriya had come, wearing a sari of a light orange colour. She was seen lying in the dark shadow at the foot of the tree, while some man was stooping down on her body and inspecting her.

Romapati stood up on hearing footsteps. His face was pale in fear; he said in a broken voice, 'Snake! She has been bitten by a snake!'

Manilal pushed him aside and picked up Haripriya in his arms. Haripriya was unconscious; the snake had left its tooth-marks on her left ankle — two crimson spots side by side.

4

Haripriya did not survive; she died on the way while being taken home.

Venomous snakes had not been seen in that forest before, but now there was no longer any reason to doubt their existence; it also became a more or less self-evident conclusion that this was the work of the gypsies; they had left snakes or snake-eggs in the forest by way of retaliation. But the gypsy gang had gone away long back; there was no way that they could be traced.

For some time after Haripriya's death Ramkishor's house was cast under a gloomy spell as if struck by some dreadful curse. Among all his children it was perhaps Haripriya whom Ramkishor had loved most, which is why he sustained a deep shock. Manilal was a cool and collected young man, but after his wife's sudden death he became somewhat unbalanced and confused. The foundations of his brief wedded life had crumbled under an unexpected earthquake.

Another person who was severely affected by this tragedy was Tulsi. It was not that Tulsi was too attached to her elder sister, rather there used to be constant conflict between the two. Haripriya used to chastise Tulsi at every opportunity and lock her up in her room. And yet on seeing Haripriya die before her eyes Tulsi seemed to have become mentally unhinged in some way. While roaming in the forest that day she had caught a glimpse of an orange sari close by and had gone in that direction, but then she had seen her sister lying in a dying state and had started screaming in fear. Haripriya had opened her eyes just once to look at her and tried to tell her some thing before she died.

Since then Tulsi had been reduced to a befuddled state. She went round the house with her eyes wide in shock as if she was seized by ghosts, staring blankly if any one questioned her. There was no doubt that her immature nerves had sustained a great shock.

Bangshidar and Muralidhar had also been shocked but not that deeply. Bangshidhar had become very quiet; in his own mind he was probably holding himself guilty for Haripriya's death and thinking that it would have been better perhaps if he had not resorted to such extreme force with the gypsies. As regards Muralidhar, although no outward change was visible in his conduct or movements, he seemed to have withdrawn within himself like a tortoise. There was one issue however on which the brothers were in perfect accord; they had both started looking at Manilal with strong detestation, as if it was Manilal who was responsible for Haripriya's death.

A month after Haripriya's death Manilal went to Ramkishor and sought his permission to leave the house. Stating that his connection with the family had been severed forever, he spoke with tearful eyes, 'I shall never forget your kindness. But I have no place in this family any longer.'

Ramkishor's eyes were also filled with tears. He said, 'You have no place? My daughter, who was destined to leave me, is gone, but am I to lose you as well? No, no, that shall not happen. Please stay. If God wills your connection with this family might be revived one day.'

Bangsidhar and Muralidhar were both present there. Bangshidhar's face darkened in anger as he got up and left the place; Muralidhar's lips curled in displeasure. Neither of them had failed to recognize what their father had hinted at.

Manilal did not depart. He went on living in the house of his erstwhile father-in-law with an even more detatched and indifferent attitude than before.

Two years passed. Normalcy was restored to Ramkishor's family once again. Only Tulsi did not regain the liveliness, which she used to display earlier. Her mind had been subjected to a severe shock, which seemed to have halted both her physical and mental development. At the age of thirteen her body and mind had remained as immature as that of a ten year old girl; even after reaching adolescence she had remained like a child.

But on the other hand her mind had undergone an odd change. For no accountable reason she had now become extremely devoted to her tutor — a man, whom she had hitherto treated with utter disdain. This — rather than pleasing the tutor Romapati, had made him feel exceedingly uncomfortable and embarrassed. Those who are accustomed to be held in disregard become discomfited if they are treated with a little warmth.

Any way, Ramkishor's household had started functioning smoothly once again when a guest arrived at the house. He was a friend of Ramkishor's youth; rather, he was a close friend of Ramkishor's elder brother, Rambinod and his ties with Ramkishor had weakened after Rambinod's untimely death, but the link of friendship had not been severed all together. His name was Ishanchandra Majumdar. He was a professor in Berhampore College and had retired lately. When Bangshidhar was about to be sent off in disgrace from the college a few years back it was he who had helped him out of the difficult situation.

Professor Ishanchandra was a lean and dry man, as if shrivelled by ascetic practices and his disposition was a little on the bitter side. His health had failed after retirement and he was perhaps financially straitened as well. He had written a letter to Ramkishor reminding him of their previous intimacy and stating: I have not seen you and your children for a long time; I do not know how long I am going to live; I am told that the climate out there is very healthy, etcetera. In his reply Ramkishor had extended his cordial invitation to the Professor: the weather here is very congenial, please come over, you shall be fully cured if you stay here for a month or two.

Ishanchandra had arrived in due course and settled down in the house. Bangshidhar was not aware of anything; he had gone for a few days to supervise harvesting in a distant paddy-field. On returning home he came face to face with Ishanchandra. Bangshidhar was struck dumb as if he had seen a ghost; his face turned very pale at first and then became flushed slowly. Drawing close to Ishanchandra he asked in a low voice, 'You here?'

Ishanchandra looked steadily at his erstwhile student for some time and then said in a dry tone, 'Yes I have come here. Do you have any objection?'

Bangshidhar drew him by his hand and said, 'Come here. There is some thing I have to tell you.'

Nobody knew what discussion took place in secret between the two, but that the exchange had not been pleasant was evident when Ishanchandra went and told Ramkishor that he wanted to go away that very day. Ramkishor made repeated appeals to him and in the end the Professor consented to stay at the fortress. One room in the fortress was fit for living; the professor had no objection to living in solitude and he consented that his meals may be delivered to the fortress every day.

Ramkishor escorted Ishanchandra to the fortress that evening and returned home after getting him properly settled there. Then he summoned Bangshidhar and a long question-answer session was held between the father and son. Suddenly Ramkishor flared up like a bundle of straw on fire and started scolding his son in a raised voice. But Bangshidhar did not say a word; his eyes reddened as he heard the abuses hurled at him while his mind boiled in futile anger.

Ishanchandra started living at the fortress. He spent the nights there all by himself. But barring Bangshidhar and Muralidhar the rest of the family-members used to call on him at the fortress during the daytime. Muralidhar had become very angry with the Professor, because by taking up residence at the fortress he had unwittingly deprived Muralidhar of his secret arbour for amorous trysts.

A fortnight passed peacefully. Then one evening as Ramkishor was on his way to see Ishanchandra and was about to climb the steps to the fortress, he noticed smoke curling up behind some trees around the well. He walked in that direction out of curiosity and saw a **sadhu* sitting under a tree with a fire lit before him.

The *sadhu*'s body was smeared with ash, he had matted hair and his face was covered with black and grey beard and a thick moustache. Ramkishor and the *sadhu* stared at each other for a long time. Then a loud, raucous laughter emerged from the *sadhu*'s throat.

Ramkishor could not visit the fortress that evening. He returned home and took to bed. A little later he had an attack of fever. Under the influence of mounting fever he started raving loudly in a delirium.

The doctor arrived. In due course the delirium stopped and the fever subsided. Ramkishor recovered gradually. But it was seen that his heart, which had been strong and sound till then, had been severely damaged.

Another fortnight passed. Ishanchandra continued to remain at the fortress. Nobody tried to drive away the *sadhu* from the foot of the tree. Once bitten twice shy; nobody wanted a repetition of the tragedy which had ensued from the conflict with the gypsies.

**sadhu*: A hermit.

LATER EPISODE

1

It was an autumn morning in Calcutta. Byomkesh and I were reading the newspaper at our Harrison Road residence after breakfast. Satyabati was occupied with her domestic chores. Puntiram, our domestic help, had gone to the market.

After Byomkesh got married I had proposed to move out from the place. I had thought that as a friend I should ensure that the newly-weds could live without disturbance. But Byomkesh and Satyabati had rejected my proposal outright; they had not let me go. So I had been living with them for the last four years. After getting to know Byomkesh very closely I had got over my lifelong regret of not having a brother of my own. Now Satyabati had filled in the combined roles of my sister and sister-in-law. And lately the prospects of acquiring a nephew had appeared on the horizon. So I was passing my days in unexpected bliss.

That morning we had split up the newspaper. I was reading the first page while Byomkesh was occupied with the inner pages. Byomkesh did not have much interest in the news items, which were printed boldly in the main section; his mind was more inclined to roam through lanes and bylanes rather than taking the main roads.

Raising his face from the newspaper, Byomkesh asked me, 'Have you heard the name of Ishanchandra Majumdar?'

I thought for a while and said, 'The name sounds familiar. Who is he?'

Byomkesh said, 'He was a professor of history. I had studied under him for some time at Berhampore. The gentleman has died.'

I said, 'If you were his student at one time, it must be said that he had become old enough to die.'

'No doubt, but his death was not natural. He died from snakebite.'

'Oh!'

'He had gone to the same place where we went for a change of air last year. And it was there that he met with his death.'

My mind went back to the pretty little town surrounded by hills in the Santhal Parganas. We had spent a few wonderful weeks there.

I recalled the faces of many acquaintances, whose memories were about to fade from my mind. Mahidhar Babu, Purandar Pandey, Dr. Ghatak, Rajani ...

Just then there was a knock on the outer door. I got up and opened the door to find the postman, who handed over an envelope addressed to Byomkesh. Since we rarely received letters from any one, I stood looking eagerly at Byomkesh after passing on the envelope to him.

He opened the envelope, read the letter and looked up with a smile. 'Can you tell me who wrote this letter?'He asked me.

I said, 'How can I? I do not have X-ray eyes.'

'It is a letter from Purandar Pandey, *D.S.P.'

I exclaimed in amazement, 'What! And I was thinking of him just now!'

Byomkesh nodded his head and said, 'I too was thinking of him. Not only that, but there is also a mention of Professor Majumdar's affair in the letter.'

'Strange!'

Byomkesh said, 'Such strange incidents do occur from time to time. We remember someone of whom we haven't thought for many days and the man appears in person before us. Experts say it is coincidence. But it involves a much deeper mystery. There is a distinct link somewhere, which we cannot see ...'

'Let it be. What has Pandey written?'

'Read it yourself.'

I read the letter. The summary of what Pandey had written was as follows—

'A mysterious incident has occurred here recently. A prosperous family lives on a hilltop at a short distance from the town. Ishan Majumdar, a friend of the gentleman who heads that family, had come here for a change of air. He has died suddenly. The cause of death is stated to be snakebite, but both the police and the doctor, who conducted the post-mortem have doubts on that score. ... Byomkesh Babu loves to get involved with mysteries; moreover winter is about to set in here; the weather is very pleasant. If he

*D.S.P.: Deputy Superintendent of Police.

cares to come down here with his friend for a few days and live as a guest at the humble abode of this poor man, it might be possible to kill two birds with one stone.'

When I finished reading the letter, Byomkesh asked, 'What do you say?'

I said, 'Not a bad idea. You do not have any pressing assignments here at this time. But Satyabati ...'

Byomkesh nodded his head and said, 'We can't take her anywhere in her present condition...'

'Quite true. But supposing she wants to come with us? Or, if she does not want to let you go? Women in this condition tend to become quite unreasonable, it is difficult to say what they would ask for at any time.'

I stopped speaking as I heard the sound of approaching footsteps.

Satyabati entered the room. Her face had shrivelled in fatigue and her body had taken the shape of a large fish bulging with eggs. She came and plumped into a chair. We remained silent. Satyabati spoke out in a tired voice, 'Send me to my brother. I don't want to stay here any longer.'

Byomkesh and I exchanged glances. He asked, 'You don't want to stay here? Why?'

Satyabati replied without warmth, 'I can't stand the two of you. I am getting angry every time I look at you people.'

I thought that this must be one of the symptoms of her present condition, otherwise why should she get angry on seeing us?

Byomkesh let off an aggrieved sigh and said, 'All right, you may go to your brother. I shall not stop you. Ajit can drop you at Sukumar's house ... And we too might make a short trip somewhere in the meantime.'

In response to our telegram Purandar Pandey had come to the railway station personally to receive us. He took us to his residence, where we sat down to consume assorted snacks with tea and enquired about old acquaintances. We were told that all those with whom we had become friendly on our last visit were still in town. Only Malati Devi was no longer alive. Professor Shom had sold his house and left the town. Then the conversation was directed towards the business that had brought us there. Purandar Pandey narrated the detals of Professor Ishan Majumdar's death. Side by side we could learn many things regarding the state of affairs in Ramkishor's family.

The details of Professor Majumdar's death were like this. —The Professor had been staying at the fortress for about a month; there was a marked improvement in his health. On the night before his death he took a stroll in the compound of the fortress after dinner; the tutor Romapati was with him at that time. Romapati went home at around half past nine; the Professor remained all by himself. Nobody knew what happened at the fortress during the night. Romapati went to the fortress again next morning. He saw the Professor lying dead near the door of his room. There were marks of snakebite on his ankle and a deep bruise behind his head stretching up to the ear. In the clenched fist of his right hand there was a shining gold coin of the *Badshahi* period.

The marks of snakebite had not been noticed by any one at first. Ramkishor suspected that some miscreant had come at night and murdered Ishan Babu; this suspicion was confirmed by the deep bruise on the head. So he sent for the police.

After the police arrived the marks of snakebite were discovered. But by then it was too late to avert the investigation. The police sent the body for postmortem.

During postmortem the poison of a cobra was found in the dead man's blood. This left no doubt that snakebite was the cause of death. But still Purandar Pandey was not totally convinced. He suspected that some underhanded trickery had been deployed.

After hearing everything Byomkesh asked, 'When it cannot be denied that death was caused by snakebite, why are you still suspicious?'

Pandey said, 'My suspicion is supported by several minor reasons. Although none of these reasons have much weight individually, considered collectively they do make some sense. Firstly, if Ishan Babu died of snakebite, how did he sustain a blow on his head?'

Byomkesh said, 'It could be that after he was bitten by the snake, he became scared and fell down, hurting his head and losing consciousness. And then he could have died while he was still unconscious. Isn't that possible?'

'Not impossible, but there are more questions. Where did the snake come from? I have had the place searched thoroughly; no trace of any venomous snake was found anywhere.'

'But you just told us that two years back Ramkishor Babu's daughter also died of snake-bite.'

'She was bitten by a snake in the forest, where snakes might be found. But how did the snake reach the fortress? It is impossible that it had crawled across the steep surface of the hill. It could of course have climbed up along the staircase, but there was no reason for it to do so. There are no rats or frogs in the fortress, then what could have drawn the snake to climb all those steps to reach there?'

'Then what ...'

'Unless someone had carried the snake to the fortress and left it there, — that could have happened.'

Byomkesh went on thinking as he said, 'Hmm, anything else?'

Pandey said, 'And you also have to bear in mind that a gold coin was found in the Professor's clenched fist. Now, where did it come from?'

'It could have belonged to him.'

'Fom the reports that I have gathered regarding the Professor's financial standing it doesn't seem possible that he would walk around with gold coins in his hand.'

'Then what is your guess?'

'I am unable to make any guesses, which is why my suspicions are growing stronger. I have now started thinking that it was not just snakebite; there must be a much deeper mystery.'

After remaining quiet for a while Byomkesh asked, 'Did Ishan Babu have any close relatives?'

Pandey said, 'There is a married daughter, her husband is a doctor and they live in Nepal. I am told that the Professor did not have good relations with his daughter or son-in-law.'

Byomkesh became engrossed in his thoughts. We sat in silence for about five minutes and then Pandey said, 'I admit that it is not possible to prove all that I have just told you, but these issues cannot be ignored either. And then there is some thing else, which you must know. Ramkishor's family is not quite normal.'

Byomkesh was startled. 'What do you mean?' he asked.

Pandey explained, 'Not a single person in the family is straight or simple. Ramkishor Babu seems like a goodnatured man from outside, but his docility is that of a tamed tiger, it is by no means his true characteristic. Also, there could be some secret mystery in his past life; why otherwise should he start living incognito in the midst of this jungle from such an early age? Then there is the elder son, Bangshidhar, — an obstinate and ruthless fellow; the way he manages the estate would make one think that he is a descendent of Chengis Khan! I have heard that he committed a few murders and had some people beaten up severely within his father's property, but there were no witnesses or evidence of any sort.'

Byomkesh asked, 'How old is Bangshidhar? Is he married?'

'Around twentysix or twentyseven. He had been married, but within two months of his marriage his wife met with an accidental death. Accidental deaths seem to occur with a strange regularity in this family.'

'Did she too die of snakebite?'

'No, she jumped down into the ditch from the hilltop or somebody had pushed her down.'

'A wonderful family! Now let's hear the rest.'

'The second son Muralidhar is full of vices. He is squint-eyed and a hunchback; his father did not get him married; so he indulges in debauchery behind his father's back. But there is one strange thing that I have noticed; both sons are dead scared of their father. Had the father been a harmless sort of person would the sons have been so scared of him?'

'Hmm — what next?'

'There was a daughter, Haripriya, a few years younger than Muralidhar. She died of snakebite. I do not know much about her character. But the son-in-law is a simple person.'

'Son-in-law?'

Pandey spoke about Manilal and then concluded his descriptions by talking briefly about Gadadhar and Tulsi. 'Gadadhar,' he said, 'is a cranky and clumsy fellow; what little wit he possesses is all bent on mischief. And Tulsi – she is a young girl whom I have not been able to read. She is not stupid or affected, nor is she precocious. And yet she seems to be somewhat strange.'

Byomkesh took his time in lighting a cigarette and then said, 'From the way you have just analyzed the characters for us it seems that you believe that any one of them could be directly or indirectly responsible for Ishan Babu's death.'

Pandey smiled and said, 'That is what I suspect – yes, but the suspicion has not yet reached the stage of belief. I cannot understand how anyone's purpose could have been served by killing the old professor. Anyway, I would suggest that you withhold your comments till we visit the fortress this evening; then you can make an on the spot survey and give me your views.'

Pandey left for office. Byomkesh asked me, 'What do you think?'

I said, 'I don't know. Everything seems somewhat smoky.'

Byomkesh said, 'There could be more to this. Like they say, there is never a smoke without a fire.'

2

The three of us set off that evening in a police car. It took us about half an hour to cover the six miles on the stone-paved road.

On reaching the well we saw that another car was already parked there. As we got down from our car; Pandey said, 'That is Dr. Ghatak's car. I wonder if any one in the family is sick.'

We learnt that Dr. Aswini Ghatak, with whom we had been acquainted on our previous visit was Ramkishor Babu's family physician. As we were proceeding towards the house we saw a thin stream of smoke emerging from the other side of the well.

Byomkesh asked, 'What's that? Where is that smoke coming from?'

Pandey said, 'A *sadhu* has set up his home there.'

'*Sadhu*! A *sadhu* in the midst of this forest! But surely he has no hopes of getting any alms here.'

'No, but I believe uncooked food items are sent to him from Ramkishor Babu's house every day.'

'Oh! How long has the *Babaji* been here?'

'I can't say. But he was here even before the Professor's death.'

'Really? Come, let's go and have a look at the *sadhu*.'

Clad only in a small piece of loincloth the *sadhu* was sitting under a tree with a fire lit before him. When we walked over and stood in front of him he opened blood-shot eyes and looked at us intently for a few moments; a strange, silent smile appeared on his bearded face, then he closed his eyes again.

We stood there uncertainly for some time and then walked away. This *Babaji* did not belong to the usual type of *sadhus*, who lived exclusively on alms. There was a distinct difference, but whether it was due to any elevation in his spiritual status or for any other reason, was some thing that I was unable to decide.

Pandey asked, 'Now where would you like to go? Would you like to meet Ramkishor Babu first or visit the fortress?'

Byomkesh said, 'Let's see the fortress first.'

As we were about to climb up the steps to the fortress the driver Bulakilal emerged from his den and saluted Pandey.

'Bulakilal, why is the doctor here? Is anyone sick?' Pandeyji asked him.

Bulakilal said, 'No sir, both the doctor and the lawyer are here. Who knows what secret talks are going on?'

'The lawyer? You mean Himangshu Babu?'

'Yes sir. Shall I notify the master that you are here?'

'Don't bother. We shall go and see him in due course.'

Bulakilal then folded his hands respectfully and said, 'Sir, I had been preparing *thandai*, if you would kindly excuse me.'

'*Thandai* – with *bhang*? Oh well. Go ahead then. We'll have a look at the fortress and come down soon.'

'Very well, sir.'

We started climbing the steps to the fortress. Pandey smiled and said, 'This old man makes excellent *bhang* and that is what keeps him occupied most of the time.'

We had to climb seventy-five steps before we reached the main entrance to the fortress. There was no gate at the entrance, it must have been missing since long, but the stone arch was still intact – unscathed by the passage of time.

The first thing that caught our attention as we walked in was a canon. At first sight it looked like the stump of a tree laid on the ground with its head tilted upwards. Exposed to sun and rain for over two centuries the ten feet long body of the canon had become rusted and covered with thick scales. It looked like a solid column of iron — unmovably heavy and nobody had obviously tried to handle it for ages. The hole for inserting the canon ball was not very large; a coconut peeled of all its skin could have possibly passed through it somehow, but even that narrow orifice was now filled with mud and earth and a few shoots of live grass had raised their head from the mouth. The sight of the canon lying on the ground as a witness to the past history of the derelict fortress seemed to touch me with a sentimental feeling. It seemed as if once a mighty warrior in it's youth, it had now been prostrated with old age and was counting days till the arrival of death with it's head raised towards the sky.

Barring the canon I could see no other movable object, which could have belonged to the past era. Enclosed by walls all around, the compound of the fortress was not more than one acre in area and it was paved with stones all over. Along the circular periphery of the compound walls there were several small cubicles, which were probably used at one time for housing the sepoys who guarded the fortress. The cubicles built in stones were in a derelict condition; at some places they had collapsed altogether, while prickly shrubs had blocked the entrance to others. Like a navel at the centre of the circle stood the main building of the fortress and stretching between the navel and the circumference lay the huge expanse of the compound.

The building was square-shaped and looked quite strong from outside. It comprised five or six rooms of varying sizes. Despite petty repairs undertaken lately, most of the rooms were not in habitable condition. Some rooms had large cracks on their walls, while some had holes in their roof through which we could see the sky. Only one room on the rear side was in good shape. Although the lime mortar had flaked off exposing the joints between large stone slabs, the room had been made habitable by fixing a new doorframe and a panelled door at the entrance.

Pandey pointed towards the door-sill and said, 'The professor's body was found lying there.'

Byomkesh kept looking at the spot for some time and then said, 'After he was bitten by the snake, he could have struck his head with the door frame before he fell down, which would explain the bruise on the head.'

Pandey said, 'That is no doubt possible. But you have just seen the entire building; it is no doubt in a derelict condition, but there is no accumulation of refuse where a snake could remain in hiding. Before the professor came to stay here carbolic acid mixed with water was sprayed thoroughly all over the place and the same thing was done twice more while he was living here ...'

'Did nobody live here before the professor's arrival?'

Pandey smiled tightly and said, 'Nobody on record. But Muralidhar ... .'

Byomkesh said, 'Hmm .. I understand,' and entered the room.

The room was about fourteen feet square and it's floor was paved with stone. Barring a bed and an easy chair there was no other furniture in the room. Presumably the other items of furniture, which might have been been provided for the use of the professor, had since been removed

We noticed something special in this room, which we had not seen in any of the other rooms. Pegs had been fixed along three walls of the room at a height of one foot or so above the floor level; the pegs were protruding about one and a half feet from the walls and at one time they were probably thick as crowbars but over the years they had become corroded and brittle.

Byomkesh asked, 'What are those pegs for?'

Pandey said, 'I think this room was either the office or the treasury of the fortress. Planks laid across these pegs could have served as shelves on which assorted articles could have been kept, including books of accounts and even boxes for storing money. As a matter of fact such pegs can be seen in many ancient buildings in Bihar even today.'

Byomkesh went on casting his eyes on the walls and the floor of the room. Then he asked all of a sudden, 'The Professor must have come here with some baggage and bedding. Where are they?'

'They are all with us, I mean with the police.'

'Did you check what was held in his baggage?'

'A few clothes, three or four books and exercise books, three ten-rupee notes and some coins wrapped in a piece of cloth.'

'And what about the gold coin found in his clenched fist?'

'That too is in police custody. Once this case is solved all those articles shall have to be handed over to his successors.'

Byomkesh went on looking all around the room for some time, but did not seem to find anything of significance. Then he sighed and said, 'Let us go. I have finished my inspection here.'

We had descended to the compound of the fortress and were proceeding towards the exit when a young man walked in hurriedly through the gate. Pandey whispered to us that this was Romapati, the tutor. He was lean and slim with a dark complexion and his face and eyes showed keen intelligence. He was in his mid-twenties and bore a somewhat diffident attitude. Pandey accosted him and said, 'Here, **Mastermashai*, where are you off to?'

Romapati smiled a little hesitantly and said, 'The doctor and the lawyer are having some urgent discussions with the master; all the elders are present there. But I could not see Gadai and Tulsi there and so I thought that they might have come here.'

'No, I haven't seen them here.' Pandey introduced us saying, 'These are my friends; they have come here on a visit.'

Romapati looked intently at Byomkesh for a while and then asked in a composed voice, 'Are you Byomkesh Bakshi, — the seeker of truth?'

Byomkesh broke into laughter and said, 'Yes. But how did you recognize me? My photographs have not been published anywhere.'

**Mastermashai*: A teacher or a tutor, addressed with respect.

Romapati became embarrassed then and stuttered, 'I … no, no, I haven't seen any photograph … but it struck me when I saw you … I have read your books .. I have been thinking for some time … if you came here the mystery could be solved …' Then he became even more confused and stopped speaking.

Byomkesh smiled pleasantly and said, 'Come, let us chat for a while.'

The canon was close by. Byomkesh dusted the surface of the canon with his handkerchief and sat down on it, inviting Romapati to sit beside him. Romapati sat down hesitantly in a corner.

Byomkesh said, 'You just said that I might be able to solve the mystery. But Ishan Babu died of snakebite, — what mystery is there to solve?'

Romapati did not reply; with his face lowered in embarrassment he started picking his fingers. Byomkesh surveyed him closely from head to toe and then said in an easy tone, 'Let it be. You were with Ishan Babu almost till nine thirty on the night that he died. What were you talking about?'

Romapati now replied eagerly, 'He had a lot of affection for me. Whenever I came to see him he used to tell me stories. That night …'

'What story was he telling you that night?'

'He was telling me the history of this fortress.'

'The history of this fortress! Really! Won't you tell us what you heard? We would love to hear the history.'

Pandey and I walked over to the canon and sat down on it. Romapati recounted the story that he had heard. Commencing from the time of Raja Jankiram he went on to narrate the story upto the period of Rajaram and Jairam during the sepoy mutiny.

After hearing the whole episode, Byomkesh said, 'Hmm, it does sound like real history, but none of this is found in the textbooks. How did Ishan Babu come to know about it?'

Romapati said, 'He knew every thing. Our master had a brother, who died at an early age. His name was Rambinod Singh, he and the professor were bosom friends. It is from him that the professor had heard all this; he knew the entire family history up to Rambinod Babu's death. He had written down everything in a notebook.'

'Written down in a notebook? Where is that notebook?'

'I can't tell you where it is now, but I had seen it. It is probably in his steel trunk.'

Byomkesh looked at Pandey, who nodded and said, 'There is a notebook carrying some thing written with a pencil. But I can't say what is written there; it is all in Bengali.'

'I'll have to go through it. Anyway —,' Byomkesh turned towards Romapati and said, 'We have learnt quite a lot from you. Now tell me, why did you again come to the fortress on the following morning?'

Romapati said, 'The professor had asked me to see him. He had told me: Let us stop here tonight; come and see me early tomorrow morning and I shall tell you the rest of the story.'

'Rest of the story—what could it be?'

'He didn't tell me that. But I guess what he meant was the history of this family dating from the sepoy mutiny to the present.'

'But why? Did he have any specific purpose in telling you all that?'

'I really don't know; he used to tell me whatever came to his mind and I too enjoyed listening to him. He told me a lot of stories about the Mughal and Pathan periods. One day he told me that a family, which had fallen prey to the crime of fratricide had no hope of being spared; however high the family's status might be it was bound to be destroyed. This is what history bears witness to.'

We looked at each other. A frown appeared on Pandey's face.

Byomkesh got up and said, 'It is getting dark. Come, let us now go and see Ramkishor Babu.'

By then the sun was had gone down behind the house on the other side of the ditch.

3

On reaching the courtyard we saw that Bulakilal was pouring *bhang* sherbet from one vessel to another; his actions were being keenly watched by Gadadhar and Tulsi.

Gadadhar gaped at us with his mouth wide open; Tulsi cast apprehensive eyes at us and then moved sideways towards Romapati and held his hand.

Romapati scolded them and asked, 'Where were you two all this time? I have been looking for you all over the place!'

Tulsi did not reply; she went on looking intently at us. A sound of gurgling laughter emerged from Gadadhar's throat. He said, 'The *sadhu* was smoking *ganja* and we were watching him.'

Romapati rebuked him,'Didn't I forbid you to go to the *sadhu*?'

Gadadhar said, 'We didn't go to him, we only stood at a distance and watched him.'

'That's enough— come, let's go home now.' Romapati moved away towing the two. I heard Tulsi asking him eagerly, 'Who are these men?'

Bulakilal handed us glasses filled with his concoction. It was excellent *bhang* sherbet, prepared with curd, black pepper, cucumber seeds and various other ingredients. That particular type of sherbet was not prepared anywhere else excepting in the north-western regions of India. Pandey praised Bulakilal's skill and said, 'This is excellent stuff! But Bulakilal, for whom did you prepare such a large quantity of *bhang*? You didn't know that we were coming here.'

Bulakilal said, 'Sir, it is for me, of course and then the *sadhu baba* has a glass or two.'

'The *sadhu baba* doesn't seem to be averse to anything. And ...'

'And – Ganpat carries away some in a pot.'

'Ganpat – Muralidhar's personal servant? Does he take it for his own consumption or for his master?'

'That I do not know, sir.'

'Well, Bulakilal, you are an old employee of this family, can you tell me which are the members having any addictive habits?'

Bulakilal remained silent for some time and then said, 'The master takes a little opium in the evening. I do not know about the others, sir.'

It was evident that he wouldn't tell us even if he knew. We finished our sherbet, made a few more complimentary remarks and started climbing the steps towards the house.

There were about seventy to eighty steps in this flight as well. The sun had set when we reached the top, but there was still plenty of daylight. Romapati was standing near the entrance; he said, 'Would you like to meet the master? Come with me.'

The room where Romapati presently took us was the drawing room.

Apart from a table and chairs there was a large divan covered by a mattress. Ramkishor Babu was sitting at the centre of the divan, with Chandmohan the estate manager sitting on one side and Manilal the son-in-law, sitting on the other side. The two sons, Bangshidhar and Muralidhar were seated at two corners of the divan facing their father. Dr. Ghatak and the lawyer Himangshu Babu were sitting in chairs drawn close to the divan. Daylight was streaming into the room through the open windows on the western side and yet the room seemed somewhat dark from where we stood.

As we were about to enter the room we heard Muralidhar saying in a sneering voice, 'The rightful inheritor gets nothing and the sly rogue grabs it all! Why should Manilal be given the fortress? Have I got no rights? I shall take the fortress.'

Bangshidhar spoke out immediately, 'Why should you take it? My claim comes first. I shall take the fortress: I'll get it repaired and live there.'

Ramkishor seemed to explode like a stick of dynamite on fire, as he screamed at his sons, 'Shut up! I'll thrash anyone who argues with me and throw him out from here. If I want to leave every thing to Manilal, what has that to do with either of you? Impudent rascals!'

Manilal spoke in a calm voice, 'But I didn't ask for anything ...'

Muralidhar twisted his face in a sneer and said, 'No, you didn't ask for anything! All you did was to brainwash our father behind our backs. You wolf in a sheep's ...'

Ramkishor was about to explode once again, but Dr. Ghatak raised his hand and said, 'Ramkishor Babu, you have become very excited, which is not good for your health. Let us stop the discussions here; we may resume our talks some other day.'

Ramkishor regained some control over himself and said, 'No, doctor, this matter cannot be left hanging any longer. I do not know how long I'll live. I want to resolve all these issues right away. Himangshu Babu, you have heard how I wish to dispose of my property. There is no need for any further discussions. Please start drawing up the deed, the sooner we can get it registered the better it is.'

'All right. I'll proceed as you want,' Himangshu Babu rose to his feet.

And it was only then that everybody seemed to notice the three of us, standing near the door, unable to either enter or retreat. Ramkishor Babu frowned in our direction and asked, 'Who is it?'

Pandey advanced and said, 'It is I. Two of my friends have come here on a visit and I had brought them to see the fortress.' He then introduced us by our names.

Ramkishor addressed us cordially, 'You are most welcome. Please come in and sit down.' It did not seem that he had heard Byomkesh's name before.

Bangshidhar and Muralidhar got up and left. Dr. Ghatak seemed a little surprised and disconcerted at first to see us, then he folded his hands and greeted us. After exchanging a few more words with Ramkishor he took his leave along with the lawyer. The three of us were then left in the room with Ramkishor Babu, the estate manager Chandmohan and the son-in-law Manilal.

Ramkishor Babu called out for the servants asking them to put on the lights and serve tea.

Chandmohan said, 'I'll go and fetch them.'

He got up and left. Chandmohan had a very dark complexion and a shrunken appearance, but his eyes were filled with shrewdness. He cast a sharp glance at Byomkesh from the corner of his eye before leaving the room.

As we exchanged courtesies I noticed that Ramkishor Babu's behaviour towards outsiders was polite and cordial. Then Byomkesh said, 'I heard that Ishan Majumdar came here and died of snakebite. I had studied under him at one time.'

'Really?' Ramkishor Babu cast a surprised look at Byomkesh, 'My elder son also — what was I saying? Yes, Ishan was my close friend. I shall never be able to get over the mortification that he met with an accidental death while living at my home.'

From the way he spoke it seemed that he was unaware that Ishan Babu's death could have been caused through any reason other than snakebite.

Byomkesh spoke in a compassionate voice, 'It is very sad. I believe he was also a friend of your elder brother.'

Ramkishor remained quiet for a while and then spoke with some emphasis, 'Yes, but my brother passed away nearly thirty years back.'

'Oh – then it was with you that he had a close friendship lately. Tell me, which of the residents of this house knew him before he visited this place? You knew him, of course, who else?'

'My estate manager, Chandmohan knew him from before.'

'Your driver is an old employee, didn't he know him?'

'Yes, Bulakilal knew him.'

'And I believe your elder son too was his student?'

Ramkishor cleared his throat and said, 'Yes.'

While this conversation was taking place I happened to look at the son-in-law Manilal. He was turning his eyes on Byomkesh and Ramkishor in quick succession just as a cat sitting by a man eating his meals looks alternately at the man's mouth and his plate. In the semi-darkness I could not read the expression on his face, but there was no doubt that he was listening to the dialogue with close attention.

Byomkesh said, 'A gold coin was found in Ishan Babu's clenched fist. Do you have any idea where it came from?'

Ramkishor shook his head and said, 'No. It's very strange. Ishan's financial standing was not good; he was most certainly in no position to walk around with gold coins in his hand.'

'Is it not possible that he found it somewhere in the fortress?'

'Yes, that is possible. Because my ancestors had hoarded a lot of their wealth inside that fortress. When the sepoys looted the place there was every possibility that a few gold coins could have fallen off here and there. In which event that gold coin is my property.'

Byomkesh said, 'Had it been your property wouldn't Ishan Babu have returned it to you? So far as I know he was not the sort of man who would have filched any thing belonging to some one else.'

'That is true. But, as you know, dire need often corrupts a man's morals. Or it could be that the snake had bitten him just when he picked up the gold coin; so the poor fellow had no time to give it to me.'

A servant came in with a kerosene lamp and placed it on a table; another servant carrying tea and assorted snacks on a tray held it before us. We politely refused the snacks but accepted the tea.

Byomkesh took a sip of tea and said, 'This place has no electricity. Ishan Babu must have been using kerosene lanterns.'

Ramkishor said, 'Yes. But a week or so before his death he had borrowed an electric torch from me. After he died everything else was found, but not the torch.'

'Really! Where could the torch have gone?'

Manilal spoke for the first time in a solemn voice, 'I think somebody must have stolen the torch during all the confusion in the morning after the incident.'

Pandey enquired, 'Who could have stolen it? Do you suspect anyone?'

Manilal had opened his mouth to reply, but was intercepted by Ramkishor, who said, 'No, no, Mani, what you are thinking is wrong. Romapati did not take it; if he did he would have certainly told us.'

Manilal did not speak any more, but kept his lips firmly closed. We understood that the matter of the lost torch had been discussed earlier and that the target of Manilal's suspicion was Romapati. This gave us a hint of some minor discord in the family.

Eventually we finished our tea and got up to leave. Byomkesh said, 'I am fortunate that I could make your acquaintance while visiting this place. You have built your house in a most attractive location. Any one who comes here would not feel like going back.'

Ramkishor Babu was delighted to hear this and said, 'Well, why don't you stay here for a few days? But I can tell you that after a day or two you would want to run away from here. We have become habituated to the loneliness, which is why we can go on living in this place.'

Byomkesh said, 'Thank you. I shall bear your invitation in mind. But if I do come again you would have to let me stay in the fortress. Your fortress has captured my heart like one of those mythical hungry stones that I have read of.'

Ramkishor said in a morose voice, 'After what has happened I am scared to let anybody stay in the fortress. Anyway, if you really decide to come we shall see what can be done.'

As we advanced towards the door I was startled to see two glittering eyes behind a black curtain. Tulsi had been listening to our conversation all this time, now she slipped off in a flash.

After dinner that night the three of us were reclining on easy chairs in the open terrace of Pandeyji's house and smoking cigarettes. During that particular period the weather was very pleasant — soothingly warm in the daytime and comfortably cold at night.

Pandey said, 'Now tell me what you think.'

Byomkesh took two or three puffs at his cigarette and then said, 'You are right – there are discrepancies, but they cannot be investigated till we move into the fortress.'

'You have already set up a preamble for that today. But is it really necessary?'

'It is necessary. The matter cannot be dealt with from so far away. I have to spend time with those people and mix with them; then only can I get to know their secrets. Today I noticed that none of them were speaking out what they had in their minds; they all seemed to be withholding some thing or other.'

'Hmm. Then you are convinced that Ishan Babu did not die from snakebite?'

'It is too early to draw that conclusion. I can only say that what seems to be apparent is not true, there is some deep and startling mystery. Where did the gold coin come from? Where did the torch disappear? Is the story that Romapati recounted to us true? Why does every one want to acquire the fortress? With the exception of the head of the house why can't anybody in the family stand the sight of Manilal?'

I said, 'Manilal can't stand Romapati.'

Byomkesh said, 'That is natural. Both are dependent on Ramkishor Babu. Perhaps Romapati also cannot tolerate Manilal. None of the family-members can stand each other. That should work to our advantage.'

Disposing the butt of his cigarette in an ashtray, he asked, 'Pandeyji, can you tell me what is Bangshidhar's level of education?'

Pandey said, 'I know that he had passed the Matriculation examination, and was then admitted to Berhampore College, but after a few months he stopped studying there and returned home.'

'There could have been some complications. Bangshidhar had come to know Ishan Babu at Berhampore – but why did he give up his studies so abruptly?'

Pandey said, 'I can find out. It didn't happen too far back. If there was any complication it should be traceable from the records of the college.'

'Yes, please try to collect this information. And how far had Muralidhar studied?'

'That fellow is an utter ignoramus.'

'Hmm, the entire family seems to have become somewhat boorish after living in the wilderness. But there is still a trace of old-fashioned courtesy in Ramkishor's behaviour.'

'But he didn't seem to be much grief-stricken at the loss of his childhood friend; rather he has set his eyes on seizing the gold coin.'

Byomkesh broke into laughter and said, 'Alas, it is the rule of this world since yore, he who has the most forever asks for more. I shall have to go through Ishan Babu's belongings tomorrow morning and also read his notebook. They might provide some clues.'

'What next?'

'Next we shall go and sit tight at the fortress. That is something which you shall have to arrange for us.'

'All right. But I have one suggestion. You should not share your meals with that family. Who can tell what is playing on their minds?'

'You may be right. Do you have an icmic* cooker?'

*Icmic cooker: A brass-lined device, similar to a tiffin-carrier in shape and size, in which different food items can be cooked on charooal fire.

'I do.'

'That's all we would need.'

We spent some time in silence. Byomkesh lit up another cigarette and asked, 'Ajit, did anything strike you when you saw Ramkishor Babu?'

'What could have struck me?'

'The moment I saw him today, it struck me that I had seen him somewhere before. Didn't that strike you too?'

'No, I am afraid not.'

'To me his face seemed familiar at first sight. But I am unable to place where and when I had seen him.'

Pandey stifled a yawn and said, 'The chances of your seeing Ramkishor Babu before today are remote. I doubt if he has set foot in any public place during the last five years. You might have seen someone with a similar appearance somewhere.'

After remaining quiet for a while, Byomkesh said, 'May be, you are right.'

4

During breakfast next morning Pandey asked, 'Are you still determined to go and stay at the fortress?'

Byomkesh said, 'Yes, do please make the necessary arrangements. We shall stay there for two or three days at the most, not longer.'

Pandey said, 'But I am not feeling very comfortable with the idea; who knows, the place could really be infested with snakes.'

Byomkesh laughed and said, 'Even so, they wouldn't be able to harm us, we know how to charm snakes.'

'Well, in that case I think I should go and speak to Ramkishor Babu. But is there any harm if instead of living in the fortress you stay in Ramkishor Babu's house?'

'No, no, living in close proximity with the family wouldn't suit my purpose. I wouldn't be able to see things from a proper perspective. The fortress would suit me better.'

'All right. I am leaving instructions at the office,— my clerk Ataullah would show you Ishan Babu's belongings whenever you ask him. He has the key to the godown.'

Pandeyji left on his motorbike at about nine in the morning. His office and residence were housed in the same building. So we were in no hurry to go through Ishan Babu's belongings. We lit up cigarettes and were idling with the newspapers when a small car arrived and stopped in front of the entrance. Byomkesh looked out from the window and said, 'It's Dr.Ghatak'

Dr.Ghatak came in looking somewhat penitent; he was obviously thankful that we had not divulged his private affairs during the previous evening and must have been convinced that we would not do so in future. He said, 'I did not get an opportunity to talk with you properly last evening, so ...'

Byomkesh received him warmly and invited him to sit down, saying, 'If you hadn't come to us we would have gone down to see you today. Tell me how you are keeping. How are all our old friends? Mahidhar Babu ...?'

The doctor said, 'They are all well.'

Byomkesh blinked his eyes and asked with a tight smile, 'And Rajani Devi?'

The doctor's ears reddened, then he broke into laughter as he said, 'Rajani is well. On hearing that you are here she wanted to know if Mrs. Bakshi has come with you.'

'Satyabati hasn't come this time. She ....' Byomkesh looked at me.

I explained about Satyabati's condition and said, 'Satyabati has driven us out of Calcutta. And we too have made up our minds that we shall not return there till we receive any good news.'

The doctor smiled and congratulated Byomkesh, but the smile was not reflected on his face. A starving man may smile on seeing another man eat, but that smile is not one of joy.

Reading his thoughts from the expression on his face, Byomkesh slapped his back and said, 'Don't fret, my friend. Very few people have the good fortune of getting what you have. Just think, side by side with the sweetness of conjugal life you are enjoying the rare thrill of making love to a woman who belonged to another man.'

I too joined in and said, 'Remember the words of Shelley : Oh wind, if winter comes can spring be far behind? Let the season of flowers be over, the fruits shall arrive on their own.'

Now the doctor's face was lit up with a genuine smile. After we had exchanged pleasantries for some time, Byomkesh said, 'Dr. Ghatak, at Ramkisnor Babu's home last evening we happened to overhear a few things about how he intends to dispose of his property and we are curious to hear the details. If you have no constraints why don't you tell us what you know about the matter.'

Dr. Ghatak said, 'Why should I have any constraints? Ramkishor Babu is not doing anything in secret. He suffered a sudden breakdown about a month back; the condition of his heart was quite bad; now he has recovered to some extent. But he is scared that if he dies suddenly at this time his two elder sons shall squander all his assets in fighting lawsuits and they might perhaps try to deprive the two minor children from their rightful shares. That is why he wants to distribute his property among his heirs during his lifetime. The property shall be divided in four equal shares; the two elder sons shall receive one share each, the remaining two shares shall be held by Ramkishor. After his death Gadai and Tulsi shall inherit those two shares as his successors, the two elder sons shall not get anything more.'

Byomkesh said thoughtfully, 'I see. What led to those hot exchanges about the fortress that we overheard yesterday?'

'Ramkishor Babu has retained the fortress in his own custody. But both Bangshidhar and Muralidhar have their eyes on it.'

'And what was all that talk about giving away the fortress to Manilal?'

'The fact is that Ramkishor Babu has decided to get Tulsi married to Manilal. You might have heard that Manilal had been married to Ramkishor's elder daughter, who died. In course of our talks yesterday Ramkishor Babu happened to mention that after his death Gadai shall inherit the dwelling house and Manilal shall inherit the fortress. By Manilal he implied Tulsi; Manilal is not being given anything separately. And that is what led to the fall out between Bangshi and Murali.'

'Hmm. But Tulsi's marriage is still a long way off. She is too young.'

'May be she is too young for marriage in the modern way of thinking, but she is not really a child; she is around thirteen or fourteen years old. Ramkishor Babu is perhaps planning to get her married soon. If he happens to die suddenly his two minor children must have a reliable guardian. He does not have the least trust in his two elder sons.'

'What little I have seen of them hardly justifies any trust in either. What sort of a man is Manilal?'

'He is a cool-headed person, which is why Ramkishor Babu has more confidence in him. But I must also say that the doggedness with which he is clinging to his father-in-law's house hardly gives the impression that he has much self-respect.'

Byomkesh stared blankly for a while and then spoke out abruptly, 'Dr. Ghatak, you should take adequate precautions about your patient.'

Taken by surprise, the doctor asked, 'Patient! Which patient?'

'Ramkishor Babu. Somebody may stand to gain if his heart stops beating before the Will is registered.'

The doctor looked at Byomkesh with wide eyes.

Dr. Ghatak left at about ten, after which we sent for the clerk Ataullah.

Ataullah was a middle-aged Muslim, with a courteous bearing, which gave me the distinct impression that he came from an aristocratic family. His slender body was cloaked in a long coat, his beard was dyed with henna, he wore kohl on his eyes and had a *pan* in his mouth. Bits of *pan* came out like spray from his mouth while he spoke in an elegant dialect. To me he seemed to be a straightforward person.

On hearing our request he had Ishan Babu's trunk and bedding brought over by two orderlies. The bedding comprised bare essentials — a cheap, threadbare mattress and a dirty, sticky pillow wrapped up in a discoloured durrie. But still Byomkesh took his time in going through the items. He shook the mattress and pressed the pillow with his fingers, but no hidden metallic items were found.

After asking the orderlies to take away the bedding Byomkesh said, '*Munshiji*, I believe there was a gold coin. Can we please have a look at it?'

'Certainly, sir. I brought it with me just in case you expressed a wish to see it.'

Ataullah took out a small wooden box from the pocket of his coat. There were many symbolic words and designs drawn on the surface of the box. The gold coin was wrapped in cotton and kept inside the box.

It was a coin of pure gold, similar in shape and size to a silver rupee of the present day. Byomkesh turned it around in his hand and said, 'There seems to be some thing inscribed on it in Urdu. Can you read it?'

Ataullah spoke in a slightly wounded tone, 'It is not Urdu, sir. It is Persian. It was not the practice in those days to write in Urdu on gold coins. If you wish I can try to read it; I am well-conversant with Persian.'

Somewhat embarrassed, Byomkesh said, 'Oh really! Then would you please read and tell me the date of this coin.'

Putting on his spectacles, Ataullah read the inscription on the coin and said, 'There is no date. It states here that this coin was printed during the regime of Nawab Alibardi Khan.'

Byomkesh said, 'Then this gold coin belonged to the period of Jankiram, not of any later date. All right Ataullah *sahib*, we are very grateful to you. You may now return to your office. I might ask for you if I need your help again.'

Ataullah said, 'Thank you sir' and left.

Byomkesh then took up the professor's trunk and sat down to examine it's contents. But the small tin trunk from which most of the paint had peeled off, yielded nothing to indicate the cause of it's owner's death. The clothes and other articles of daily use held in the trunk seemed to indicate that the professor was either a man of stringent means or of extremely frugal habits. There were two books with torn covers; one of which was a book on political economics composed by Shyam Shastri and the other was an English translation of *Shair-i-Muktaksharin*. These books gave us some indication of the Professor's knowledge and interest in history.

In addition to the two books we found a very old, leather-bound notebook. The notebook was perhaps about thirty years old, it's cover had become loose and the pages were discoloured and about to be dislodged. A few lines were written on some pages in a haphazard manner, some times in pencil and some times in ink. The handwriting was not very good, but it was the same handwriting all through. Those who are occupied with teaching usually keep an all-purpose notebook of this sort at hand, so that they can jot down whatever comes to mind at any time.

Picking up the notebook with great care, Byomkesh and I sat down on a table. He then went on turning the pages of the notebook one after another as I looked on.

The first two or three pages were blank. Then it was written on a page –

If the presiding deity of history
could have spoken in the voice of men
he would then have said in tune
with the drum-beats of the *Muharram* —
earn wealth, go on earning wealth.

Byomkesh frowned and said, 'It does sound like the drum-beats of the *Muharram*, but what does it mean?'

I said, 'It seems to suggest that one should concentrate solely on earning wealth. This Ishan Babu was perhaps a cynic at heart.'

Byomkesh examined the writing some more and then turned the page. Only a few dates were noted on the next page. They were various dates from history, such as the year of commencement of the Hijra era, the date on which Sashanka Deb died and so on. He had probably noted these dates for reference while teaching his students. There was similar jotting of dates on a few more pages, but it is unnecessary to go into all those details here.

After that there were a few more blank pages. Then abruptly a long composition had been recorded, which began as follows —

'I heard the history of Rambinod's family from him. During the sepoy mutiny the looters might not have been able to take away the hoarded wealth from the fortress; at least that is what Rambinod believes. He had gone down to see the fortress. He has high hopes that if he ever becomes rich he would buy that fortress and take up his residence there.'

Thereafter the entire episode starting from the life of Jankiram up to the period of Rajaram and Jairam was written down exactly as we had heard from Romapati on the previous day, — without a single variation. After we had finished reading the whole account, I commented, 'At least we can be sure of one thing now; Romapati did not tell us a false story.'

Byomkesh said, 'Romapati had no doubt told us the correct story, but where is the proof that he had heard it from Ishan Babu on the night that he died? He could very well have heard it a couple of days earlier.'

'That is true. Then …'

'Then – nothing. What I mean to say is that we cannot exclude any possibility at this stage. In other words, there is no evidence to establish that Romapati had heard the first part of the story that very night and had gone there on the following morning to hear the rest.'

After turning the pages for some time we came to a page where a few words were written in a tone of deep anguish …

— Rambinod is no longer alive. My one and only true friend is gone.

He died such a terrible death! The scene is glued to my eyes like a nightmare.

Byomkesh kept his eyes fixed on the writing for some time and said, 'Terrible death? Does not seem like a natural death then. We have to investigate this matter.'

Noticing a baffled look on my face, he smiled and recited in a soft voice, 'Wherever you see ash my friend, blow hard and in the end, you may lay your hands on hidden gems.'

There was no further writing on the pages appearing on the front portion of the notebook. It could be that after Rambinod's death the notebook had remained unused for a long time or it might have been misplaced. Thereafter when the writing was resumed it had been commenced from the back page.

The first words were written in ink, which had got smudged on the yellow page. On the top of the page it was written –

Ramkisor's eldest son Bangshidhar has been admitted to the College. Once again I came in contact with the family. I had not kept in touch with them after Rambinod's death.

At the bottom of the same page it was written –

Bangshidhar has committed a grave mistake.

I am trying to save him.

After all he is Rambinod's nephew.

Byomkesh said, 'We shall probably get to know the details of Bangshidhar's misdeed in a few days. But what is this?'

It was observed that the writings on the remaining pages of the notebook were all in red and blue pencil.

Byomkesh turned over the pages a few times and then said, 'Ajit, would you please check the trunk and see whether there are any red and blue pencils in it.'

I did not have to search too long; a red and blue double-ended pencil was found at the bottom of the trunk.

Byomkesh said, 'Good, now it is clear that whatever is written hereafter were written by Ishan Babu after he arrived at the fortress; they depict the last chapter of his life.'

The first writing was like this –

I could find no secret chamber in the fortress.

This is very strange! Where had the gold and jewels been hidden?

I am certain that they were not stored in any open room. Surely there must be a secret chamber somewhere. But where? Had the sepoys been able to trace the secret chamber it would not have remained secret any more; they would have smashed the door before leaving; then it would have been exposed to one and all. This would seem to indicate that the sepoys had been unable to trace the secret chamber.

Byomkesh said, 'The Professor's reasoning is not very logical. Rajaram's family did return to the fortress after the sepoys had left. They could have repaired the damaged treasure-chamber, which is why nothing is visible at this time.'

Byomkesh turned the page and read —

Someone is trying to scare me and drive me away from the fortress.—Could it be Bangshidhar? But I am not going to leave this fortress that easily. Earn wealth! Go on earning wealth!

I asked, 'Why the drum-beats of the *Muharram* once again?'

Byomkesh replied, 'Perhaps the Professor had become excited by the smell of gold.'

The last entry in the notebook appeared after a few pages. We looked at it in amazement. Three lines were written in either Urdu or Persian, below which there were just three words written in Bengali – '*Who is Mohanlal*?'

Byomkesh sighed deeply and said, 'Quite true. Who is Mohanlal? It is beyond our powers to find an answer to this question. Let us call Ataullah *sahib*.'

Ataullah arrived and deciphered the writing, which, he told us, was in Persian language. He said, 'Sir, the dead man seems to have been well-versed in Persian, but his language is a bit old-fashioned. He has written: If Jairam or I do not survive, our entire wealth shall remain in the custody of Mohanlal.'

'In the custody of Mohanlal ?' Byomkesh asked.

'Yes sir, that is what is written here.'

'Hm. All right Ataullah *sahib*, you can take away the rest of the stuff. I would only like to keep this notebook with me.'

We lit up cigarettes and reclined on easy chairs. After a while I asked, 'What did you conclude after reading the notebook?'

Byomkesh went on playing the *tabla* with his hands on the armrests of the easy chair and said in rhyme with the sound he was making, 'Earn money, go on earning money!'

'Jokes apart, tell me what you think.'

'Not everything is clear to me till now. But if anyone had murdered Ishan Babu I can see what was the motive of the murder.'

'What was the motive?'

'The eternal motive – money.'

'What could be the significance of all those words written in Persian?'

'He did not write them himself. What I mean to say is that the handwriting was his own, but the composition was not his, it belonged to Rajaram. Ishan Babu had come across it somewhere in the fortress and then copied it in his notebook.'

'Then?'

'Then he died.'

5

It was well past midday when Pandeyji returned home. Taking off his helmet he wiped sweat from his forehead with a handkerchief and said, 'The job is done, but the old man was quite difficult at first.'

Byomkesh asked, 'Difficult? Why'

Pandey said, 'We are late for lunch. I'll tell you while we eat. Did you find out anything?

Byomkesh said, 'Yes, I'll tell you while we eat.'

As we sat down for lunch Byomkesh said. 'You tell me first. Yesterday Ramkishor Babu seemed half-inclined to let us stay there, why did he have a change of heart today?'

Pandey said, 'After we came back last night somebody told him that you are a famous detective. That scared him.'

'Why should he be scared on that account? If his conscience is clear ...'

'That is precisely what I had to tell him in the end. I said, what does it matter if Byomkesh Babu is a detective, why should you be afraid? Do you have anything to hide? Then the old gentleman consented very quickly.'

I said, 'Then Ramkishor Babu is really trying to hide some thing?'

Pandey said, 'That is what I suspect. But it has nothing to do with Ishan Babu's death. It is some thing else. Any way, I have made all arrangements so that one room in the fortress is ready for your occupation today itself. If you wish you may shift there this evening or you could go there tomorrow morning.'

Byomkesh said, 'We'll go this evening.'

'Very well. There is some thing else that I have arranged for you. My personal orderly Sitaram shall stay with you.'

'No, no. That wouldn't be necessary.'

'It is necessary. Sitaram shall not be in uniform, he would go with you as your servant. He is a very careful man, on top of which, he has a special qualification; he knows the art of snake charming. And I can assure you that he shall be of a lot of help to you. You would need someone for fetching water from the well, washing your clothes, cleaning your utensils etcetera. It is better that you do not avail of the services of Ramkishor Babu's servants.'

In the end Byomkesh acceded to the suggestion. Pandey said, 'Now tell me what you have learnt.'

Byomkesh narrated the full details of the mystery that he had unravelled from Ishan Babu's notebook. After hearing him, Pandey commented, 'Hm, I have a strong urge to find out the identity of Mohanlal, but it would be impossible to locate his addresss after a hundred years. And then, Ishan Babu had written in the end that someone was trying to scare him and drive him away from the fortress. He suspected Bangshidhar. But what do you think could have actually happened? How was the attempt made to scare him?'

Byomkesh shook his head and said, 'We can't find answers to any of those questions now. Let us see if we can solve the mystery of the fortress after we land up there.'

That afternoon the three of us and Sitaram reached the fortress on the peak of the hill in a police van. Pandeyji had decided to get us settled there and return home. Sitaram was to remain with us. He was around thirty-five with a tall slim figure, a coppery complexion and a moustache which made him look like a wild cat. A remarkable feature of his appearance was that he looked like a perfect gentleman when he was dressed in decent clothes, but if he wore a loincloth he could easily pass as a servant. While travelling with us he was wearing a short *dhoti*, which reached barely up to his knees and carried a country-made towel on his shoulder. In other words, he looked like an all-purpose servant.

We had quite a bit of baggage with us, — bedding and suitcases, rice, pulse, vegetables assorted eatable items, an *icmic* cooker and various other supplies. Sitaram and Bulakilal started carrying the baggage inside the fortress. Pandey said, 'Come, let us pay a visit to the owner of the house.'

The owner of the house was seated in the front verandah alongwith his son-in-law Manilal. He greeted us warmly although he seemed a little aggrieved that we had made separate arrangements for getting our meals cooked. He then commented humorously that being city-dwellers we were unlikely to feel comfortable in the midst of the forest and hills. But his eyes remained constantly alert and watchful.

While these pleasantries were being exchanged I noticed that the other residents of the house had become both wary and restive on our arrival. Bangshidhar and Muralidhar were roaming in circles around us like roving kites, but never coming close to us. Romapati stretched out his neck from the house once, but moved away on seeing us. Chandmohan, the estate manager, was seated at the other end of the verandah; he was smoking from a *hookah* and casting sharp glances at us from the corner of his eyes. Hiding behind a cluster of jasmine plants, Tulsi watched us like a curious squirrel and then ran off when she knew that we had noticed her. After a while I saw her peeping out from behind a pillar.

They had all come to know that Byomkesh was a famous detective and that he had come to live in the fortress with some deep-rooted intentions; this seemed to have affected their peace of mind in different ways. Gădadhar perhaps was the sole exception; his shallow intelligence had not been stirred by the news of our arrival; we did not see him anywhere.

When we got up to leave Ramkishor Babu said to Byomkesh, 'Please remember that you are my guests; you must not hesitate to let me know if you need anything.'

'Certainly'.

Manilal received some signal from the master of the house and accompanied us obviously with the intention of reaching us up to the fortress.

While climbing down the steps, Byomkesh asked, 'How did Ramkishor Babu know that I was a detective?'

Manilal said, 'I told him. I knew you by name and I had read a few books written by your friend here. The master was very agitated when he heard this. And later when he came to know that you wanted to stay in the fortress he became very scared.'

'Why?'

'There was this mishap only the other day.'

'So you people are scared that we too might be bitten by snakes. Oh, by the way, didn't your wife also die from snakebite?'

'Yes sir.'

'This place must be infested by snakes.'

'Must be. But I haven't seen any myself.'

After reaching the courtyard we started climbing up the steps to the fortress.

Manilal abruptly spoke out to Byomkesh, 'Please excuse me, sir, but since you people are from the police I am feeling curious to know some thing. Is it quite certain that Ishan Babu's death was caused by snakebite?'

There was a brief exchange of glances between Byomkesh and Pandey.

And then Byomkesh enquired, 'Why? Is there any doubt on that issue?'

Manilal hesitated a little and then said, 'No – but – nothing can be said.'

Pandey said, 'Barring snakebite what else could be the cause of death?'

Manilal said, 'That is some thing which I too can't make out. I had seen the marks of snakebite on Ishan Babu's foot, just like the marks on my wife's feet.' Manilal let out a deep sigh.

We reached the entrance to the fortress. Manilal said, 'I'll leave you here. The master is not keeping good health; I do not like to leave him alone too long. I shall come to see you tomorrow morning.'

Manilal folded his hands respectfully and took his leave. The sun had set. A thin slice of moon seemed to smile at us for a moment from the top of Ramkishor Babu's house before disappearing behind it. We walked into the compound of the fortress.

Byomkesh said, 'Only this morning I had asked Dr. Ghatak to keep a close watch on his patient; but now I find it was an unnecessary advice. Till the deed for transfer of title of the property is registered Manilal shall stand guard on his father-in-law like his shadow.'

Pandey's lips twisted in a wry smile, as he said, 'Very true. Also, they now seem to have some misgiving about Ishan Babu's death, but we shall remain close-lipped.'

'Of course'

We crossed the compound and proceeded towards the building. Pandeyji was carrying a long, bulky torch in his hand; it not only threw a powerful and far-stretching beam of light, but could also serve as a handy instrument for beating up someone. He lit the torch lighting up the path in front of us and said, 'I am going to leave this torch with you; you might find it useful. Now, let me go and see what arrangements have been made for your stay.'

We found that the room with the pegs on the walls had been prepared for our stay. Two iron cots, a table and a few chairs had been laid out in the room to cover up it's bareness to some extent. Sitaram had lit up lanterns, made our beds and was boiling water for tea on a kerosene stove, while our meals were being cooked in the *icmic* cooker. We were amazed by the speed and zeal of his activity.

Hot, steaming tea was served shortly. Pandey took a sip of tea and asked, 'Did you find any thing, Sitaram?'

Sitaram said, 'I have made a round of the fortress, sir. There is no snake here.'

It was a positive statement. Pandey sighed in relief and said, 'Thank God. Anything else?'

'Barring the steps there are no other means of access to the fortress. There are steep rocks outside the walls.'

Byomkesh looked at Pandey and asked, 'Do you know what that means?'

'What?'

'If any assailant wants to enter the fortress he shall have to come up by the steps, ...in other words through the courtyard. Bulakilal could probably catch a glimpse of him.'

'Hmm, you are right. We shall have to interrogate Bulakilal. But not today, it's quite late. Sitaram, I don't have to explain your duties to you. Look after these gentlemen and keep your eyes and ears open.'

'Yes sir.'

As Pandeyji got up to leave, he told us, 'I shall come some time tomorrow. Be careful.'

We walked down with Pandeyji up to the entrance of the fortress. Byomkesh switched on the torch from the top, lighting up the entire flight of steps and Pandeyji walked down. After a while we heard the sound of the police van being driven off. On the other hilltop we could see lights flickering dimly in Ramkishor Babu's house.

We returned to the fortress and stood in the open compound. The stars had appeared in the sky, a pleasant breeze was blowing from the direction of the forest. As if guessing our wish Sitaram had brought out two chairs and placed them in the compound. We sighed contentedly and sat down on the chairs.

As I sat in the darkness split by stars many strange, imaginary scenes floated across my mind. Like the well-remembered prince of the stories heard in childhood and his close friend and constant companion, the two of us seemed to have wandered far, far away from the king's domain and arrived at a fairyland, where a beautiful princess was lying asleep in an enchanting palace. Of course there was no sleeping princess here, but maybe, there was a priceless jewel, glittering on a cobra's head, guarded by invisible ogres. Who knew what strange mystery lay hidden within the four walls of this old fortress like a precious pearl held inside an oyster shell?

Byomkesh lit a cigarette with a flash, breaking through the romantic web of my thoughts. He said, 'Ishan Babu was right, there must be a secret treasure-chamber somewhere inside this fortress.'

I said, 'But where? How can we dig up this large fortress to find out the hiding place?'

'No, no, that's out of question. But I think Ishan Babu had been able to locate the hiding place; there could be no other way to explain the gold coin clutched in his fist.'

I turned his statement in my mind and asked after a while, 'If that be so, there must be a lot more gold coins in the same place.'

'Possibly. But what is more important is that if he could trace the hiding place we should be able to find it as well.'

Byomkesh got up and started pacing up and down. After pacing for some time he muttered 'Oh' and stumbled. He was about to fall down, but somehow managed to regain control.

I jumped up, exclaiming, 'What happened?'

'Nothing. I had stumbled over some thing.' He switched on the torch pointing it at the ground.

What had escaped our notice in daylight was now clearly visible. Someone had dug up a square tile of stone and then tried to put it back with inexpert hands. But the stone had not been set in level with the surface, one of its sides was a little raised and it was there that Byomkesh had struck his foot and stumbled.

When I observed the loose stone, I exclaimed in excitement, 'Byomkesh! Could the secret chamber be located under this loose stone?'

Byomkesh shook his head and said, 'No, this stone is at the most fourteen inches in size. Even if there was a hole under it no human body could pass through such a narrow gap.'

'But still ....'

'No, my friend, it's not what you are thinking. The access to the secret chamber can't be located in an open courtyard. Any way, we shall get this stone lifted tomorrow morning and have a look at it.'

Byomkesh moved the torch all around, but it did not appear that the stone paving had been disturbed anywhere else. The canon was installed close by; its base had become embedded in earth through accumulated dust and clay. We could see no loose soil or stone there either.

Sitaram arrived and reported that our meals were ready. I looked at my wristwatch; it was a quarter to ten. We had not noticed how the time had flown.

We went in and sat down to take our meals. I had no idea that kedgeree and mutton curry cooked in an icmic cooker could taste so delicious. Sitaram had also made some omlets, so our dinner was a sumptuous affair.

After we had finished eating, Sitaram sat down in a corner of the verandah and had his meal. He then stood near the door and said, 'Sir, if you permit me, I could take a round of the place.'

Byomkesh said, 'That's fine. But where are you going to sleep?'

Sitaram said, 'Don't worry sir. I shall roll out my bedding near this door.'

Sitaram left. We lowered the wick of the lamp and stretched on our beds. The door was left open, because we would otherwise have felt stifled in the windowless room.

I had started feeling somewhat drowsy when I was roused by Byomkesh's voice, 'You know I don't quite like those pegs.'

'Pegs! Which pegs?'

'Why are there so many pegs on these walls? Pandeyji did offer an explanation of some sort, but I still have my doubts.'

It was pointless to wonder about pegs at this late hour of night. I checked the time on my watch; it was well past eleven. Sitaram had not yet returned from his round.

'Go to sleep. You can think about the pegs tomorrow.' I said and turned over in my bed.

6

I had fallen fast asleep but was roused by a loud sound like a bomb exploding near my head and sat up in a hurry. For a moment I could not remember where I was.

When I did become conscious of the time and place, I saw Byomkesh focussing the torch towards the door where several broken pieces of some thing looking like an earthen pot were lying scattered on the ground. Then he ran out very fast from the room with the lighted torch in his hand, saying, 'Ajit, please come.'

I got up in my dishevelled clothes and ran after him, not realising if he was chasing anyone or only trying to escape from danger. I simply ran in the direction towards which his torchlight was focused.

After running out from the compound Byomkesh threw the torch light on the steps. As I drew near him I saw a man running up. When he reached us I saw that it was Sitaram.

Byomkesh asked, 'Sitaram, did you see any one climbing down the steps?'

Sitaram said, 'Yes sir, as I was climbing up I collided against some one. I tried to grab him, but he evaded my hands and ran away.'

'Could you recognize him?'

'No sir, I could not see his face in the darkness. But he swore out some filthy words when I collided with him, from which I could guess that he must have belonged to a lower class of some hindi-speaking community.—But what has happened here, sir?'

'That I don't really know yet. Come and see.'

We returned to the room. The broken pieces of an earthen pot were lying scattered near the door. Byomkesh pointed the torch towards them and said, 'Look. I was still awake and when I heard light footsteps outside I thought that you had returned. Then there was a loud sound … .'

Sitaram picked up one of the broken fragments of the pot and smelt it. He then said, 'Sir, please sit down on your beds with your feet up.'

'Why? What's the matter?'

'Snake. Someone must have carried a snake in an earthen pot covered with a clay plate and thrown it down at this place. Would you please give me the torch, sir, so that I can take a look around. The snake must be somewhere here.'

We promptly sat down with our feet up on the bed; it was pointless to act foolhardily with a snake loose in a dark night. Sitaram walked out with the torch and started looking for the snake.

Byomkesh raised the wick of the lantern and said, 'Now I can understand what method was deployed to scare Ishan Babu away from this place.'

'But who could be the person?'

'It is difficult to say that at this time. It could be Bulakilal or Ganapat or it could even be the *sadhu baba*.'

Just then we heard Sitaram's loud laughter. He raised his voice and said, 'Sir, please come and see. There is nothing to fear.'

We walked over very carefully to Sitaram. At a corner of the verandah a brownish snake was lying, twisted into a coil. It had been injured and hence unable to escape, but it started whirling it's body under the bright light of the torch.

Sitaram laughed and said, 'Sir, this is a harmless snake. It seems that someone has tried to play a joke with us.'

'Joke, indeed! Now, what can be done with the snake?'

'I'll take care of it sir.'

Sitaram brought a brass lid with several small holes on its dome and placed it on the snake. He said, 'Let it stay here tonight. Tomorrow we can decide what to do with it.'

We returned to the room. Sitaram started laying his bedding near the door. It was exactly two o' clock.

Byomkesh said, 'Sitaram, you can now tell us where you were and what you were doing till so late in the night.'

Sitaram said, 'Sir from here I went down to the courtyard. I found Bulakilal fast asleep in his room from the effects of *bhang*. I had intended to collect some information from him, which is why I had become friendly with him in the evening. But even after shaking him for some time with both hands I could not rouse him from his slumber. I then thought that I might as well go round to see if the *sadhu baba* was awake.

'The *sadhu baba* was awake and happy to see me. He asked me several questions – about your identities and the purpose of your visit to this place and so on. I told him that you had come here for a change of air.'

'Good. What else did you talk of?'

Sitaram said, 'There was a lot of useless talk, sir. Then in a roundabout manner I raised the topic of the professor *sahib*'s death. The *sadhu baba* flared up in anger. I found that he was very bitter with the master of the house and his manager. He went on saying, they shall be ruined, they shall be ruined.'

'Really! The *sadhu* seems to be a most ungrateful person. What else?'

'Then the *sadhu baba* prepared a *chillum* of *ganja* and offered me a little portion with his blessing.'

'You took the *ganja*?'

'Yes sir. I couldn't refuse some thing which the *sadhu baba* had offered me with his blessing.'

'That is true. What happened next?'

Then the *sadhu baba* spread his blanket on the ground and prepared for going to sleep. So I took leave of him. On my way back I collided with that man on the steps.'

Byomkesh said, 'Now tell me some thing, Sitaram. On your way back did you happen to see Bulakilal?'

'No sir, I did not see him. But while passing through the courtyard I could hear the loud noise of snoring from his room.'

'All right. So now it is seen that who-so-ever else the person carrying a pot with the snake might have been, it was neither Bulakilal nor the *sadhu baba*. I doubt if he would think of paying us a second visit tonight. So let us try to get some sleep.'

When we woke up next morning we found that the snake covered with the lid was dead; it must have been hurt severely when it was hurled down with the earthen pot. Sitaram carried it on the tip of a stick and threw it outside the rampart of the fortress. We too climbed up on the rampart and made a round. We observed that although the rampart was broken at several places, there was no other access to the fortress save and except through the front entrance. There was a steep decline right below the rampart.

At about eleven in the morning Byomkesh and I set about for Ramkishor Babu's house, leaving Sitaram at the fortress. Romapati greeted us respectfully at the front verandah and said, 'Please come in. The master is just about to start off for the town.'

'Oh, is that so?'

We were hesitating to step inside when Ramkishor Babu came out of the house, clad in a dhoti and a *kurta* of tussore silk with a *chaddar* wrapped around his shoulders. On seeing us he said, 'Ah, here you are! – How do you like the place? Did you have a comfortable night? I hope you were not inconvenienced in anyway?'

Byomkesh said, 'We had no inconvenience at all. We spent the night in perfect comfort. Are you going out somewhere?'

'Yes, I have to see my lawyer in connection with the registration of some documents. But now that you are here, I could go a little later ... .'

Byomkesh said, 'No, no, you are going out for some urgent work, we wouldn't like to hold you up. We were just taking a stroll, we did not come here for any work.'

'Well—all right then. Romapati, please serve them tea and snacks and look after them. We shall be back by the evening.'

Ramkishor went out of the house, followed by his son-in-law Manilal, who was carrying a large stack of documents. While passing us Manilal greeted us politely with a smile.

Byomkesh spoke to Romapati, 'Don't bother about tea. We had tea just before coming here. Is the document for division of the property going to be registered today?'

'Yes sir.'

'Thank God, at least one worry is about to be over. I have a lot of things to discuss with you, but that can wait. Now, can you tell me where I can find Ganpat?'

Romapati was a little surprised as he asked, 'Ganpat, you mean Murali-da's servant? He must be in the house, although I did not see him this morning. Should I go and fetch him?'

Just then Muralidhar came out to the verandah and looked distinctly flustered on seeing us. The squint in his eye became even more prominent

Byomkesh approached him, saying, 'Oh, you are Muralidhar Babu? *Namaskar*. Would you please call your servant Ganpat. I need to talk to him.'

There was an odd change in Muralidhar's facial expression, registering a combination of fear and outrage. He asked in a piercing tone, 'What have you got to do with Ganpat?'

'I want to ask him a few questions.'

'He – I have granted him leave. He has gone home.'

'Is that so? When did you grant him leave?'

'Yesterday. Yesterday afternoon.'

Without waiting for any further questions Muralidhar walked back hurriedly inside the house.

Byomkesh and I looked at each other. There was a worried expression on Romapati's face. He drew close to Byomkesh and then said in a lowered tone, 'Yesterday afternoon. But I had seen Ganapat in the house till yesterday evening … .'

Byomkesh nodded his head and said, 'That is entirely possible. Because Ganpat could not have left for home till midnight. Any way, the estate manager Chandmohan should be at home. We would like to meet him.'

Romapati said, 'He must be in his room.'

'Right, would you please take us there?'

Chandmohan's room was located at the extreme end of the house. On reaching near the door of his room we saw that with his face to the wall, he was filling tobacco in several bowls of the *hookah* arranged in a row. Most probably he was making arrangements in advance to serve his needs for the whole day. Byomkesh nodded at Romapati, indicating that he should leave us there. As we entered the room Byomkesh lightly closed the door behind us.

Chandmohan sat up apprehensively at our abrupt arrival; his cunning eyes were filled with a sudden gleam of dismay. He blurted out, 'Who is it? Oh … it's you!'

Byomkesh sat down at one end of the bed and said, 'Chandmohan Babu, I want to ask you a few questions.' His voice did not sound at all smooth.

Getting over the initial impact of apprehension, Chandmohan started wiping his hand on a towel and asked, 'What questions?'

'It is a very old affair. How did Rambinod meet with his death?'

Chandmohan's face seemed to shrivel, as he said in a broken voice, 'I cannot say anything — I am only the estate manager of this family.'

Byomkesh spoke in a stern voice, 'Chandmohan Babu, you know who I am. It wouldn't do you any good if you try to conceal things from me. There is proof that you were present during Rambinod's death. Now tell me in detail how Rambinod died.'

Chandmohan cast a sharp, oblique glance at Byomkesh and then slowly walked to the bed and sat down. He said in a dry, resigned voice, 'Since you are compelling me to speak I have no option but to talk. I can only tell you what I know.'

He wiped his face with the towel and started speaking —

'In the year 1911 we were in Monghyr. Rambinod and Ramkishor were then trading in *ghee*, which they used to supply to various markets in Calcutta. They had a huge store-house of *ghee*. I was their employee and I used to sit at the store-house, while the two brothers used to make to and fro trips to Calcutta.

'Suddenly Monghyr was struck by bubonic plague. People started dying in large numbers and families started disappearing overnight. Those who survived left their homes and fled to other places. Rambinod and Ramkishor, who were both in Monghyr at that time, had a big problem on their hands. They had goods worth about sixty to seventy thousand rupees stacked in their godown, which they could not leave behind and go away, as the whole lot would have been stolen. So the three of us conferred among ourselves and decided to live in a hired boat on the Ganges; every day one of us would take turn in coming to the town and checking the godown before going back to the boat. The rest, we thought, we should leave in the hands of fate. Luckily the godown was not too far from the Ganges.

'We were soon joined by one of Rambinod's boyhood friends, Ishan Majumdar, who was then a teacher at Monghyr School; the same Ishan who died through snakebite the other day. We did not have any boatmen. We rowed the boat ourselves. It was a fairly large boat. We cooked our meals on the boat and slept there at night. There were some sandbanks on the riverbed, where we occasionally spent our nights. Our only contact with the town was maintained through a single visit during the day by one of us for checking the godown.

'After we had spent ten to twelve days in this manner Rambinod was struck by the plague one day. He had gone to the town and came back with fever. We rowed the boat to one of those shallow patches on the riverbed and took Rambinod down. Apart from the fact that there was no cure for plague, where could we find a doctor or procure any medicine in the middle of the river? Rambinod died the very next day.'

Byomkesh asked, 'What did you do then?'

Chandmohan said, 'We did not dare stay there any longer. We gave up our vigil over the godown and rowed our boat to Bhagalpur.'

'Did you cremate Rambinod's body?'

Chandmohan again wiped his face with the towel and said, 'We did not even have any wood to cremate him. His body was left floating on the Ganges.'

Byomkesh got to his feet and said, 'Come, Ajit, let us go. I have finished my work here.'

As we walked out of the house, I asked, 'What was your impression? Did Chandmohan tell us the truth?'

'He told us a few lies, but that did not make much difference.'

As we were about to go down the steps we saw Tulsi had set up her playhouse under the shade of a tree close by. She was deeply engrossed in her play and did not notice us.

When Byomkesh went and stood close to her, she looked up with wide eyes. Byomkesh addressed her with affection, saying. 'You are Tulsi, aren't you? You have such a charming face.'

Tulsi went on staring intently at Byomkesh's face.

Byomkesh said, 'We are staying at the fortress. Why don't you come to see us? Come some times, I can tell you a lot of stories.'

Tulsi went on looking at him without uttering a word.

We left the place.

7

It took us some time to recover our breath after climbing all those steps to the fortress. Then Byomkesh lit a cigarette and said, 'Ramkishor Babu has gone to get the documents registered. Once that happens there is bound to be a shake-up at the house; Bangshi and Muralidhar would probably choose to move out and set up separate homes in the town. We have to make sure that we finish our investigation before that happens.'

I asked, 'Byomkesh, have you been able to come to any conclusion yet? The more I get to see the situation here the more complicated every thing seems to me.'

Byomkesh said, 'Some hazy pictures are tending to appear on my mind's screen. They are not small pictures; they seem to depict many incidents, involving several people and their various impacts. The drama was commenced a hundred years back and it is not over yet. By the way, I had forgotten about the loose stone, which we discovered last night. Come, let us go and see if there is any tunnel under it.'

Walking back to the spot we found that lime and brick-dust had coagulated on the stone and it's surface was not as smooth as those of the adjoining stones. Byomkesh said, 'It seems that this particular tile was removed and then put back in the wrong way. Come, let us lift it and see.'

We tried to lift the stone with our fingers, but it did not budge. Sitaram was then called. He was a smart man; he used a cooking skewer to prise open the stone with ease. There was no hole or tunnel under the stone; it was packed with lime and brick-dust. Byomkesh examined the reverse side of the stone and said, 'Look here, some thing is written on this side in Urdu or Persian!'

I noticed that a few lines in some strange language had been engraved on the surface of the stone. The engraving was not very deep; moreover having gathered dust and mud over the years, it had become almost imperceptible. Byomkesh suddenly exclaimed, 'It seems to me.... Hang on, let me fetch Ishan Babu's notebook.'

Byomkesh had retained Ishan Babu's notebook. He now brought it over and after opening the page containing the Persian writing he started comparing it with the inscription on the stone. I too joined in the scrutiny. We could not of course decipher the meaning of the inscription, but we could easily see that the two writings carried the same type of strokes.

Byomkesh said, 'It's done. Let's go.'

We put the stone back in it's proper place and returned to our room. Byomkesh asked, 'What do you now make of the situation?'

'I would rather that you explain it to me.'

'Cast your mind to what happened a hundred years back. On hearing that the sepoys were on their way, Rajaram moved his family out of the fortress. Only he and his son Jairam remained at the fortress and together they concealed all their gold.

'But after hiding his wealth Rajaram was filled with the apprehension that should he and his son both die at the hands of the sepoys, how would his wife and family members find the treasure? So he wrote down some clue on the stone, using a language, which was not accessible to everybody. Then he rubbed mud and dust on the stone to make the writing indistinct so that it did not catch the sepoy's attention easily.

'When the sepoys arrived they found nothing. In their anger and frustration they killed both the father and son and went away. Later when Rajaram's family-members returned to the fortress they too were unable to trace out where Rajaram had hidden his treasure. The clue written in Persian language on the stone escaped everybody's notice.'

I said, 'Then you believe that Rajaram's treasure is still hidden in this fortress?'

'That is what I think. Unless of course the sepoys had tortured Rajaram and Jairam to find out the hiding place, in which event there is nothing left here.'

'What happened next?'

'Then after the expiry of a hundred years Professor Ishan Majumdar arrived here. He was a scholar of history and conversant with the Persian language; moreover he had heard the chronicle of the fortress from his friend Rambinod. He started his search, not openly, but in secret. I do not know how far his covert search had progressed, but he had found one clue – the inscription on the stone. He had carefully copied it out on his notebook and then put back the stone upside down so that nobody could detect it.

Then – what happened next is what we have to find out.'

Byomkesh stretched out on the bed and went on staring at the ceiling. My mind was filled with many jumbled thoughts. Pandeyji was probably not coming this morning. ...How was Satyabati keeping in Calcutta? ... What had prompted Byomkesh to talk with such affection with Tulsi? ... The girl was said to be about fourteen years old, but she looked as if she was just ten....

A shadow fell on the door. Turning my head I saw that it was Tulsi, accompanied by Gadadhar. I could read both apprehension and eagerness on her face; she must have felt scared to come on her own, which is why she had brought her brother with her. But Gadadhar did not show any signs of fear or hesitation. He had a top and a piece of string in his hand and wore an ear to ear smile on his face. On seeing us he laughed and said, 'Hey, hey, Tulsi shall be married to our **Jamai Babu*, hey, hey, hey ... .'

Tulsi turned with lightning speed and slapped his face. Gadadhar stood stunned for some time with a sulky look and then went off with a grim expression, winding the string on his top. I realised that he was accustomed to being slapped regularly by his younger sister.

Byomkesh spoke affectionately to Tulsi inviting her to come inside, but Tulsi refused to enter; she remained standing by the door, holding on to the doorpost. Byomkesh then got up, took her hand and made her sit down on the bed.

But Tulsi was still unable to get over her apprehension; she looked like a doe driven to desperation by a hunter. Then Byomkesh started talking softly to her as if he was of her age. He made a few funny remarks, which made her smile and he talked about games that little girls enjoyed, about the make-believe marriage of dolls and other childish games, which gradually helped her to overcome her fear. She responded initially with a few 'hmm's and 'no's and then started talking freely.

Soon we had set up an easy friendship with Tulsi. We found that she had a simple mind, but her intelligence was quite sharp. Her nerves, however, were still highly strung; the slightest provocation could cause her nervous reactions to exceed normal limits. Byomkesh had made a correct diagnosis of her nature, which is why he had succeded in drawing her out by treating her with affection.

It is not necessary to reproduce the entire conversation that we had with Tulsi that day. A part of what we learnt from her has been written earlier; the rest is reproduced below.

**Jamai Babu*: Elder sister's husband.

Byomkesh asked, 'Did you get to know Ishan Babu, your father's friend who had come to live here?'

Tulsi said, 'Oh yes. He used to tell me such wonderful stories. He did not sleep well at night; so I often came to him in the late hours of night and heard his stories.'

'Really! Did you come to see him on the night that he died?'

'No. They had locked me up in my room that night.'

'Kept you locked in your room?'

'Yes. Because I wander around whenever and wherever I feel like, they keep me locked up at every opportunity that they get.'

'Who are they?'

'Everybody. My father, my two elder brothers, *Jamai Babu*.'

'Who locked you up that night?'

'Father.'

'Hm. And last night you were locked up by your second brother?'

'Yes, but how did you find out?'

'I can find out everything. Now, tell me something else. Do you remember your sister-in-law, the lady whom your eldest brother had married?'

'Why shouldn't I? She was very pretty. My sister was very jealous of her.'

'Oh! Do you know why your sister-in-law committed suicide?'

'No, I don't know that. My elder sister had locked me up in my room that night.'

'Oh.'

Byomkesh looked meaningfully at me. After talking of other matters for some time Byomkesh asked, 'Tell me, Tulsi, whom do you love most in your house?'

Tulsi replied unhesitantly and without any embarrassment. '*Mastermashai*. And he too loves me very much.'

'And don't you love Manilal?'

Tulsi's eyes seemed to be on fire 'No.Why is he so jealous of *Mastermashai*? Why does he go on reporting about *Mastermashai* to my father? If he marries me I shall throw him down from the top of the hill!'

Tulsi ran out from the room after she said this.

We went on looking at each other's faces for some time. Then Byomkesh sighed deeply and said, 'Poor girl!'

As we were preparing to get up for our bath after about half an hour Romapati peeked from outside and asked in an embarassed voice, 'Did Tulsi come here?'

Byomkesh said, 'Yes, she has left a little earlier. Please come in and sit with us for a while.'

Romapati entered the room and sat down hesitantly.

Byomkesh said, 'Romapati, do you remember that you told us on the day that we arrived here that the problem of Ishan Babu's death shall now be solved. In other words, you are convinced that there is some problem involving Ishan Babu's death. Right?'

Romapati remained silent. Byomkesh continued, 'Let us presume that Ishan Babu's death was mysterious, that some one had murdered him. Now I am going to ask you some questions and I want you to answer them in a straightforward manner. Do not hesitate to tell me the truth. Just think that you are responding as a witness under oath in a court of law.'

Romapati said in a subdued voice, 'All right.'

Byomkesh said, 'You are quite familiar with every member of the household. Can you tell me, who is the one person among them, who is capable of commiting murder?'

Taken by surprise, Romapati remained quiet for some time and then said in a shaken voice, 'I should not speak against them as they have provided me shelter in their house, but if the situation so demands perhaps every one of them is capable of committing murder.'

'Every one? Even Ramkishor Babu?'

'Yes.'

'Bangshidhar?'

'Yes.'

'Muralidhar?'

'Yes. Their nature is most violent ... .'

'What about the Chandmohan, the estate manager?'

'Perhaps not. But if ordered by the master he could employ someone to commit a murder.'

'Manilal?'

Romapati's face darkened. Grinding his teeth he said, 'He doesn't have the guts to commit a murder with his own hands. All he can do is to harm people by informing maliciously against them.'

'And you? Can you commit murder?'

'I —!'

'Let it be. — Did you steal the torch?'

Romapati said in a bitter voice, 'I know that I have been slandered. I also know who has spread the slander. But you tell me, sir, if I had to steal any thing why should I steal just a torch?'

'In other words, you didn't steal the torch. Forget it. Are you aware that Tulsi's marriage has been fixed with Manilal?'

Romapati's face hardened, but he said in a controlled voice, 'I know. That is what the master wishes.'

'Nobody else wants it?'

'No.'

'You do not want it either?'

Romapati got to his feet and said, 'I live in this house as a mere dependant of the family. How can my wanting or not wanting be of any consequence? But if this marriage does take place it would end in sheer disaster.'

After saying this, he walked out of the room without speaking another word.

Byomkesh went on looking towards the door for some time and then said, 'This young fellow has guts!'

8

When Sitaram served us tea that evening, Byomkesh said, 'Sitaram, there is something I want you to do for me. About two years back a group of gypsies had set up their tents here. I want you to find out from Bulakilal, which members of Ramkishor Babu's household used to visit the gypsies' camp frequently. Please try to collect as much information on the subject as you can.'

Sitaram said, 'Very well, sir. Bulakilal has now gone to town with his master. I'll talk to him when he comes back.'

When Sitaram left the room, I enquired, 'Why this interest in the gypsies?'

Byomkesh said, 'Poison. Don't we have to find out where the snake-poison came from?'

'Oh!'

Pandeyji arrived just then. He was carrying a binocular, which was hung from his shoulder by a leather-strap. Byomkesh said, 'Hello! What shall we do with a binocular?'

Pandeyji said, 'I brought it for you, in case it comes to some use. I couldn't come this morning as I got stuck up in some work. On my way here just now I came across Ramkishor Babu, whose car had developed engine trouble while he was returning from town. Bulakilal was sitting at the steering wheel, Ramkishor Babu was seated in the car and the son-in-law Manilal was pushing the car from behind.'

'What happened then?'

'I had their car towed here by my van.'

'Was their work in the court completed today?'

'No, some work is still left. They would go to town tomorrow again. Now tell me – is there any fresh news?'

'There is plenty of news.'

Pandeyji became quite excited as he heard the latest news. When everything had been recounted to him, he said, 'Now there is no further doubt. Ishan Babu had been able to find the treasure-chamber, which is why he had been murdered. But the question is: who could have murdered him?'

'Starting from Ramkishor Babu and ending up with the *Sadhu Baba* – anyone could have murdered him. But that is not the only question. There is another question as well.'

'What is it?'

'Where did the poison come from? Snake-poison is not available everywhere. And then we have to consider that some particular instrument was used for injecting the snake-poison into the victim's body so that it left marks exactly similar to those of a serpent's teeth.'

'A hypodermic syringe ... .'

'A syringe used for injections leaves a very small mark, which vanishes in a minute or two. You had noticed the marks on Ishan Babu's feet. Did they seem to you like the mark of injections?'

'No. And moreover there were two marks side by side.'

'That is immaterial. When a patient is lying unconscious is there any problem in pricking a needle twice in two spots side by side?'

'That is true. What was the other question?'

'If Ishan Babu had been able to find the treasure-chamber where could it be located?'

'Must be in this fortress.'

'Not just in the fortress, but somewhere within this building. Why is Muralidhar trying to scare us away from here by using snakes?'

Pandeyji looked sharply and asked, 'Muralidhar?'

Byomkesh said, 'He could have other designs. But the fact remains that before Ishan Babu's arrival nobody had any knowledge regarding the location of the treasure-trove. Thereafter one other person in addition to Ishan Babu came to acquire this knowledge and it was he who murdered Ishan Babu. But I have a feeling that the murderer has not been able to remove the treasure till now.'

'How did you come to that conclusion?'

'You have seen that nobody is happy that we are staying in the fortress. What could be the reason?'

'I understand. Then we have to find the treasure-chamber first. But have you been able to think of any particular place where it could be located within this building?'

Byomkesh smiled and said, 'A suspicion has been roving in my mind since yesterday ... .'

I said, 'The pegs!'

Just then Sitaram came in to remove the teacups. Byomkesh looked at him and asked, 'Has Bulakilal come back?'

Sitaram nodded his head and left with the teacups and plates on a tray. Pandey asked, 'Did you send him anywhere?'

'Yes, it has some thing to do with Bulakilal.'

'All right, now tell me about your suspicion.'

Byomkesh said, 'Those pegs. I am being constantly plagued with the suspicion that what seems to be the obvious purpose is not the sole reason why they were installed; in fact, they were meant to serve as the tools for a hoax.'

Pandey went on surveying the pegs and said, 'Hm. What do you suggest?'

Byomkesh said, 'I was thinking that we could try to move and turn them with our hands and see what happens. Now that you are here, it is better that we try out the exercise in your presence. If the treasure-chamber is unearthed, only the three of us shall know about it, none else shall be allowed to share the knowledge at this time. Ajit, please close the door.'

The room became dark when I closed the door. We then lit up both the lantern and the torch and commenced our investigation. There were fifteen pegs in all. We started pulling, pushing and turning each of them with our hands. The pegs were rusted, but they remained firm, not budging even by a hair's breadth.

Suddenly Pandey exclaimed, 'Here! This one is moving, — just a little —!'

We ran over and stood beside him. The peg was fixed in the middle of the wall facing the door. Pandey was holding the peg and pushing it inward, but we could not see if it was moving or not.

Pandey said, 'I can't manage this on my own. Byomkesh Babu, please lend me a hand.'

Byomkesh got down on his knees and started pushing the peg with both hands. Very slowly the square piece of stone started receding inside. Then a dark hole appeared behind it.

I focussed the torch light on the hole. It was around three feet by three feet in size and led to a narrow flight of steps going down.

Pandey was very excited. He took out a handkerchief to wipe his forehead and exclaimed, 'Well done! The treasure-chamber has been found! — Byomkesh Babu, it is you have discovered it and you shall lead the way.'

Byomkesh entered first with the torch in his hand. He was followed by Pandeyji; I went in last carrying the lantern. At the bottom of the steps there was a room as wide as the room on the upper floor. Along one wall of the room there was a row of tall pitchers of clay, each pitcher carried an urn-shaped clay pot on its top and each pot was covered by a plate of clay. At the other end of the room there was a small furnace, to which the pipe of a blower was still connected. The leather skin of the blower had dried and flaked off, but it could still be identified as a blower. There was nothing else in the room.

We were breathing very rapidly, excited at the prospect of finding many priceless treasures, which the tall pitchers might yield. But first we had to check the remaining area of the room. As Byomkesh cast the torchlight all around I caught sight of a shining object in one corner. On reaching the spot I found that it was an electric torch. I picked it up and tried to turn it on, but found that it was already switched on and that its battery had run down.

Byomkesh said, 'This torch provides indisputable proof that Ishan Babu had been able to find this room.'

We then started checking the earthen pots one by one. They were all empty, except one, which had some crumbled powdery stuff at its bottom. Byomkesh picked up a handful of the stuff and examined it; then he wrapped it up in his handkerchief and put it in his pocket as he said, 'This could be salt, lime or some thing quite different.'

Thereafter the pitchers were examined one by one. But alas, no priceless treasures were found! They were all empty; there was not even a single paisa in any of them.

We looked at each other with baffled eyes. Then we set about in another thorough search of the room, but we could find nothing.

In the end we climbed up the steps and closed the secret door. Then I opened the outer door to find Sitaram strolling outside. Byomkesh told him in an exhausted voice, 'Sitaram, would you please prepare another round of tea for us.'

We pulled chairs and sat outside. Pandey had become quite dejected. He looked at Byomkesh and asked, 'What do you think happened? Where could all the treasure have disappeared?'

Byomkesh said, 'There are three possibilities. First, the sepoys could have looted every thing. Second, the person who murdered

Ishan Babu could have removed the treasure that very night. Third, Rajaram could have hidden the treasure somewhere else.'

'Which of these possibilities seems most probable to you?'

Byomkesh waved his hands in the air, smiled and recited the concluding line of the poem *Balaka*, 'Not here, somewhere else; somewhere else, at some other place.'

While sipping his tea Byomkesh asked Sitaram, 'Did you get to see Bulakilal?'

Sitaram said, 'Yes sir. He was repairing the engine. I could have a few words with him.'

'What did he say?'

'Sir, Bulakilal is an idiot. After dusk he has *bhang* every evening and then goes to sleep like a log; he knows nothing about what happens during the night. But he told me that during the daytime almost every member of the house used to visit the gypsies' camp. Even Bulakilal himself went there a few times.'

'Why did Bulakilal go there?'

'To get his palm read. The gypsy girls are supposed to be experts in palmistry, they can recount the past and forecast the future very accurately. They told Bukalilal that he would shortly be appointed as the Governor's chauffeur.'

'Which other resident of the house used to visit the gypsy camp?'

'The master of the house, his two elder sons, the son-in-law, the estate manager, everyone used to go there. And the two young children used to roam around the place all the time.'

'Hmm, any thing else?'

'Nothing else, sir.'

As it was getting late Pandeyji got up to leave. Byomkesh handed over the small bundle tied in his handkerchief and said, 'Please get a chemical analysis of this stuff done and see what you find. There is no reason to feel disappointed with what we have uncovered so far. At least we are now certain that Ishan Babu was murdered, the rest too shall become clear gradually.'

While putting the small bundle in his pocket, Pandeyji said, 'Oh, there was a letter for you in today's mail; I am sorry that I had forgotten to give it to you till now. Here,' he handed over the letter to Byomkesh and said, 'I'll see you tomorrow.'

We walked with Pandeyji up to the steps and after he had left we came back to our room. Byomkesh opened the letter and read it. I asked, 'Is it from Satyabati?'

'No, it is a letter from Sukumar.'

'What is the news?'

'There is no fresh news, but everything is fine.'

9

The night passed peacefully.

Next morning Byomkesh sat down with Ishan Babu's notebook. Sometimes he read it, sometimes he raised his eyes upwards and moved his lips soundlessly, without uttering a word.

Pandeyji had left the binoculars with us on the previous day. I picked it up and asked, 'What is the topic of your research?'

Byomkesh replied briefy, 'Mohanlal.'

On hearing the name 'Mohanlal' I suddenly remembered the lines from the 'Battle of Plassey,' which I had read long back. I started reciting, '*Again and yet again the roar of the canon, putting the water of the Ganges in turmoil —*'

Byomkesh looked up at me with reproachful eyes. But I continued reciting, '*stand by, heretic, stand by and turn around, Mohanlal shall roar and behold, death shall strike you to the ground!*'

When I noticed that the reproach in Byomkesh's eyes was about to assume a violent expression, I went out of the room quietly. If someone could not bear to hear a few lines from a poem, which inspired bravery, it was not proper to force it down his throat.

I was greeted by a bright, golden autumn morning as I came outside. I still had the binoculars with me and I raised it to my eyes as I climbed up on the rampart. The view all around was beautiful. Through the binoculars the distant mountain-peaks had drawn closer to me; I could see waves of sunlight toying with the crest of the woods. And then as I went on turning the binoculars I eventually had them focussed on the front porch of Ramkishor's house. I could see every detail of the house very clearly. Ramkishor came out of the house, ready to leave for the town, accompanied by his two sons and his son-in-law. They climbed down the steps. Soon the motorcar drove off. Gadadhar, Tulsi and their tutor Romapati remained in the house.

On returning to the room I found Byomkesh still studying the notebook resting on his lap; he was bent like a hen sipping water. Occasionally he would look up and mumble some thing to himself. I said, 'Look, Ramkishor Babu and his party have just left for town.'

Without paying heed to me, Byomkesh continued his imitation of a hen, sipping water. Then he abruptly asked me, 'Mohanlal was a valiant warrior, wasn't he?'

'That's what I have heard.'

Byomkesh did not speak another word. From his behaviour I had the distinct impression that he would devote the whole morning to the notebook. Rather than wasting time in such inactivity I asked, 'Why don't we go and have a chat with the *Sadhu Baba*? He could probably read our palms.'

Looking up absent-mindedly, Byomkesh said, 'Not now, may be in the evening.'

I spent a part of the afternoon lying in bed and dozing. I thought that Ramkishor Babu was absolutely right when he had told us that we would feel stifled after living for a couple of days in this wilderness.

I must have fallen asleep but when I woke up it was around a quarter to three. Byomkesh was not in the room. I went out and saw him strolling on the rampart. Although the sun was not very strong, I failed to see how he could enjoy walking on the rampart at that hour. Hoping that he had probably found some new clue, I walked out towards him.

When he caught sight of me Byomkesh seemed to emerge from a trance and said in a mechanical voice, 'I need a drill.'

'A drill?' I noticed a worried and distracted look on his face; an expression with which I was quite familiar, as it usually indicated that he had discovered some clue. 'Did you find any thing?' I asked.

Now Byomkesh seemed to recover his senses fully as he spoke in a somewhat embarrassed voice, 'No, no, nothing. You were sleeping soundly, so I decided to come out and enjoy the natural sights with the binocular. But there was nothing to see. – Here, you can see for yourself.'

Byomkesh had placed the binocular on the rampart. He now handed it over to me and then stepping down from the rampart, he walked back slowly towards the room. I was a bit surprised. What had happened to Byomkesh today?

I looked all around. The environment around me seemed to be dozing in the warm air. I raised the binocular to my eyes and went on turning it in many directions till it was focussed on Ramkishor Babu's house.

There was a similarity between watching through a binocular and eavesdropping; the former was somewhat like eavesdropping with one's eyes. Ramkishor Babu's house had come as close as ten feet to me; I could see everything around it, but nobody could see me from the house.

There was no one near the entrance to the house, but the main door was wide open. I raised the binocular. The roof of the house was enclosed with knee-high parapet walls and the staircase was at the rear end of the roof. Romapati was sitting on the parapet with a hand on his cheek; I could see him in profile. There was nobody else on the roof. Romapati seemed to be engrossed in his thoughts.

Suddenly he looked up in surprise. Tulsi came up by the staircase, her face and eyes filled with secret excitement. Drawing close to Romapati with quick steps, she brought out her right hand, which she had hidden in her sari and showed him something. She was holding some black object in her hand, which looked like a pencil or a fountain pen.

I could see all this quite clearly through the binocular, but I could not hear what they were saying; it was like watching a silent movie of the olden days. Romapati was saying something in an agitated manner and waving his hand, while Tulsi had her arms around his neck and seemed to be beseeching him and trying to put the black object into his hand.

Just then a few more actors made their appearance on the stage. Ramkishor Babu came up by the staircase; behind him came Bangshidhar and Muralidhar, followed by Manilal.

Everybody looked angry; Romapati rose to his feet and stood motionless in apprehension. Bangshidhar's face became distorted in anger as he scolded Tulsi and then snatched away the black object from her hand. Tulsi seemed to argue vigorously for some time, but then she gave up and went down the staircase with a tearful face. After this Ramkishor and his two sons surrounded Romapati and they seemed to be scolding and abusing him, while Manilal stood by silently, frowning at Romapati and chewing his lower lip.

All of a sudden Bangshidhar slapped Romapati very hard on his face. Ramkishor intervened and then pointed his finger towards the staircase. Romapati went down the staircase followed by the others.

In the absence of dialogues it was not possible to understand the significance of this strange scene, which I had just witnessed. I waited for another ten minutes, but could not see any further action; whatever occured thereafter must have happened inside the house beyond my vision.

I walked back to the room and narrated what I had just seen to Byomkesh. He listened attentively and then said, 'Ramkishor Babu and his party have then returned from the court. You could not identify the object in Tulsi's hand?'

'It looked like a fountain pen.'

'We might get to know soon. Romapati is most likely to come here.'

But Rompati did not come; the one who came was Tulsi. She came in flying like a dry leaf blown by a storm and got stuck to our doorpost. She looked like some one, who had lost her senses; her eyes were red with weeping. On seeing Byomkesh seated on the bed she came running in and casting herself on his lap, she started crying loudly, 'They have driven away my *Mastermoshai.*'

'They have driven him away?'

It was not easy to stop Tulsi's crying. However, she calmed down eventually through Byomkesh's tender comforting; her cries were reduced to sobs and it was then that we could get to know what had actually happened.

Jamai Babu had two fountain pens; one was his own and the other was gifted to him during his marriage. ... now what would *Jamai Babu* do with two fountain pens? So today in *Jamai Babu*'s absence Tulsi had taken out one pen from his drawer and gone to give it to her *Master Mashai*.... because *Master Mashai* did not even have a single pen... but *Master Mashai* had refused to accept the pen, rather he had become angry and ordered her to take it back and keep it in its proper place... just then the other members of the family had arrived and they had called *Master Mashai* a thief .... Tulsi told them so many times that *Master Mashai* had not stolen the pen, but nobody listened to her... in the end they beat up *Master Mashai* and threw him out of the house.

There was no discrepancy in Tulsi's story with what I had witnessed through the binocular. We tried to console Tulsi; we told her that her *Master Mashai* would come back again, there was no cause for worry, if necessary, we shall go and speak to her father and so on.

We were startled when we heard the noise of someone clearing his throat; turning back, we saw Manilal standing by the door. As soon as she caught sight of him Tulsi ran past him at a darting speed.

Byomkesh said, 'Please come in Mani Babu.'

Manilal stepped into the room and said, 'The master sent me in search of Tulsi. She is very naughty; I hope she did not bother you too much.'

Byomkesh said, 'She did not bother us at all. We understand that her tutor has been sent away, — that is what she had come to tell us.'

Manilal looked a little uncomfortable as he said, 'Yes, Romapati has been sent away by the master. None of us were at home; he had opened my drawer with a false key and stolen a pen. It was an expensive pen.'

Byomkesh extended his hand and asked, 'Is it the one which you are carrying in your breast-pocket?'

'Yes,' Manilal took out the pen and handed it over to Byomkesh.

It was a Parker pen, an expensive item. Byomkesh has a fancy for pens. He opened the cap and also opened the rear end to examine the mechanism of filling ink. He then returned the pen to Manilal and said, 'It's a very good pen, a pen worth stealing. Does anyone else in the house own a fountain pen?'

Manilal said, 'No. Reading or writing is not much in vogue in this house. Only the master uses a quill and an inkpot for his writing.'

'Hmm. Tulsi was telling us that it was she who had taken out the pen from your drawer.'

Manilal spoke with regret, 'Tulsi is lying. Romapati always had this bad habit. Only the other day an electric torch .... '

I started saying, 'But the electric torch .... '

Byomkesh spoke out before I could finish the sentence, 'An electric torch is a trifling article. Whatever else Romapati might be, he does not lack intelligence. Do you think he would ruin his future prospects by stealing a torch?'

Manilal went on looking at Byomkesh for some time and then said, 'I am feeling rather confused after hearing you; who knows he might not have stolen the torch after all. But today – my pen —? Then did Tulsi really —!'

I said with some force, 'Yes, Tulsi is telling the truth. I .... '

Byomkesh again interrupted me and said, 'Manilal Babu, we should not meddle in your family issues. We have come here for a few days for a change of air. What have we got to do with all these affairs? You have done what you thought was right. And there ends the matter.'

'Still—it is not right to falsely accuse anyone —' Manilal stepped towards the door as he said this.

Byomkesh asked, 'Was your work at the court completed today?'

'Yes. All that had been left was the signing of the documents and it was completed very quickly today.'

'So, now there is nothing to worry.'

'No, sir.'

After Manilal had left Byomkesh went to the door and looked up and down; he then came back and said, 'You had almost let the cat out of the bag.'

'What! How did I do that?'

'First you were about to blurt out that the lost torch had been found.'

'Yes.'

'Then you were about to tell him that with your binoculars you had seen what happened on the roof.'

'Yes, but what was the harm in telling him?'

'Telling anything to Manilal is the same as telling it to all the other inmates of the house. The wolf in sheep's clothing, whom we are searching for, would have come to know that we have located the treasure-chamber and that we are also keeping round-the-clock watch over his movements with a binocular. Wouldn't the quarry have been scared off?'

This had not struck me at all and I felt quite silly.

Sitaram served us tea. Pandeyji arrived a little later. He had brought a lot of fresh foodstuff for us. Sitaram went to fetch them from the car. We exchanged information while sipping our tea.

On hearing what we had to report, Pandeyji said, 'The fish has started escaping from the net. Romapati has left today; Bangshidhar and Muralidhar might leave tomorrow. We have to haul up the net quickly. Oh yes, I have been able to gather information regarding Bangshidhar's misdeed at the college.'

'What was it?'

'He had quarrelled with another boy; then the dispute was settled. But Bangshidhar had fostered a strong grudge in his mind; during the celebration of the *holi* festival he had mixed *datura* seeds with *bhang* and given it to the other boy to drink. The boy had almost died and only just managed to survive.'

Byomkesh remained quiet for a while and then said, 'Hmm. Then Bangshidhar is well-versed in the administration of poison.'

'That he is. He is not only headstrong, but also has a habit of carrying a grudge.'

When it struck five, Byomkesh said, 'Come, let us go down and have a talk with the *sadhu.*'

10

When we reached the coartyard we found Bangshidhar coming down the steps from Ramkishor's house with firm steps. On seeing us he seemed to slow down for a moment; but instead of stopping he walked straight on, as if he was going to take the road to the town.

Byomkesh said in a soft voice, 'Bangshidhar was going to meet the *sadhu baba*, but he changed his mind on seeing us.'

Bangshidhar had not gone very far. Pandeyji called out, 'Bangshidhar Babu!'

Bangshidhar stopped and stood where he was, casting his eyes on the ground.

We walked over to him. Pandeyji asked in good humour, 'Where are you off to in such haste?'

Bangshidhar replied briefly in a rude tone, 'I am going for a stroll.'

Pandeyji smiled and said, 'But you have just come back from the town. Do you have to go for a stroll again?'

I could see the veins on Bangshidhar's temple start swelling, as he said in a truculent voice, 'Yes, I do. You may be a police officer, but you cannot stop my movement.'

Pandeyji's face hardened. He said in a stern voice, 'Yes I can. You had poisoned some one at the college hostel; that case has not been closed yet. Criminal suits are never time-barred. I can arrest you if I deem fit.'

Bangshidhar's face shrivelled in fear. Had I not seen it happen before my eyes I would have never believed that extreme rudeness could turn to such intense alarm so fast. He cast quick looks all around him like a trapped animal and the next moment he retraced his steps towards the direction that he had come from.

Pandeyji laughed softly and said, 'Now we have seen the might of Bangshidhar. Let's go.'

We walked down to the place where the *sadhu baba* was sitting. A thick cluster of trees all around made the place look quite dark. The *sadhu* was seated before a small fire. A quiet but meaningful smile spread on his face when he saw us. He waved his hand signalling us to sit down.

Pandeyji started the conversation with him in Hindi; as he was wearing his police uniform, the *sadhu baba* started talking with him enthusiastically.

The conversation was pursued on general topics for some time. We all concurred about the greatness of an ascetic's life as compared to the lowliness of the mundane existence of a family man. Seemingly pleased with our reactions the *sadhu* then brought out some *ganja* from his cloth-bag and started preparing it for consumption.

Pandeyji asked, 'How do you get *ganja* in this remote place, father?'

The *sadhu* looked upwards and said, 'The Almighty provides it, my son.'

With the help of his pincers he picked up a small piece of burning coal from the fire and placed it on the bowl of his hookah. I took this opportunity to have a close look at the pincers. I realised that *sadhus* could live without fear in wild forests because they were not totally weaponless. If one knew how to make proper application of these pincers they could probably be used for killing a wild animal. And then again their pointed ends could serve the purpose of picking up a very small piece of hot coal, as I had just seen with my own eyes. The *sadhus* must be accomplishing several tasks with the help of this single implement.

The *sadhu baba* now started taking a puff from the bowl of *ganja* with great force. The arteries and veins of his throat and temple swelled up. After inhaling for a full minute, he put the empty bowl face down on the ground.

Then came the operation of exhaling the smoke. The *sadhu* took about three minutes to complete this task. Smoke emerging from behind his beard and moustache filled the air with a sweet aroma.

The *sadhu* exclaimed loudly, '*Byom! Byom Shankar!*'

Just then we heard footsteps and turned back to see a man walking in our direction. He came to a sudden halt on seeing us. We could then see that it was Ramkishor Babu. He too recognized us at the same time and said in a faltering voice, 'Oh — it's you—!'

Byomkesh said, 'Come and join us.'

But Ramkishor said in a somewhat despondent voice, 'No, no. You people are talking with the *sadhu baba*, please carry on. I had only come to pay my homage to him.' He saluted the *sadhu* with folded hands from where he stood and left.

Turning towards the *sadhu* I could see the same strange smile on his face. If the smile could be analysed it would have been difficult to state how much of it was spiritual and how much was roguery, — probably the two qualities were present in equal proportions.

Now Byomkesh spoke in Hindi, '*Sadhu baba* you have been here for a fairly long time. Do you know that a man died here of snakebite the other day?'

The *sadhu* said, 'I know. There is nothing that I do not know.'

Byomkesh enquired, 'Did you see anyone going to the fortress that night?'

'Yes, I did.'

The same smile, - a strange mixture of spiritualism and roguery, had reappeared on his face. Byomkesh was about to ask him some more questions, but again we could hear the sound of footsteps from behind. We turned our heads. The *sadhu* also looked sharply in the same direction. But no one came forward; probably the person had noted our presence and retreated from a distance.

As Byomkesh was about to question the *sadhu baba*, he placed a finger on his own lips and said in fluent Bengali, 'Not now. Come to me at midnight. I shall tell you then.'

I stared in amazement. But Byomkesh got to his feet in a flash and said, 'All right, father. We shall come at midnight. Let's go Ajit.'

After coming out from the tree coverage we saw that it had grown dark. Byomkesh and Pandeyji looked searchingly all around, but there was no one anywhere.

Pandeyji said, 'I'll have to take leave of you from here. It would have been good if I could stay till midnight. But that is not possible. I'll come tomorrow morning.'

Pandeyji left.

While returning to the fortress I asked, 'Byomkesh, the *sadhu baba* is a Bengali?'

'Of course.'

It was around seven in the evening when we returned to the fortress. We placed our chairs in the open compound and sat down.

The *sadhu baba* must be knowing some thing. But what could he know? Could he have seen Ishan Babu's murderer entering the fortress that night? But the steps leading to the fortress could not be seen through the tree cover where the *sadhu* stayed — particularly in a dark night. Then did the *sadhu baba* have a habit of roaming about the place during the late hours of night? ... Those pincers were no trifling weapon; if poison was applied to the sharp points of the pincers ....

I addressed my questions to Byomkesh. But all I heard in response was a sound emerging from his throat as if he was trying to suppress a cough.

We finished our dinner by ten and again sat down in the open compound. We had to remain awake for a further two hours. Sitaram finished his meal and went out, probably for a smoke. The lantern had been placed in a corner of the room, it's wick lowered.

The hands of the clock were moving towards eleven. Our excitement was mounting ...

'Byomkesh Babu!'

We were both startled out of our thoughts by this whispered address. Then I saw a shadowy figure standing a little away from us. Byomkesh got to his feet and said, 'Romapati! Come, come.'

We escorted Romapati to the room. Byomkesh raised the lantern wick and inspected him from head to toe. He then said, 'I see that you haven't had any thing to eat. – Sitaram!'

Within five minutes Sitaram cooked a preparation of several eggs and placed it before Romapatii. Rompapati started eating without a word. His face was pale, his eyes had shrunk into their sockets; his half-sleeve shirt was torn in many places and he had no sandals on his feet. While eating he said, 'Then you must have heard everything. Who told you?'

'Tulsi. Where were you all this time?'

'In the forest at first and then behind the fortress.'

'Did they beat you very hard?'

With one hand Romapati lifted the shirt from his back. We could see red, swollen bruises all over his skin.

Byomkesh's face became hard.

He asked, 'Bangshidhar?'

Romapati nodded his head.

'Why didn't you go to the town?'

Romapati did not reply; he went on eating in silence.

'What would you gain by staying here?'

Romapati said in a low, indistinct voice, 'Tulsi.'

'Do you love Tulsi?'

Romapati remained silent for a while. Then he spoke very softly, 'Every body hurts her, keeps her locked up, nobody loves her. If I am not here she would die.'

When Romapati finished eating, Byomkesh pointed his hand towards his own bed and said, 'Lie down and get some sleep.'

Romapati let out a sigh of exhaustion and stretched himself on the bed.

Byomkesh looked at his face for a long time and then started interrogating him.

'Romapati, do you know who murdered Ishan Babu?'

'No, I don't know who committed the murder, but I do know that he was murdered.'

'Do you know who killed Harpriya?'

'No, she tried to tell me—but she couldn't.'

'Do you know why Bangshidhar's wife jumped down from the hill?'

After remaining silent for some time, Romapati said, 'I do not know, but I did have my suspicions. Haripriya, the elder sister couldn't stand Bangshidhar's wife; Haripriya also possessed a very malicious nature. She probably put on a mask of ghosts and scared Bangshidhar's wife ... .'

'Mask?'

'Haripriya had a Japanese mask. The day after that incident I found the mask at the edge of the forest. I thought that it might have been blown down there by the wind. So I picked it up and gave it to Haripriya; she took it from me and tore it up.'

'Does Bangshidhar know about the mask?'

'I didn't tell him any thing.'

'You must have seen the *sadhu baba*. What do you think of him?'

'Somehow I can't feel any devotion towards him. But the master has a lot of regard for the *Sadhu*. Uncooked food items are sent to him from the house every day.'

'Did Ishan Babu tell you any thing about the *sadhu baba*?'

'No, he didn't even go to see him. He was rather ill-disposed towards *sadhus* in general.'

Byomkesh looked at his watch and said, 'It is midnight. Romapati, please go to sleep. We are going out for a while.'

Romapati looked up and asked, 'Where?'

'Not very far; we shall be back soon. Come Ajit.'

We went out carrying the big torch.

No lights were on in Ramkishor Babu's house. While passing by the courtyard we were greeted by the loud sound of Bulakilal's snoring.

The tree-cover where the *sadhu baba* had set up his temporary abode was also enveloped in darkness, with only a soft glow emerging from the fire covered by ashes. The *sadhu baba* was lying in front of the fire, but the posture in which he was stretched out did not seem quite natural.

Byomkesh threw the powerful light of the torch on his face, but the *sadhu baba* did not wake up. Byomkesh put his hand on the *sadhu*'s arms and shook him, but failing to get any response, he sighed deeply and exclaimed, 'Oh!'

The torchlight was flashed all over the *sadhu*'s body and then came to rest on his feet. There were two marks of snakebite on the upper part of the ankle.

11

Byomkesh said, 'So Rambinod did meet with his death at long last.'

'Rambinod!'

'You seem utterly amazed. Don't tell me that you hadn't guessed it all this time!'

Wood had been added to rekindle the fire. The *sadhu*'s corpse was stretched out before the fire, already stiff. We two were sitting on our haunches a little away from the fire, facing each other.

Byomkesh said, 'Do you remember that Ramkishor Babu appeared somewhat familiar to me when I saw him for the first time? What had really happened was that I had seen the *sadhu* just a little earlier. There is a resemblance in the appearance of the two brothers; I couldn't catch this in the beginning, but I did when I saw Ramkishor for the second time.'

'But Rambinod had died of the plague!'

'Rambinod was struck by the plague, but even before he died the others dumped him on a sandbar on the river and fled. I had guessed this from what I heard from Chandmohan. Then Rambinod survived.'

'Where was he for all these years?'

'That I do not know. Perhaps he had developed some apathy towards worldly matters in the beginning and moved around all over the country with other *sadhus*. Then he must have traced Ramkishor to this place and arrived here. But all that can wait. We have to take some steps for guarding the body. Ajit, let me stay here, while you can take the torch and go and fetch Sitaram. Also, if you can, you may try to wake up Bulakilal and bring him here as well. Let the two of them stand guard over the body.'

I said, 'And you are going to stay here all alone? No, I can't agree to that. Either we'll both stay here or we'll leave this place together.'

'You are scared that I shall be bitten by the snake? But this snake is not of such breed, my friend. It does not strike persons who are awake. Any way, since you want it that way, let's both go.'

When we reached the courtyard, Byomkesh said, 'Let's wake up Bulakilal first.'

We succeeded in waking up Bulakilal after repeated shoving and pushing. Byomkesh then informed him of the *sadhu*'s death and asked, 'Did the *sadhu baba* have *bhang* tonight?'

'Yes sir, he had one pot of *bhang*.'

'Who else had *bhang* tonight?'

'A servant had been sent from the house; he carried a pot of *bhang*.'

'All right, now go and guard the *sadhu*'s body. I shall send Sitaram to join you soon.'

Bulakilal walked off with disjointed steps. Even though he was awake, he had still not got over the befuddling effect of *bhang*.

When we reached the fortress we found Sitaram was awake and waiting for us. On hearing the news his eyes became wide for a second; then he quietly walked down the steps.

Romapati was fast asleep on the bed. We did not wake him, but sat outside. It was twelve thirty.

Byomkesh said, 'We shouldn't sleep tonight. At least one of us should stay awake. Ajit, you better sleep for a couple of hours, after which I can wake you up and get some sleep myself.'

But I did not feel at all inclined to get up from my chair; my mind was in a highly agitated state.

I asked, 'Byomkesh, who killed the *sadhu baba*?'

'The same person who killed Ishan Babu.'

'But who was it?'

'Why don't you tell me? Can't you guess?'

That very question had been whirling in my head all this time. Very softly I said, 'If the *Babaji* was Rambinod, who could have killed him? One suspect is of course Ramkishor Babu —'

'He would kill his brother?'

'He had left his brother in a dying state and fled. The same brother had now come back, perhaps he was demanding his share of the property.'

'All right, let us presume that Ramkishor Babu murdered his brother. But why did he murder Ishan Babu?'

'Ishan Babu was Rambinod's bosom friend; he had recognized the *sadhu* and probably threatened Ramkishor: better divide the property without posing any hindrance, otherwise the whole scandalous affair shall be disclosed. There were only two people who could identify the *sadhu* as Rambinod,— Chandmohan and

Ishan Babu. Chandmohan was under his master's thumb, so the problem could be solved if Ishan Babu was removed from the scene —'

Byomkesh suddenly slapped my back and said, 'Ajit! What's happened to you? You have started talking with logic. Has enlightenment dawned at long last? But no more; please go to sleep now. I shall wake you up exactly at three a.m.'

As I was about to leave, he spoke to himself in a lowered voice, 'Is Romapati asleep or just pretending to sleep?—Any way, it doesn't matter, I shall stay awake.'

Pandeyji arrived at around eight next morning. He had received the news of the *sadhu*'s death at the foot of the steps, now he was furnished with the rest of the information. Byomkesh said, 'You may take the body and leave. But you'll have to come again — and listen — '

Byomkesh took Pandeyji a little away and spoke to him in a low voice for some time. Pandeyji said, 'All right, I shall be back by ten. Don't let Romapati leave the room.'

Byomkesh and I went to Ramkishor Babu's house at around nine thirty. Ramkishor Babu was seated on a divan in the drawing room, Manilal sat next to him. Bangshidhar and Muralidhar had been pacing in front of the divan, but they both disappeared as soon as they saw us. Some family conference had perhaps been in progress, but it came to a halt on our appearance.

Ramkishor's cheeks had become shrunk, his eyes had sunk into their sockets, but outwardly he appeared to be unaffected. He greeted us with a thin smile and said, 'Please come, take your seats.'

We pulled up chairs and sat close to the divan. Ramkishor cleared his throat and said in a normal voice, 'Now the *sadhu baba* has been bitten by a snake. It is gradually becoming impossible to live in this place. Bangshi and Murali have decided to move out within the next few days; the rest of us had thought of remaining here. But if the snake-attacks go on spreading in this manner ... .'

Byomkesh said, 'Snake-attacks in the winter season — strange!'

Ramkishor said, 'Then we had another disturbance last night. Till now no thief had ever entered this house –'

Manilal said, 'This was not a common thief.'

Byomkesh asked, 'What happened?'

Ramkishor said, 'Ever since I have been unwell Manilal sleeps in my room at night. At about 12 last night — Mani, you better tell them what happened. By the time I was awake the thief had escaped.'

Manilal said, 'I am a very light sleeper. It was quite late last night when I was awakened by the sound of footsteps outside our bedroom. It is the practice of this house not to bolt any door at night; even the main door is closed lightly without bolting it from inside.

'It seemed to me as if someone was trying to push open the door of our bedroom very softly from outside. My bed is at some distance from the door; I got up soundlessly and tiptoed across to the door. The lights in the room had been put off, but even in the darkness I could see that the door was opening inside very slowly. It was then that I acted very foolishly. If I had only waited a little longer the thief would have entered the room and I could have grabbed him. But instead I tried to pull open the door from inside. The thief was very much on his guard; he ran off with hurried footsteps.'

Ramkishor said, 'It was then that I woke up.'

Byomkesh said, 'The person whom you took to be a thief, could it have been Tulsi? I have heard that she has a habit of roaming around at night.'

Ramkishor's expression became stern as he said, 'No, it was not Tulsi. I had locked her up in her room last night.'

Byomkesh asked Manilal, 'You could not recognize the thief?'

'No. But —'

'You think it was a known person?'

'Yes.'

Ramkishor said, 'Now there is no point in trying to hide or dodge the truth. You are aware that I had thrown out Romapati yesterday. Manilal believes that it was Romapati who had come here with some purpose.'

Byomkesh asked, 'Can you tell me the exact time when this incident occurred?'

Ramkishor said, 'At exactly a quarter to twelve. I keep a watch under my pillow and I had checked the time.'

Byomkesh sent a meaningful glance in my direction. I kept silent; at a quarter to twelve Romapati had been lying on Byomkesh's bed.

Ramkishor spoke with mixed feelings of regret and seriousness, 'Some thing more has come to my attention this morning. Romapati had not taken his belongings; they were still lying in his room. This morning we searched the room. We found this article in his tin suitcase.' He took out a gold hairpin from his pocket and gave it to Byomkesh.

It was a two-folded pin, similar to the steel pins which women commonly use for tying their hair, but it was made of pure gold and was a little longer and thicker in size with sharp points like needles. Byomkesh turned it around in his hand and then looked at Ramkishor, who said, 'This belonged to my elder daughter Haripriya; it had been missing since her death.'

After returning the hairpin Byomkesh looked squarely at Ramkishor and said, 'Ramkishor Babu, it is now time to have a showdown.'

Ramkishor seemed to be taken by surprise, as he asked, 'Showdown?'

'Yes. It is necessary to find out who is responsible for the death of your elder brother Rambinod Babu.'

Ramkishor's face became pale. He opened his mouth to speak, but no words came out from his mouth. Trying to regain control over himself with great difficulty, he said in a choked voice, 'My elder brother —! Whom are you talking of?'

Byomkesh said, 'You know whom I am talking of. There is no point in this play-acting. We know that the snakebite was not a real snakebite. Your brother was murdered last night.'

Manilal blurted out, 'He was murdered?'

'Yes. Did you know that the *sadhu baba* was your father-in-law's elder brother, Rambinod Singh?'

By then Ramkishor had regained control over himself. He screamed in a sharp voice, 'This is a lie! My elder brother died of the plague many years back. From where did you pick up all these cock and bull stories? Can you prove that the *sadhu* was my elder brother? Do you have any witness?'

Byomkesh said, 'There was a witness. Ishan Majumdar. He too was murdered.'

Ramkishor now exploded in anger. He yelled loudly, 'Lies! All lies! This is all police trickery! Get out from my house! I want you to clear out from the fortress this very moment! There is no place for police spies on my property.'

Just then Muralidhar's scared face was seen outside the window. He shouted, 'Father, the police have surrounded the house.' The next moment he was seized and dragged away by policemen.

Hearing footsteps I looked towards the door to see Pandeyji, dressed in his full uniform, as he made his entrance slowly into the room, followed by Dr. Ghatak, carrying his medical bag.

12

Pandey said, 'Ramkishor Babu, I have a warrant for searching your house. Do you want to see it?'

Ramkishor looked up fearfully, his face turning pale and then asked in a broken voice, 'What does all this mean?'

Pandey said, 'There have been two murders on your property. The police believe that both the culprit and the proof of his crime exist in this house. We want to conduct a search.'

Ramkishor's face became blank. 'All right, do as you wish,' he said and leaned back on a cushion.

Pandeyji said, 'Doctor.'

Dr. Ghatak was ready. In less than two minutes he gave an injection to Ramkishore, checked his pulse and said, 'Nothing to worry.'

Peeping out through the window I saw that the place was filled with policemen. Several constables had blocked the entrance to the steps.

Inspector Dubey entered the room, saluted and said, 'Sir, all residents of the house are in their respective rooms. They have been asked not to leave their rooms.'

Pandey said, 'Good. We need two neutral witnesses. Ajit Babu and Byomkesh Babu, I would request you to kindly stay with us all through the search to make sure that the police does not resort to any illegal action.'

Manilal had been standing by us all this time. He now asked, 'Should I also go and stay in my own room?'

Pandey turned towards him and said, 'Manilal Babu! No, no, let us check your room first.'

Manilal said, 'Please come.'

Pandey, Dubey, Byomkesh and I followed Manilal and entered his room. It was a fairly large room with a bed on one side, in addition to an almirah, a cabinet and a few other items of furniture.

Manilal said, 'Please go ahead and see what you wish.'

Byomkesh said, 'There is not much that we have to see. You have two fountain pens; if you would just let us have a look at them, it would serve our purpose.'

It seemed as if a mask had been dislodged from Manilal's face for a few moments. I remembered what Byomkesh had told me about a wolf in sheep's clothing; it now seemed to me that a cruel beast had just discarded it's disguise and come out with all its ferocity; for a moment I had a glimpse of a truly terrible face. Then Manilal went to the cabinet and opened a drawer; taking out the Parker pen from the drawer he quickly removed the caps at both ends; gripping the pen like a dagger he raised his eyes towards Byomkesh. I cannot describe the deep malice and fury held in those eyes. Exposing his canine tooth, Manilal screamed, 'Here is the pen! You want to have it? Come, come and get it from me.'

We stood speechless like statues. Pandey took out his revolver from the holster.

Manilal laughed out loudly like a hyena. Then he inserted the nib of the pen into his left elbow and pressed down the ink-filled syringe with his thumb.

Back in the drawing room, Byomkesh said to Ramkishor Babu, 'You had nourished a viper in your breast. But now we are getting out from here; we have no inclination to avail of your hospitality even for a moment longer. All I am carrying from your house is this phial containing snake-poison.'

Ramkishor Babu went on looking at us with anxious, bewildered eyes. After reaching the door Byomkesh turned back and said, 'Let me tell you some thing more before I leave. Your ancestors had hidden a lot of gold. I know where that gold is. But I have no wish to get involved in what is not my business. You are free to enjoy your ancestral wealth. Come Pandeyji. Ajit, let us get away from here.'

That afternoon, half-reclined on an easy chair in Pandeyji's residence, Byomkesh was narrating the story. The listeners were Pandeyji, Romapati and I.

'I'll tell you the story very briefly. You may ask me if you find any omissions.'

Pandeyji said, 'Let me give you some information first. It's about that white, powdery stuff, which you had given me for testing; the chemist's report has arrived. Here it is.'

Byomkesh frowned after reading the report, 'Sodium Tetra Borate, Borax. I know that colloquially it is said to have some link with gold, but does it serve any other purpose?'

Pandey said, 'I do not know exactly. Perhaps it was needed for preparing some medicines in those days.'

Handing back the report to Pandeyji, Byomkesh said, 'Let it be. Now listen to the story.

'Manilal seemed to be a nice person from outside, but he possessed a monstrous nature; he was as cruel as he was greedy. After his marriage he made up his mind to seize the entire property owned by his father-in-law. He was not well-treated by his brothers-in-law, nor did he care for his wife. But what he had succeeded in doing was to win over his father-in-law through his servile behaviour.

'Manilal had his first stroke of luck when some gypsies came and set up their tents in the property. He collected snake poison from them in secret.

'It is not clear why he murdered his wife at the outset. He might have disclosed his scheme to his wife in a weak moment or it could be that Haripriya had happened to catch him unawares in the process of filling poison in the fountain pen. Whatever may have been the actual reason, Haripriya had to be removed first. And yet this involved a major risk, as it terminated the relationship with his father-in-law. But Manilal had cast such a strong influence on his father-in-law that he was quite convinced that Ramkishor would never think of bringing their relationship to an end. Manilal had his eyes on Tulsi.

'Any way, there was no hitch after Haripriya's death. Manilal received a firm assurance from Ramkishor that Tulsi's hand would be given to him in marriage. He kept waiting patiently. Once the marriage was solemnized he could get rid of his brothers-in-law one by one. Two years passed; Tulsi had almost reached a marriageable age, when Ishan Majumdar made his appearance. The *sadhu* arrived a few days later. But no contact was established between these two persons; neither man knew till the end that he had come so close to his friend.

'Ramkishor Babu always suffered from a guilty conscience that he had deserted his brother in a dying condition. When he recognised the *sadhu* he had a heart attack and he almost died.

'After he had recovered to some extent he may have said to his brother, — What has happened cannot be undone, but if the truth is now disclosed I shall be disgraced. Rather let me set up an *ashram* for you at my cost at any holy place of your choice.

'But Rambinod had his brother under his clutch; he refused to budge from the place. He continued to squat under the tree and curse his brother.

'This is what I guess. If Ramkishor ever speaks out what actually transpired you shall find that my guess is not very far from the truth. But Manilal became worried when his father-in-law got indisposed; if his father-in-law died suddenly all his plans would have come to naught; his brothers-in-law would have thrown him out of the place immediately. He then started instigating his father-in-law to make separate settlements in advance for his two elder sons. For Manilal this had a distinct advantage that even if Ramkishor succumbed to heart-failure, he would have had control over half the property as the legal guardian of the two minor children. Thereafter he would have married Tulsi and Gadadhar would have died of snakebite.

'Ramkishor had complete trust in Manilal, apart from which he was afraid that after his death his two elder sons would deprive their minor siblings from their rightful shares of the property. So he acceded to Manilal's suggestion and started consulting his lawyer.

'Meanwhile another event was taking place at the fortress; Ishan Babu was occupied in a treasure hunt. First he found out the Persian inscription on the stone. He carefully copied the writing in his notebook and continued his search. Then, while moving the pegs in his bedroom with his hands, he found that one of the stones was loose. He had no trouble in realizing that the treasure-chamber was located under that stone.

'But the stone was very heavy; Ishan Babu was old and sickly. How could he remove the stone and enter the secret chamber? He was not pure at heart; dire need might have corrupted his morals. He did not inform Ramkishor about his discovery, but started looking for an accomplice.

'Two able-bodied men used to call on him regularly, Romapati and Manilal. Ishan Babu chose Manilal, because he was the stronger of the two and also because he was not on good terms with his brothers-in-law, — some thing which Ishan Babu had already found out.

'Perhaps the arrangement was to share the treasure on half and half basis. But Manilal had made up his mind to grab the whole lot; why should he allow his father-in-law's wealth to pass to other hands? On the particular night the two of them removed the stone and got down into the treasure-chamber.

'Before they could start searching the clay pots and pitchers Ishan Babu found a gold coin on the floor. Manilal thought that the pitchers and the pots must be filled with gold coins. Without wasting any time he struck a heavy blow on Ishan babu's head with the torch. Ishan Babu fell down unconscious, after which it was not difficult to prick his feet with the pen.

'But the mind of a murderer is always beset by a sense of haste. Manilal carried Ishan Babu's body upstairs. I think some distraction might have occurred just at that time from outside. Muralidhar had been trying to scare Ishan Babu away from the place; he could have been hurling stones from outside at that very moment. Manilal became apprehensive and shut down the secret door. He could not go through the clay pots; also the torch remained lying in the underground chamber.

'It is possible that Manilal had not come to know till the end that there was no treasure in the secret chamber. Before the stir created by Ishan Babu's death could die down we took up residence at the fortress; so Manilal had no scope of conducting his search. But he had no dearth of patience; he waited calmly and went on coaxing his father-in-law so that the fortress could be included in Tulsi's share.

'Manilal had a suspicion from the very beginning that we had not gone there only for a change of air; but there was nothing that he could do about it. And then a series of incidents occurred yesterday, which made him really nervous. Tulsi stole his fountain pen and went to present it to Romapati. I cannot say if there was any poison in the pen at that particular time, but it was only natural that Manilal should be deeply concerned about his pen. Moreover, he could not stand Romapati — can any man tolerate his future wife's favourite? So he seized this opportunity to get Romapati thrown out of the house. Any way, not much harm had been caused till then, but something else occurred at dusk. When we were sitting with the *sadhu baba* and listening to his tall declarations, — *there is nothing that I don't know* etcetera, — it was at that very moment that Manilal was coming to see the *sadhu*. Overhearing the *sadhu*'s bluster from a distance he became convinced that the *sadhu* must have seen him going up to the fortress on the night of Ishan Babu's death and that he was about to divulge that very fact to us at midnight.

'Manilal was scared that everything was about to be ruined. There was a witness to his crime. It did not strike him that the *sadhu baba* knew nothing about Ishan Babu's death. He decided that he would get rid of the *sadhu* before midnight.

'After we came back the *sadhu baba* had a pot of *bhang*. Thereafter Manilal carried another pot of *bhang* for him mixed with some drug. The *sadhu* drank it without hesitation, because he did not mistrust Manilal. Then he fell fast asleep under the effect of the drug; Manilal arrived in due time and sent him to the land of eternal repose.'

I asked, 'Tell me some thing. If the *sadhu baba* did not know anything, why did he ask us to see him at midnight?'

Byomkesh said, 'He asked us to see him because he wanted to tell us his own story and reveal his true identity to us.'

'There is some thing else that I wanted to ask you. What do you think of the thief who had broken into Ramkishor Babu's house last night?'

'It was an imaginary thief. On his return after murdering the *sadhu* Manilal might have stumbled at the door while entering the bedroom; the noise woke Ramkishor Babu. So the invented thief made his appearance. Ramkishor Babu takes opium regularly; opium-smokers do not wake-up easily, so Manilal was not worried. But when Ramkishor did wake up, Manilal quickly invented a story. This served to heap more suspicion on Romapati's head while absolving Manilal all together. The same purpose was served by hiding Haripriya's hairpin of gold in Romapati's suitcase. If there was any cause to suspect anyone the suspicion would have fallen squarely on Romapati.'

Byomkesh lit a cigarette.

I asked, 'When did you realize that Manilal was the culprit?'

Byomkesh said, 'In the beginning I could not even make out the nature of the weapon used in the killings. I had my first suspicion when Tulsi mentioned about the fountain pen. And when Manilal handed over the fountain pen to me everything became clear in a moment. He told us himself that nobody else in the house had a fountain pen. Such a simple weapon! Just think. Carry it in your pocket in style all the time, nobody would suspect.'

After a brief silence Pandeyji said, 'But the mystery of the hidden treasure is still not unravelled.'

Byomkesh smiled.

A motorcar arrived and stood at the gate and a horn was blown. From the window I saw Ramkishor Babu and Doctor Ghatak alighting from the car.

On entering the room Ramkishor Babu folded his hands together and said, 'I beg all of you to please forgive me. In my rank stupidity I had misunderstood every thing. Romapati, my son, it is you whom I have hurt the most. Please come back home with me.'

Romapati rose to his feet shyly and touched Ramkishor's feet in obeisance.

13

Ramkishor Babu was cordially invited to sit down. Pandeyji went inside presumably to order some tea and snacks for the visitors.

Dr. Ghatak smiled and said, 'Too much excitement is not good for my patient. I have brought him here only on his insistence; otherwise he should have stayed in bed.'

Ramkishor spoke in a heavy voice, 'Excitement! Doctor, if I can remain alive after going through all that has been happening from this morning, I should have no further cause for fear.'

Byomkesh said, 'There is actually no further cause for fear. Not only is your peril now over, but you are also in the hands of a good doctor. You see I know what a competent physician Dr. Ghatak is. But please tell me some thing, are you still not prepared to acknowledge the *sadhu* as your elder brother?'

Ramkishor Babu seemed genuinely remorseful as he bowed his head. Then he said, 'Byomkesh Babu, I am already feeling deeply mortified, please do not put me in further embarrassment. Believe me, I had literally fallen at the feet of my elder brother, but he refused to re-enter family life. Then I offered to build a temple for him at Hardwar, where he could stay in utmost comfort as the head priest and sole beneficiary. But my brother did not listen to me. If he did, he wouldn't probably have met with such an unnatural death.'

He sighed deeply.

Pandeyji returned. In his hand he had the gold coin, which we had seen earlier. He handed it over to Ramkishor Babu and said, 'Keep it. This belongs to you.'

Ramkishor accepted the gold coin and eagerly examined it, before raising it to his forehead as a mark of respect. He then said, 'This is an heirloom. My ancestors had left all their wealth for us, but it was only because of our ill fortune that we weren't able to find it. Byomkesh Babu, have you really been able to trace it?'

'I believe that I have been able to trace the wealth, but I haven't seen it with my own eyes.'

'Then – then —!' Ramkishor Babu gulped in dismay.

Byomkesh smiled and said, 'It is held within your property. Why don't you search it out yourself?'

'Do you think I had left out anything in my search? Ever since I bought the fortress I searched it from top to bottom, but I found nothing. In my utter disappointment I had thought that the sepoys must have taken away everything with them. But if you really have been able to trace it, won't you please tell me where it is. I promise that I shall not deprive you; you shall get your share. I accept these two gentlemen as arbitrators, Pandeyji and Dr. Ghatak; I shall pay you whatever they consider as fair and justified. You have already done me a very big favour, even if you want a half-share ... .'

Byomkesh said in a dry tone, 'I don't want any share. But I have two conditions.'

'Conditions! What conditions?'

'My first condition is that you shall get Tulsi married to Romapati. And the second condition is that you shall transfer the title of the fortress to Romapati as a dowry by executing a deed in his favour.'

I had no idea that Byomkesh had been playing a matchmaker's role unknown to all of us. We were quite amazed on hearing his terms. Romapati moved a little away from the rest of us, blushing in embarrassment.

Ramkishor pondered over the matter for some time with his head bowed. Then he looked up and said, 'All right. I do not dislike Romapati. I know him; he is a good lad. If I try to get Tulsi married elsewhere, who knows, I might get landed up with some other rascal, — which I would not want at all.'

'And the fortress?'

'I shall execute a deed for transfering the title of the fortress. You want that Tulsi and Romapati should inherit all the ancestral wealth, isn't it? It shall be done.'

'You shall not go back on your word?'

Ramkishor spoke with some hauteur, 'I àm a desecendent of Raja Jankiram. I never go back on my word.'

'Fine. Dusk has already set in and it has become dark. I shall call on you tomorrow morning.'

Next morning we reached the fortress again. There were four of us – Byomkesh, Pandeyji, Sitaram and I. Only Ramkishor and Romapati were present from the other side. Bulakilal had been ordered to ensure that nobody came to the fortress. He was standing guard at the courtyard.

Byomkesh said, 'It took Ishan Babu just two weeks to find what you had been unable to trace for years. Because he was a historian, he knew where to search. First he found the inscription on the stone, which stated – *In case Jairam or I do not survive, our entire wealth is left in the custody of Mohanlal.*

'This inscription was written by Rajaram. But who was Mohanlal? Ishan Babu failed to grasp this. Perhaps there wouldn't have been any trouble if he had understood the meaning of the inscription and disclosed his findings to Ramkishor Babu instead of trying to steal the entire treasure for his own use.

'Then Ishan Babu succeeded in locating the treasure-chamber and he concluded that the treasure was held there. We now know that save and except a single gold coin, which had rolled down accidentally on the floor, there was nothing else in the secret chamber. Rajaram had removed every thing. Let me mention here that the sepoys had failed to locate the chamber; if they had succeeded in doing so, not a single earthen vessel would have remained intact.

'Any way, the question was — who was Mohanlal? Mohanlal, in whose custody Rajaram had left all his wealth. If we think a little deeply we can realize that Mohanlal could not be a human being. Barring Rajaram and Jairam no one else was in the fortress at that time; Rajaram had sent off everybody. Then in whose custody did he leave his wealth? What sort of a creature was Mohanlal?

'I too was unable to make any sense in the beginning. Then, suddenly one day, Ajit started reciting the lines from *The Battle of Plassey — *again and again the roar of the canon – the roar of Mohanlal.* The canon — Mohanlal. In those days canons were often named after valiant warriors. The identity of Mohanlal, in whose custody the treasure was held,— flashed through my mind like an electric spark. There is Mohanlal!' — Byomkesh pointed his finger at the canon lying on the ground.

By this time all of us had become quite excited. Ramkishor spoke out in a breathless voice, 'What! The gold is buried under the canon!'

'Not under the canon. In those days most people used to bury their gold in the ground; but Rajaram did not do such a bungling job. He had poured the gold into the barrel of the canon and sealed up the ends. Can't you see dry grass sprouting from the mouth of the canon? A hundred years back the sepoys had seen just such dry grass shooting out from the canon; they had never thought that the entire barrel of that derelict canon could be filled with solidified gold.'

Ramkishor said in impatient tone, 'Then why are we wasting time? Come, let us start removing the earth from the mouth of the canon and take out the gold coins.'

Byomkesh said, 'Gold coins? There are no gold coins any more, Ramkishor Babu. Rajaram had used his brains with such dexterity that even if the sepoys had traced the gold they wouldn't have been able to lift it away from here.'

'What are you saying? I do not understand anything!'

Byomkesh said, 'Pandeyji, do you remember that we had found a furnace and a blower in the treasure-chamber? There was also some Borax powder in an earthen pot. Now, do you understand what was done? Rajaram had melted all his gold coins and poured the molten gold down the barrel of that canon. So, now— there is a solidified column of gold inside the canon.'

*The Battle of Plassey: 19th century classic Bengali poem.

'Then – then ...?'

'If you dig up the earth from its mouth you may be able to see the gold, but you wouldn't be able to take it out.'

'Then what is the way out?'

'You can think of way outs later. You'll have to procure oxy-aceteline devices from Calcutta for cutting through the outer shell of the canon. It is about three inches thick; you can't cut it with ordinary chisels. However, for the time being we can dig up the earth from the mouth of the canon and check whether my guess is correct. Sitaram !'

Sitaram was carrying a hand-drill machine and other tools in his hands. On receiving orders from Byomkesh he mounted the canon like he was astride a horse, while the rest of us gathered below. Sitaram started digging up the earth from the mouth of the canon with great zeal.

After he had dug up to a depth of around one foot, Sitaram said, 'Sir, I cannot dig any more. It's a hard surface.'

Byomkesh ordered, 'Start with your drill!'

Sitaram inserted the drill into the mouth of the canon and then started twisting it. After he had twisted the drill only a few times flakes and thin shavings of gold started flying out from the mouth of the canon and falling all around. Meaningless sounds emerged from our lips while we stood by in amazed excitement.

Byomkesh raised his hand and said, 'That's enough, Sitaram. Stop.'

Then he turned to Ramkishor Babu and said, 'Now we have proof that my assumption was not wrong. Ramkishor Babu, you should install a sturdy door at the entrance to the fortress and post proper guards. And till such time as the entire gold is recovered, I would suggest that you should live here with your family. Do not leave all that gold loosely exposed and unwatched.'

It was almost one o' clock in the afternoon when we reached Pandeyji's residence. We were told that a telegram had arrived in Byomkesh's name. Our faces became pale. What tidings did the telegram carry? Who could have sent it? — Was Satyabati all right?

Byomkesh's hands shook a bit as he tore open the cover. Standing very close I stared at him anxiously.

While reading the contents of the telegram his face assumed an odd expression. Then he looked up at me, cleared his throat and said, 'Gold! Gold – there as well!'

'Gold?'

'Yes, I have got a son.'

It was six months later. Calcutta was getting ready for the advent of summer. Byomkesh and I were reading the morning newspaper after sharing the pages. Satyabati was squatting on the floor with her son and a bowl of milk, which she was trying to feed him, resulting in a keen wrestling match between mother and son.

Just then there was a knock on the outside door. Satyabati prepared to escape inside with her son. I opened the door to find Romapati and Tulsi. Romapati was wearing a silk *kurta* and *dhoti*; he had a shy smile on his face and was carrying a square box in his hand.

It was difficult to recognize Tulsi. In this short time she had blossomed into a lively, young girl. We had been invited to her wedding, but were unable to attend the function. Now we were meeting them after six months.

Tulsi blew up a storm as soon as she entered the room. On being introduced to Satyabati she picked up the baby from her arms, kissed his cheek and ran all around the room with him. Then she dumped the child on Romapati's lap, caught the edge of Satyabati's sari and dragged her inside. The sound of their cheerful exchanges and laughter reached our ears through the curtain.

Tulsi's true character seemed to have been held suppressed for all these years, but had now been set free. The gushing flow of a mountain spring had been released in full force.

When the room became a little quiet Byomkesh asked Romapati, 'What are you carrying in that box? Is it a gramophone?'

'No. I have got something specially made for you.' He then brought out some thing from the box at which Byomkesh and I went on staring in rapt admiration. It was an exact model of the fortress made of gold. Around two pounds in weight it was an exquisite instance of craftsmanship, showing every minute detail of the fortress including even the canon at the exact place.

We exclaimed in amazed voices, 'Wonderful!'

The rest of the morning was spent in eating, chatting, banter and jokes. We were told that Ramkishor Babu's health had improved, Bangshidhar had built his house on the landed property which he now owned; Muralidhar was living in a house which he had purchased in the town; Ramkishor Babu was still living in the house on the top of the hill with Gadadhar, Tulsi and Romapati.The fortress was being repaired thoroughly; Tulsi and Romapati would eventually live there.

They left in the afternoon. When it was time to say goodbye, Byomkesh asked, 'Tulsi, what sort of a man is your *Mastermashai*?'

Tulsi cast a sidelong glance with a feigned frown at her erstwhile tutor and said, 'Horrible.'

Byomkesh said, 'Hmm. But there was a day when you had placed your head on my lap and wept for him. Do you remember?'

Now Tulsi was overcome with shyness. She covered her blushing face with the edge of her sari and mumbled softly, 'Never!'